Asher's lips were on hers as she unlocked her door.

He backed her up against the wall, stealing desperate, hungry kisses. She ran her fingers through his hair, loving the feel of the slightly longer waves that fell into his face. Her tongue teased his bottom lip, and he trapped it with his teeth as he unzipped her coat, pulled it free of her body, and tossed it to the floor. Lifting her, he wrapped her thighs around his waist and steadied her against the wall. "I can't believe you dragged me out tonight," he said.

She should stop him.

But she never had before. Not the first time, six years ago, and not one time since…

Maybe
THIS
CHRISTMAS

ALSO BY JENNIFER SNOW

Maybe This Kiss (novella)
Maybe This Time
Maybe This Love
Maybe This Summer (novella)

Maybe
THIS
CHRISTMAS

JENNIFER SNOW

FOREVER
NEW YORK BOSTON

Copyright © 2017 by Jennifer Snow
Excerpt from *Maybe This Time* copyright © 2016 by Jennifer Snow
Cover design by Elizabeth Turner. Cover photography by Claudio Marinesco. Cover images © Shutterstock. Cover copyright © 2017 by Hachette Book Group, Inc.

Forever
Hachette Book Group
1290 Avenue of the Americas
New York, NY 10104
forever-romance.com
twitter.com/foreverromance

First Edition: September 2017

Forever is an imprint of Grand Central Publishing. The Forever name and logo are trademarks of Hachette Book Group, Inc.

The publisher is not responsible for websites (or their content) that are not owned by the publisher.

The Hachette Speakers Bureau provides a wide range of authors for speaking events. To find out more, go to www.hachettespeakersbureau.com or call (866) 376-6591.

ISBNs: 978-1-4555-9492-4 (mass market), 978-1-4555-9490-0 (ebook)

Printed in the United States of America

OPM

10 9 8 7 6 5 4 3 2 1

"Find what you love, and let it kill you."

—*Charles Bukowski*

Acknowledgments

I am forever grateful to Stephany Evans—the first person to believe in me—and to my editor, Madeleine Colavita, who has helped me grow as a writer with each book. A big thank you once again to Ray and Brijet Whitney for their hockey research help. You guys are wonderful. My family continues to be my greatest support system and I couldn't do this without them—Reagan and Jacob, I love you! And a big hug to my readers of this series who love the Westmores as much as I do—especially Becca Johnson, who shared her family's Christmas candy recipe with me. It is now a Westmore tradition.

XO,
Jen

Maybe
THIS
CHRISTMAS

CHAPTER 1

Asher Westmore hated surprises almost as much as he hated parties. Which everyone who'd just jumped out of their hiding places, yelling "Congratulations," should know. He turned to face his best friend.

Wide-eyed and innocent was not a look that Emma Callaway could pull off.

"This is why you were so adamant about coming here?" Asher asked, removing his baseball hat and shaking the snow from it as he ran a hand through his short brown hair.

I should have known, he thought, pushing his hair back and replacing the hat. Emma hated the Grumpy Stump—the local watering hole in Glenwood Falls—almost as much as he did. She certainly wouldn't have turned down *his* suggestion for the evening to come here unless something was up.

"Your mom is impossible to say no to," she said through gritted teeth. "Just fake a freaking smile and let's get through this as quickly and painlessly as possible." Her own fake smile was already in place.

It was too late for *painlessly*. The bright multicolored holiday lights covering every surface in the bar made him squint as he glanced around at the familiar faces. It seemed everyone in town had braved the first snow-storm of the year to come celebrate with him, which sent *quickly* flying headfirst into a snowbank as well. Every-one would want at least a few minutes of his time, as he was rarely back in his hometown. "This is premature," he hissed, but he did let his mouth twitch in the best version of a smile he could muster, as everyone continued to stare and applaud.

"You're two games away and the Devils are honoring you in New Jersey. People wanted to be a part of this," Emma said, as his brothers and their significant others approached.

"Hey, man," his oldest brother, Ben, said, hugging him first.

Winded by the rib-crushing hold, Asher said, "You could have warned me."

"Where would the fun be in that?" Ben asked, moving away and handing him his half-finished beer. "Started without you." He slid an arm around his fiancée, Olivia, who held back, offering him a small wave in greeting.

Her, he liked. Or at least, the fact that she valued per-sonal space as much as he did.

"Yeah, what took you two so long?" Abigail, his other brother Jackson's fiancée, asked, moving in to hug him next.

He squirmed uncomfortably. He wasn't a hugger. Which they all knew damn well.

When she released him, she shot what he guessed were supposed to be knowing looks between him and Emma.

She didn't know shit.

Despite what everyone thought they knew, he and Emma were not a couple. They were far too smart to ruin a perfect thing by messing around with feelings and commitments.

"The roads were terrible," Emma lied.

He hid a grin behind his hand. *He'd* been terrible. Refusing to leave her condo, trying everything in his power to charm her clothes off.

Okay, so maybe Abby knew a little something. Or at least she wasn't completely in the wrong about why they were late.

"The roads…right," she said with a wink. "You know, a triple wedding next year would be so much fun."

His mouth went dry, and he looked at Jackson to call off the attack. Just because his brothers had found women they wanted to spend their lives with didn't mean he was desperate to settle down anytime soon.

In two games, less than a week from now, he was going to be honored for his one thousandth game on NHL ice. While most players were slowing down at this point, at thirty, Asher was pushing back the clock. Hockey was everything that mattered to him, everything he'd known since he could stand in a hockey net, bubble-wrapped for his protection, and dive to block his brothers' unmerciful slap shots. Growing up the youngest brother of two NHL-crazed siblings, and even a sister who could play when forced, he'd learned two things: he never wanted to be a goalie, and if it meant playing in the NHL someday, he'd take every ill-timed body shot his brothers could send flying his way.

And he'd made it to NHL, just like his oldest brother, Ben. And just like Ben, he'd made it to a thousand career games.

Almost.

"Come on, we have a table in the back," his sister, Becky, said, waving the group along. "Mom's waiting there so we don't lose it." She rolled her eyes at him. "I can't believe all of these people are here to see you," she said.

He held out his arms. "What can I say? They know greatness when they see it."

"So you're saying they're here to see Ben?" The smart-assery in the Westmore family was strong.

He shoved her gently toward the back of the bar. "Shouldn't you be pregnant or something?"

She swung around to face him. "Newsflash—your new niece is almost a year old. Visit more, maybe," she said with her normal teasing tone, but there was a flicker of hope that he actually would reflected in her eyes.

A small wave of guilt washed over him, but only a small one. It wasn't his fault he'd been drafted to the Devils and not the Colorado home team like his brother.

The wooden bar floor was sticky beneath his hiking boots as they made their way to the reserved table. Asher hoped it could be blamed for his apparent limp as he shook hands along the way with people he hadn't seen in years. Unfortunately, the intense pain in his knee wasn't as easy to hide as his disdain over this premature celebration.

"Are you going to let me look at your knee before you head back?" Emma whispered.

Just once he wished something would escape his friend's sharp eye. "Nothing to look at. I feel great," he said, shoving her gently ahead of him through the thick crowd of well-wishers. "Besides, there's only one ache I'd like you to help me with," he whispered, the smell of her peppermint-scented body lotion making him want to lick her like a candy cane. And he would have, if hundreds of eyes weren't watching his every move. He avoided any and every kind of media attention that didn't have something to do with hockey.

His personal life was private...even from his family. He preferred it that way. And just because he was in his small hometown, surrounded by familiar faces, didn't mean there wasn't someone in the crowd who wouldn't love a shot of him that they could sell to the tabloids.

Pre-Olivia Ben had provided the gossip rags with enough content. Asher kept his head down and his nose clean.

But it was a challenge not to reach out and squeeze Emma's perfectly round ass, hugged tight by a pair of dark skinny jeans, when she turned to glare at him over her shoulder. "I'm a good therapist. I can help," she said.

That was the problem. She was a good therapist. One who would tell him to stay off of the damaged ACL in his right leg.

Not happening.

At least not until he'd reached his milestone...two games way. "I'm fine. Besides, you have enough to worry about," he said with a smirk.

Even her furrowed brow and narrowed eyes were sexy as hell. "Such as?"

"Such as trying not to look guilty as shit around my mom."

* * *

Right. An evening with Beverly Westmore, the woman driving Emma's widowed father to the brink of insanity since he'd moved into the house next door. Not that Emma was letting her father off the hook. He was as much to blame for their petty bickering as Beverly. She just wished the two could get along.

Normally, their harmless feuding over property lines and what color to paint the fence separating their backyards wouldn't bother her. But being as crazy, unrequitedly in love with Beverly's son as she was, the conflict between the families was a concern.

She tucked a strand of short blond hair behind her ear. She had always worn it shoulder-length, but just that day had chopped off the locks to a chin-length bob that framed her face, and she was still getting used to the new style.

She wondered what Asher thought of it. In the few hours since he'd been in town, he'd yet to mention it. She sighed. What did she expect? Her best friend wasn't exactly the most observant. At least not when it came to anything above her waist. If she changed the look of her ass, he'd definitely notice, she thought wryly, feeling his eyes on it as she walked in front of him.

He better cut that out before his mother saw him.

Beverly gave her the briefest of smiles as they

reached the table, then immediately her attention was all on Ash.

"I saved you a seat next to me," she yelled above the holiday music blaring from the speaker directly above them. She moved in one spot, along the long line of empty chairs near the wall. One and only one.

Emma took a seat across from them. She couldn't blame the woman for wanting her son's undivided attention. Traveling ten months a year with the Devils, Asher was rarely in Glenwood Falls. Even the off season seemed to end prematurely, with preseason training camp and living in New Jersey, so the Westmore siblings were rarely in one place at the same time. She knew it was tough on Beverly to hardly ever see the baby of the family.

Not seeing Asher was hard on Emma, too, but she knew the life of a pro athlete. Her days as a prosnowboarder had meant a lot of traveling and dedication to that sport as well. She understood Asher's commitment to the one thing in his life he was truly passionate about.

She just wished he'd open his eyes and heart to the idea of a different kind of commitment.

Her cheeks felt warmer at the thought and she prayed the twinkling red and green Christmas lights draped from the ceiling above the table could be blamed for the glow.

Jackson took a seat next to her. "Thanks for getting him here," he said, shrugging out of his leather jacket and draping it on the back of his chair.

"It wasn't easy." Nor was it the way she really wanted to spend the evening. She'd been excited when his schedule had brought him to Denver, thinking that maybe this visit might be different, that it might be the opportunity she was waiting for to open up to him about the feelings she had.

Feelings she hoped he shared.

Over the last several months, their conversations had grown a little deeper whenever they Skyped. His contract with the Devils was up at the end of that season and he wasn't certain of a renewal. He was worried for the first time in his career, and she'd done her best to reassure him that he was still one of the team's VIP players and they'd be stupid not to re-sign him. Talks had eventually turned to his future plans after hockey, and the truth about how she felt about him was constantly just a deep breath away.

She wanted to be what was next after hockey. In fact she wasn't sure she could wait until his pro athlete days were over, and he'd been giving her signs lately that she might not have to. Of course, he'd never confessed feelings…but she knew she meant a lot to him. And she was ready to find out just how much.

Unfortunately, she'd need to grow a set before actually taking the plunge. So far, gripping fear made her nauseated the moment she saw an opportunity in the conversation—a long pause, a soft glance from him—and she always choked.

That seemed to be the tagline of her life in recent years.

One that needed to change.

Once an Olympic gold medalist, she knew what it meant to go after her dreams, to work hard and put in the extra effort when everyone else called it quits—and getting Asher to realize his feelings for her would be no different. He required patience, determination, and persistence. He needed someone in his life who understood what it took to be great and supported him.

That was her.

Looking across the table at him laughing at something his mother had said, relaxed for the first time since they'd walked in, her chest ached with a longing that seemed to get stronger every day. The deep-set dimples when he smiled transformed his usual serious, strong-looking face, making her heart race. His light blue eyes, square jaw covered with stubble, perfectly straight nose, and dentist-enhanced smile rivaled those of a *GQ* model.

He glanced her way and winked, the simple gesture sending her pulse racing. Resisting the urge to crawl under the table and wedge herself between mother and son took all Emma's strength. He was only there for one evening, then gone again the next night on a red-eye flight and there was so much to say…so much to find out.

She bit her lip as she stared at the mouth she was craving. Her gaze drifted lower to his sculpted chest and arms, barely contained by the fabric of his black T-shirt, and her palms were sweating. His chiseled features and linebacker build made him one of the hottest players in the NHL. Women flocked to him like bees to honey and she wasn't immune to his good looks and charm. Maybe she should have blown off this party and let him take her clothes off the way he'd been determined to do. Talking to Ash about anything was always easier when he was naked.

"Whatever you're thinking—do *not* do it." Ben's voice next to her made her jump.

"What?" she asked, as he took a seat on the other side of her and handed her a gin and tonic—her usual.

Being sandwiched between the two older Westmore brothers was a place most women would kill to be, but as much as she liked Ben and Jackson, they couldn't compare to Asher.

"I see that look on your face. In fact, I've seen it for a while now." Ben touched her shoulder as he turned in the chair and leaned closer, so no one could hear. "Look, Em…I'm not going to pretend to know what you and Asher have, but I do know exactly where his head is right now. It's on that thousandth game this week."

She took a sip of her drink and nodded. "I know that." Probably better than any of them. The siblings were close but she knew Asher didn't confide in anyone the way he did her.

"Good. Keep it in mind, because we both know that Asher is a 'thinks with his head' kind of guy. He's not about to let feelings—his own or anyone else's—get in his way of this goal he's set for himself." He kissed her forehead as he stood, his gaze landing on his fiancée out on the dance floor with Abby and Becky.

She swallowed hard, hearing Ben loud and clear. And just like that, whatever courage she'd thought she'd summoned vanished.

CHAPTER 2

⤨

$\mathscr{A}$sher's mind might be on the game, but his lips were on hers hours later as she unlocked her door and they stepped inside. He backed her up against the wall, stealing desperate, hungry kisses. Removing his baseball hat, she ran her fingers through his hair, loving the feel of the slightly longer waves that fell into his face. Her tongue teased his bottom lip, and he trapped it with his teeth as he unzipped her coat, pulled it free of her body, and tossed it to the floor. Lifting her, he wrapped her thighs around his waist and steadied her against the wall. "I can't believe you dragged me out tonight," he said.

She should stop him.

But she never had before. Not the first time, six years ago when they'd had far too much to drink at her birthday party and both claimed it was a terrible idea to add *bene-fits* to the friendship, but did it anyway. And not one time since…which was practically whenever he was in town and they were both unattached. Since discovering she had more than friendly feelings for him the year before, she made sure she always was. "Your family would have hunted you down," she said pressing her body closer to his, squeezing his waist with her thighs. Her body burned for him, and the scent of his aftershave at his neck was intoxicating.

She loved the smell of him—all man, cool, strong, and solid—the way she imagined ice would smell if it had a scent.

"That's why I have you," he said, kissing her neck. "You're supposed to protect me from the crazies when I come home."

The feel of his warm lips against her cool flesh made her shiver, and she swallowed hard, desperate to keep the mood light. "So, I'm your bodyguard now?"

"Yes. All one hundred and ten pounds of you." His hands unbuttoned her jeans and a second later his freezing-cold fingers found her warm flesh between her thighs.

She sucked in air. "Cold!" she said trying to yank the hand free.

"Well, warm it up," he teased, kissing her again as he stroked along her folds, which were dampening quickly from his touch.

She'd never been able to resist Asher. Even before her realization that he was the only man on the planet that she couldn't live without, her attempts to keep her body from craving his were futile.

Her best friend was freaking hot as hell. A hockey player shaped more like a bodybuilder, with broad shoulders and thick chest and stomach. His six-pack abs were perfectly sculpted from hours on the ice and hitting the gym. His life revolved around hockey and turning his body into the best equipment he had.

And damn, his *equipment* was unparalleled. She returned the favor of the cold touch, as she slipped her hand beneath the waistband of his jeans.

He didn't seem to notice or care about the chilling effect as he instantly hardened beneath her hand.

The fact that he always seemed as ready and wanting of her as she was for him still baffled her. Flat-chested and athletically built, she wasn't exactly a Victoria's Secret model. At five-foot-nothing and a hundred and *fifteen* pounds, with short blond hair and average features, she didn't turn many heads in town. She was a plain Jane, and given the supermodels flinging themselves at the hockey god daily, she was shocked that he could even fake a hard-on for her.

Asher didn't seem to share her opinion of herself, and his desire and eagerness for her made her feel sexy, despite the reality in the mirror.

"Bedroom?" he asked, the sound coming from deep in his throat as his light blue eyes searched hers. Westmore eyes—all three brothers had them, the only real feature they shared.

She nodded, then, remembering the medical textbooks sprawled across her bed from her late night studying, she shook her head. "Couch."

He shook his head, biting her bottom lip before saying, "Too small."

"Table?"

"Too hard."

"You're starting to sound like Goldilocks," she said.

He shrugged, letting his grip on her thighs relax as he lowered himself to his knees. "I can't wait any longer, floor it is." He laid her on the soft tan carpet. "I can't believe you dragged me out to that thing," he said again. "We could have been doing this all night. Now I have to make up for the missed hours."

Make up for missed hours. Asher's appetite for sex was insatiable. Neither of them would be getting any sleep before he went back to Denver for his game the following night. She swallowed hard when his lips found her neck and his hands slid beneath the bottom of her sweater. His fingers inched higher over her stomach to the base of her padded bra. He pulled back slightly and sent her a look she'd seen before.

"Shut up, don't say it."

"You're smoking hot without the padding," he said anyway, reaching behind her to unclasp the bra, letting his hands roam beneath it. "More than a handful is just a waste." He flicked his thumbs over the hardened nipples.

Then why was every model and actress on the planet a D cup? She pushed aside her insecurities as his hands massaged her breasts. Who cared? Whether he meant the words or not, what he was doing with those handfuls was making her wet. "Ash…take my clothes off."

He sat straighter, leaning his weight on his knees on either side of her. "Oh, so now you want sex?" he asked with a grin, sliding her sweater and bra up over her head.

"I always want sex." *With you,* she almost had enough courage to add. Instead she sat up and reached for his sweater and T-shirt together, pulling them off quickly.

A sigh actually escaped her.

Asher's body was perfection. She trailed a hand along the ripped abs, down along the oblique muscles disappearing at the top of his jeans. Her eyes took in the smooth, sculpted, hairless chest and shoulders that she knew by heart. She'd caressed every inch of him so often, she could identify his body in the dark in a room full of muscular men. Yet, each time she saw him naked, he took her breath away. She could appreciate how much work was involved in keeping in top shape and his dedication to his training and health was as much of a turn-on for her as were the droolworthy results.

He was dedicated to his health until it came to his injured leg…but she'd deal with that later. "Why are you so disgustingly perfect?" she asked, kissing his chest.

He laughed. "Jealous of my muscles?" he asked, shoving her gently back onto her back and reaching for the button on her jeans.

No. *Jealous of anyone else who ever got to enjoy them.* They didn't fool around when one or both of them were involved with someone else, and while Ash was far from a manwhore, with an appetite for sex like he had, he must be far from celibate.

She pushed the annoying thoughts aside as he unzipped the zipper and she lifted her hips to allow him to remove her jeans. She wiggled the fabric down her legs as he tugged both denim and silk down her thighs together. He suddenly wasn't wasting any time.

He lowered his own jeans and underwear, and she'd barely gotten a glimpse of his erection before she felt it pressed between her legs.

He groaned as his body made contact with hers and he

pushed himself deeper inside, knowing she was ready for him.

They never worried about protection when they were being exclusive to one another and she was on the pill, so they didn't have to worry about consequences neither was ready for.

She clung to his shoulders as he rocked his hips, moving in and out of her body. She arched her back, bringing them even closer.

It had been months since the last time they were together, when she'd gone to visit him in New Jersey and they hadn't left his bedroom the entire time. She knew this first time would be hard and fast…and they'd play with one another later. A lot.

She grabbed the back of his head, pulling him down to her. His lips crushed hers and she could barely breathe as the rocking of his hips became faster, more desperate. She felt her desire swell as she hung on to him, her nails biting into the flesh at his shoulders. She could hold him forever and it wouldn't be long enough.

She tried to push her emotions aside and just enjoy the in and out of his cock, pulsating in her tight folds. Focus on the feel of him pulling out and entering. Every last inch of him, hitting all the right places…over and over.

Her muscles throbbed around him and she clenched them. Asher moaned at the extra sensation of her tightening and releasing, and he broke away, struggling for breath. Smoothing her hair away from her face, he stared into her eyes. "Emma…you're so fucking incredible," he said.

I love you.

God! It was on the tip of her tongue, yet refused to be said.

Did he even feel the slightest bit the way she did? Their hips rocked together in a steady, desperate rhythm. His gaze was locked on hers, and he took her hands and lifted them above her head, interlacing their fingers as he pushed deeper inside of her.

The way he looked at her took her breath away completely and she grasped his hands and pressed her body closer. It had to mean something, this connection that went beyond the physical when he made love to her, the way he took her with such passion and intensity…He had to have feelings for her.

Right?

He quickened his pace, and she felt her body ache for release. "Asher…make me come…" she panted, closing her eyes.

"Open your eyes. Look at me," he said against her lips, kissing her softly.

She opened them and he pulled back to stare at her once more. Eye contact with him as he gave her such pleasure filled her with a whirlwind of sensations.

"Emma, I…" He started then paused.

Her heart was about to explode. Love, fear, desperation made a tornado around her as she waited for him to continue.

What? Say it, Asher…

He didn't. Instead, he held her hands even tighter and released a moan as he throbbed inside of her.

She came the moment he did, the intensity of her orgasm overshadowing her disappointment. Releasing her own cry of satisfaction, she forgot all other thoughts as she savored the orgasm rippling through her.

If Asher Westmore could make her feel this incredible

when he wasn't in love with her, he'd unravel her completely if he ever were.

*   *   *

Asher rested his palms against the bathroom sink and swore under his breath. The sun was about to come up, he had to be back in Denver for practice in five hours, and the pain in his leg was unbearable.

Opening his travel bag on the counter, he rummaged through until he found what he was looking for. Shaking out three prescription painkillers, he tossed them into his mouth, then turning on the tap, he washed them down, just as the sickly tasting powder started to dissolve on his tongue. Wiping his mouth with a towel, he glanced inside the bottle before tucking it away again. Four left. They wouldn't even get him through the morning and two-hour drive back to Denver. His tolerance to the painkillers had built up so quickly that it was taking triple the dosage these days to get any kind of relief. And he didn't have time to see a doctor in town. No time and no desire to have rumors spread about a possible injury. The team's doctors were the only ones he trusted—along with several in Tijuana, Mexico. Unfortunately, the Devils weren't playing the Kings or the Sharks for several weeks, so a quick trip across the border was out of the question.

Maybe Emma had something.

Opening the medicine cabinet, he scanned the bottles. Nonprescription headache medicine was as strong as it got. Useless on his pain. They'd stopped working for him six months ago.

He closed the door and the click echoed on the bath-room walls. Shit. That would wake the dead.

"You okay?" Emma asked, knocking softly on the semi-closed bathroom door before entering a second later.

He turned, folding the hand towel over the rack. "Yeah. Sorry, I was looking for an aspirin. Headache." He pulled her into him. He couldn't be in the same room with her without wanting her body pressed to his. Especially when she looked so damn cute wearing a Devils jersey, her hair wild from their hours of sex, her lips puffy and pink and her cheeks slightly red from stubble burn.

Unfortunately, she was not only cute as hell, but smart and perceptive. "When are you going to come see me about your leg?" she asked, not buying the headache lie. "Some simple exercises and regular therapy…"

"Shhh," he muttered, burying his face in the top of her head, breathing in the scent of her gingerbread-scented shampoo. She was the only reminder of the holiday season he enjoyed. All of the tacky commercialism annoyed him, and other than spending whatever time he could with his family every year, he avoided all of the usual festivities and preparations.

"Asher, you have to deal with the injury." She pushed against his chest.

He held her tighter. "Are you wearing underwear?" he asked, sliding a hand under the jersey to discover the answer.

She sighed at his avoidance but then grinned and wrapped her arms around his neck. "What would be the point?"

Lifting her, he placed her onto the counter next to the sink and stood between her knees. Tucking her new shorter blond strands behind her ears, he kissed her. "Great haircut, by the way," he said, moving away just an inch.

She looked surprised. "You actually noticed?"

He laughed. "I'm not *always* staring at your ass."

She smiled. "Just most of the time?"

"Just most of the time." He kissed her again. This one was long and hard. He could feel himself thicken in his boxer briefs, and the pain in his leg was overshadowed with a different ache. He slid his hands upward on her thin, muscular thighs, digging his fingers into her flesh as they wrapped around to cup her bare ass.

He didn't need painkillers. He just needed his best friend's body.

But did he need more than that?

The way she'd looked at him that evening had felt different. She'd acted the same as always, but there seemed to be an underlying tension. She appeared to be searching for something in his kiss, in his eyes, in his arms…And he wasn't entirely sure she'd find what she was looking for.

He pulled back slightly. "This is still good, right? You and me?"

She frowned. "Having sex?"

He nodded slowly. She said it casually enough. He loved the fact that she never referred to it as making love, instead calling it what it was. Maybe he was reading things wrong.

Or maybe he was the one starting to question the good thing they had. Wondering if it had gone on too long. Wondering if at thirty, he should be looking for something more. Wanting more. From her?

She traced his bottom lip with her finger as she licked her own lips. "The sex is amazing."

Yes, it was. But…"I just mean, you're not looking for… more?"

Her expression clouded to something unreadable for a lightning bolt of a second before she said, "Yes, I am looking for more…"

His stomach did an involuntary lurch, and he couldn't tell if it was a bad lurch or a good lurch.

"…more sex," she added with a wicked little grin before he had time to decipher the meaning.

Relief…or was it disappointment, flowed through him. Lifting her from the counter, he carried her back to bed. "More sex I can do."

As for anything else, he wasn't sure.

CHAPTER 3

⌒∾⌒

$\mathcal{T}$he soft chords of her mother's guitar woke Emma a few hours later. It felt like only minutes since she'd last closed her eyes, but now the sun was casting its glow across the tan bedsheet draped over her. The vaguely familiar sound of one of her new favorite country songs made her roll to her side to face Asher. He was sitting in her window seat, the guitar on his lap, his gaze somewhere out the window.

The sight alone—him sitting there with nothing on but his jeans, strumming the strings of Clare's prized possession, a Gibson guitar her mother had owned since she was fifteen—made Emma's heart race.

And the husky, deep sound of his voice singing the sexy, romantic lyrics to a song he'd teased her about liking the night before made him impossibly irresistible.

Few people knew of his other talent—the ability to play anything just by hearing the song once. But he'd confessed his secret to her the first day they'd met almost ten years ago.

He'd accidentally backed his truck into her snowboard leaning on the side of her tailgate in the local sporting goods store's parking lot. Seeing who it was, she'd called him a dumb jock under her breath as she'd inspected the board. The Westmore brothers had a reputation in the town as local gods, and it had annoyed her that her equally impressive skills on a snowboard were always overshadowed by the Westmore boys' accomplishments on ice.

In his flushed, equally annoyed state, he'd used the confession about his guitar skills as a way to try to redeem himself in her eyes and convince her he was much more than everyone in town thought.

It had worked. Without really knowing her, he'd hit a chord with her.

He'd also paid for a replacement board and insisted she owed him at least a coffee for the insult. Coffee had turned into lunch, then a walk in the park, then dinner at Dale's Pizzeria on Main Street, and eight hours later, she knew enough about him to write a book.

And she'd realized she'd been dead wrong about him being a dumb jock. He'd actually graduated high school head of his class, despite studying while on the road playing Major Junior League hockey, and while hockey was his main focus, he was arguably a better musician. At least at that point in his career.

When the Westmores were hockey-obsessed kids, their mother had insisted that he and his brothers take at least one non-hockey-related extracurricular activity. Ash had picked guitar…and he had to work very little at it to be good.

She smiled now, loving the sight and the sound of the twangy, off-tune instrument.

Her mother would play the same guitar for her and her younger sister, Jess, every night before bed, telling them stories about her year in country heaven, playing the local bars and writing songs for some of Nashville's finest stars. She'd get a dreamy, far-off look in her eyes whenever she spoke of those days, before she'd met their father, before she'd had them…and Emma had always felt a tug of heartache in her chest that her mother hadn't realized her dream of becoming a country star back then.

Clare's encouragement had been part of Emma's own driving force to succeed, to follow her dreams and not let anything stand in the way. Her mother had pushed her to keep trying, to get back up when she fell, and she'd been so proud of what Emma had accomplished with her snowboarding career.

She wondered what her mom would think about her giving it up.

She swallowed a lump in her throat as Ash glanced up at her and stopped playing. "Good morning."

"Don't stop," she said, grabbing her blanket as she climbed out of bed. Wrapping it around her body, she went to sit next to him.

He turned slightly to face her and continued strumming, singing the lyrics in a smooth flawless tone that made shivers dance down her spine. His eyes met hers and her heart thundered in her chest.

Damn, the guy may be a star athlete, but he missed another calling with music. He was certainly hot enough holding that guitar.

He tore his gaze from hers as he finished the song and

checked the clock on the bedside table. "I have to go," he said, setting the guitar on the stand a second later.

"What would happen if you didn't?" she asked as he pulled her to her feet. She moved into his open arms, breathing in the scent of him, savoring the feel of his big, strong arms wrapped around her tiny frame as long as she could. The Devils' next game against Colorado wasn't until New Year's Eve…sooner than usual, but still too long.

He'd be playing on Christmas Eve in Phoenix, and she knew they would probably toast on New Year's Eve through Skype. As they did most years…So why did the thought depress her so much more now?

He kissed her forehead and didn't answer the question he knew she really wasn't expecting an answer to.

* * *

Knocking once on the Colorado team's doctor's office door, Asher entered the tiny room with the crammed desk and examination table. It was nine a.m. and no one else was around yet, but the Avalanche players would be arriving for early morning practice soon. His own team was scheduled for practice at noon, and he needed a pick-me-up before he could even entertain the thought of getting on the ice.

The dip in temperature being back in his hometown that week had his knee all kinds of messed up. Jersey had yet to see snow, and the East Coast was enjoying unseasonably high temperatures for mid-November, for which he was grateful. The cold made his knee feel a million times worse.

Fooling around with Emma the night before hadn't been a great idea, either—though only his knee thought so. The rest of him was feeling great. He always did after spending time with her. That could be a problem if he let himself think about it for too long, so he pushed the thought aside. He had one thing to think about that day: beating his brother's team and getting one step closer to his milestone game five nights from now in New Jersey, on his adopted home ice.

At first he'd been disappointed when he hadn't gotten drafted to play in Colorado with Ben. Every young player dreams of wearing their hometown colors someday, but the Devils had offered him a solid contract and a good place to cut his blades, and he'd been happy to re-sign with the team five years ago when his first seven-year contract had expired. He only had six months left on his current contract and hoped to renew once more. He wanted to finish his career where it started. They had no reason to trade him—he was one of their VIP players, and the team felt like family. He was getting older, though, and his body wasn't bouncing back from injuries as fast as it used to…Still, he believed he was a strong asset to his team.

Playing opposite Ben in Colorado twice a season was always exciting—for them and for the fans. The atmosphere in the stadium would be electric, and he knew the fans were happy for him and his success, even though he wore the opposing team's colors.

And that evening, one game away from his milestone, would be off the charts…if he could even stand up on his skates.

"Hey, Seth, how are you?" he said, closing the office door behind him.

"Hey, man…I'm good. How's the knee?" He frowned, noticing Asher's slight limp.

Mornings were by far the worst, after hours of rest… not that there'd been much the night before. An image of Emma's perfect, tight little body straddling him flashed in his mind, and he shook his head. Nope, hadn't exactly been resting.

"Or should I even ask?" Seth continued. "I'm guessing you're not here this early to shoot the shit." A tightness was undeniable in his old high school friend's voice, as he pushed his thick, dark-rimmed glasses higher on his nose.

Seth had always been a wannabe athlete, watching from the sidelines. His severe asthma and poor eyesight made sports a challenge. Despite being a spirited player, he was always picked last for teams and had never excelled at individual competition, either, coming in last at track and field. By high school, he'd finally accepted his fate and had focused on studying hard to graduate with scholarships, going into sports medicine in college instead. Asher had always liked the guy, and he knew the Avalanche players were lucky to have Seth looking after them.

"Sure I am," he said. "After I get an injection…and possibly one for the road." He climbed up onto the table and lifted the leg of his gray sweats. The knee was visibly swollen, and the inflammation was the main cause of the pain. A damaged ACL was torture, and unfortunately one of the most common injuries in the sport, besides concussions. He'd been skating on the damaged knee for almost a year and knew he had to take some time to let it heal, but not yet.

Two more games.

Seth moved closer to examine the knee. "Who have you been getting the injections from in Jersey?" He frowned, seeing the bruising at the various injection sites around the knee.

Thank God he'd been able to keep Emma's attention away from the knee the night before, otherwise he'd have caught some serious shit from her. He'd narrowly escaped a lecture about how self-medicating to dull the pain wasn't solving the bigger problem. He knew that, and he didn't feel good about the way he was handling things, but he just needed to hang on a little bit longer.

Asher shrugged. "Just the team's doctor." And several walk-in clinic doctors just outside of New Jersey. Luckily the medical systems weren't tied together, so no one doctor saw all the frequent cortisone injections he was getting. Or hell, maybe they just didn't give a shit. The Devils had been close to a Stanley Cup win the season before, getting taken out in the second round by the Avalanche. Everyone was expecting one this year. Doping a player to ensure that it happened certainly wasn't a new thing in sports.

"Bullshit." Seth called him out on the lie. "No one's giving you this much."

Asher's mouth went dry. Lying to his buddy made him feel like an ass, especially when it had been Seth who had helped him that summer with enough injections to make it through training camp. With Seth's help, Asher had been able to hide the extent of the injury from the Devils' doctor long enough to get clearance to play that season. Their deal had been that he'd help him through camp, then Asher had to come clean with the team and take the necessary time off to let the ACL heal properly before it could be damaged beyond repair.

Asher hadn't lived up to his end of the bargain. "It was feeling better after camp, and it's just been acting up again the last few weeks." Man, the stack of lies kept piling up.

Seth shook his head, but readied a needle. "I'm only doing this one last time, and only because tonight is game 999 and I know how bad you want this, man." He tapped the needle and gave no warning as he hit the site next to Asher's knee.

"Jesus." Asher winced slightly at the tiny prick on the sensitive skin, but almost immediately relief flowed into the joint as Seth removed some of the excess fluid building up around the injury. The draining of the knee was disgusting, and Asher had to look away as Seth retracted the needle.

"Does the team know what a wimp you are about needles?" Seth asked, tossing it into a safe disposal unit.

"It's not the needle, man, it's that disgusting shit you pull out with it that makes me gag."

"That disgusting shit will keep coming back until you take care of yourself," he said, taking a second needle and injecting the cortisone.

"I will. Next week, I'll take a much-needed vacation." For now, this would get him through practice and the game that evening if he didn't push too hard. Normally, he was all in, every game, but this one and the next, he planned to take his intensity down a notch.

His one-thousandth career game was a big milestone, one not every player reached. Especially not so young. His brother's award plaque on his mother's fireplace mantel taunted him almost as much as it motivated him…the same way Ben's Stanley Cup win did. His older brother was always just one step ahead all of the freaking time. Being born last, Asher's need to catch up had only magnified over the years. This year, he would reach the milestone and lead his team to the cup. And he'd have accomplished both earlier in his career than Ben had.

But one thing at a time…

"Thank you. I feel good as new." He pulled the leg of his sweats back down, bending and straightening the leg several times.

"You're not, though," Seth warned. "Not even close. You've been playing with this ACL damage for too long. I have no idea how you're doing it or what kind of crap you're taking to manage the pain, but I shouldn't be helping you like this."

"You're a good man."

"No." Seth's irritation was evident in his voice. "I'm a doctor who is going against my better judgment *and* I'm your friend. I care about your long-term career, not just these milestone moments. That's why I mean it when I say no more, Ash. This is it." He removed his plastic gloves, balled them, and tossed them toward a trash can less than two feet away. Missed. Sighing, he bent to pick them up and place them in the trash.

Asher nodded as he slowly climbed down from the table. "No problem. This was all I needed, and I appreciate you helping me out. Again. I promise I'll rest up after Tuesday's night's game. I'll take all the recovery time I need then."

Seth didn't look convinced. "Okay, man. I really hope you do. Either way, I'm out."

"Fair enough." He understood and respected that. His friend had put his neck on the line enough.

"Good luck out there tonight. If anyone's going to beat my team, I'll be less angry about it if it's you."

* * *

Emma shivered as she ran across the street to check her mailbox. November should not feel this cold. It happened every year—winter hit when no one was looking. She used to love the first signs of the winter season. Her muscles would spring to life at the dip in temperatures followed by early morning frost, and the anticipation of months ahead on the slopes had been like a drug-induced high.

Things hadn't felt like that for years. Now winter brought with it a sense of dread, a reminder of what she could no longer do.

The snowboarding accident three days before she was set to leave for the Winter Olympics in Sochi had destroyed much more than her ability to compete. Her spirit had been crushed.

When the Olympic committee had announced the new Slopestyle competition in that year's games, she'd known it was her sport. The discipline was a mix of BMX and skateboarding crossing over onto the slopes. The course was made up of obstacles such as rails and jumps, and Emma had been stoked when she'd made the elite team of athletes to attempt the competition. The jumps and tricks were exhilarating and gave her a new sense of passion for her sport.

Snowboarding had been as natural to her as walking, and she'd been excited about a new challenge.

Then she'd gotten cocky.

The weather had been mild for a week, and her coach had ordered a no-training day until the slopes were in better shape. But there was one stunt she'd yet to perfect: the double flat-down handrail. She struggled with picking up enough speed as she left the half-pipe on the course right before the obstacle, and she couldn't do a double axel before landing without the extra height.

She didn't need the stunt. She could do the single with precision and ease. But she didn't want to just final in the division. She'd wanted the gold medal around her neck. Again.

Going out on the slopes that day was the worst decision she'd made in her life.

She was moving too fast on the icy packed slope when she hit the first ramp. More speed didn't help as she hit the half-pipe, and her landing was unsteady. She should have dropped, rolled away from the flat-down handrail, but at the speed she was cruising, she knew she could hit the stunt.

Adrenaline soared through her as she did.

Then pain replaced that sensation as the impact of the hard crash on the end of the rail broke her femur in her left leg and her right collarbone in two different places, and dislocated three disks in her spine.

She'd missed the Olympics and had immediately lost all of her sponsors as soon as word of her accident spread. The look of disappointment on her coach's face as he'd left the hospital room to join the rest of the U.S. team on the flight to Russia had made her wish for death. The deep, dark void dragging her spirits to unhealthy thoughts while being medicated to dull the aching in her entire body had nearly killed her.

To be so close to something she'd worked so hard and long for and to have it taken away when the goal was just within sight had been devastating.

She hadn't thought she'd recover from it.

If it hadn't been for her family and Asher she might not have—though both had had very different ways of helping her through it. While Ash's method had been to encourage healing and getting back out there, her father and sister had called it a new opportunity to move on with a real career. They'd never believed she'd make it as far as she had with snowboarding, and they'd almost acted validated when she'd gotten hurt. But they'd been there to help her through it, and in time, she'd realized they'd been right.

A life in professional sports was uncertain, something she couldn't build a future on. She thought of Asher and Ben—in their thirties, they were starting to wind down, and most players retired by forty—and while they'd never have to worry about money once they hung up their skates for the last time, what about a sense of purpose? Would they feel fulfilled living in the limelight of their past accomplishments? She wasn't sure that was possible for men who possessed the drive and determination needed to be where they were.

Emma had simply dealt with the heartbreak of retirement earlier in her career and had made some tough decisions. Now she was in a good place. She opened the mailbox and retrieved her mail, her heart nearly stopping when she saw the envelope on top.

A letter from the University of Florida's physical therapy doctorate program.

No longer feeling the biting wind, she tore open the letter and skipped past the first cordial paragraph, searching for the word *accepted* or *denied*.

We'd like to offer you enrollment in our winter semester starting January 10...

Wow. January 10. Only eight weeks away. She'd been hoping to enroll for the following fall semester, but could she be ready to move to Florida that quickly? Excitement rose in her chest, but she forced herself to think logically. She'd need to give notice at the clinic...but they were enthusiastic about her plans to pursue her PhD—they could benefit from a more skilled doctor in the field.

Her sister would need to take over more responsibility in looking after their father, but this school and this program had been Jess's idea, so she knew her sister would encourage her to accept the earlier start date.

She bit her lip, clutching the letter as the wind nearly stole it from her hand. Her only real hesitancy came from thoughts of Asher. She hadn't mentioned her plans to him yet, thinking she had months before the fall semester started...but she'd have to tell him soon if she was going to accept the January enrollment.

She wasn't sure how he'd take it. He was always supportive of her life choices, but she knew he still believed she should return to the slopes. He didn't hide the fact that he thought she'd walked away too soon, too easily. And she couldn't help but feel as though her moving on with a new passion and a new career was somehow disappointing to him. But maybe the idea of her being in Florida, closer to New Jersey, might appeal to him...

It certainly was a pro for her when she'd been deciding which schools to apply to—not that she was making a life-changing decision based on a guy who'd made it perfectly clear that she should expect nothing more than mind-blowing sex from him several times a year. Sigh. She'd been almost certain he'd been about to say the words she'd longed to hear.

Her cell phone rang as she went inside, and her sister's number lit the call display. "Hey, Jess," she said, going into the kitchen, where she tucked the letter inside a physical therapy textbook. She'd been studying like crazy, reading through her undergraduate course textbooks and reviewing her notes, wanting to be ready for the program, should she be accepted.

"Well? Did you hear anything yet?" Jess asked.

Her sister's timing was uncanny. It was like they shared a connection she'd expect twins to have, despite being two years apart in age. Her sister was the youngest and, unfortunately, the one with her life figured out.

Emma hesitated.

If she told Jess the truth, her sister would be there within minutes to help her pack her things, and she wasn't sure she could make the January timeline work just yet. Though it was certainly tempting. "Um…I'm sure I will soon."

"Have you checked the mail today?"

Obviously, her sister knew something she wasn't saying. "Tell me you haven't been harassing your professor friend at the university." She knew letting Jess contact her friend from college to put in a good word for her had been a mistake. In fact, mentioning her interest in the doctoral program to her sister in the first place had been a mistake. Emma had been considering the program at the University of Colorado, but Jess had insisted that the program in

Florida had a better sports medicine division. When Jess got her teeth into something, she was like a dog with a bone. Relentless and determined. Unfortunately, after researching their program, Emma had had to concede that her sister was right this time. Their sports therapy program especially appealed to her, and it was one of the top programs in the country.

"Of course not," Jess said now, sounding slightly offended, as if harassment wasn't in her wheelhouse. "I just *happened* to talk to him the other day…"

Right.

"And he mentioned that the department was sending out their replies to applicants that week…and knowing that mail takes about three days from Florida to Colorado…Whatever, it's simple deduction, Emma. Did you check your mail or not?"

If she continued lying, her sister would be there in three and a half minutes anyway wrestling the mailbox key from her, and Emma wouldn't stand a chance against her sister's taller, bigger frame. "Fine. Yes. I got the letter."

"Okay, I'm in the car…"

She heard the call switching to Bluetooth. Unbelievable.

"Don't open it until I get there."

"What makes you think I haven't opened it already?"

"Because you're not excited or depressed, just your usual annoyingly casual self."

Head journalist and reporter for the *Glenwood Times*, Jess expected everyone to have a fire under their ass all the time the way she did. Chasing local stories that could be shaped into exciting, newsworthy fodder on a daily basis was the perfect career for her high-strung, type-A sister.

Hell, to Jess, grocery shopping was a mission not to be taken lightly.

Well, Emma had that fire and she was excited…she just approached big decisions a little more cautiously than Jess. And unfortunately, she couldn't shake thoughts of Asher and what he'd think from her mind.

"I opened it," she said.

Silence.

"Jess?"

"I'm holding my breath," came her anxiety-filled whisper.

She would regret this instantly, she just knew it. "I got in."

The high-pitched squeal that followed had her immediately disconnecting the call. She couldn't deal with Jess today. She loved her sister, but she was exhausting. Her input on Emma's life after snowboarding was driving Emma mad. She knew Jess thought she was being helpful, but she was a little too much, too often. She'd practically filled out Emma's application to attend the University of Colorado for her bachelor's degree in physical therapy while Emma was still recovering in the hospital, and it had been Jess who'd encouraged her to attend school year-round, instead of taking a break during the summer months, to complete the degree a year early.

Emma glanced at the time on her microwave. It was after two p.m. She'd taken the day off knowing that following a night with Asher, she'd need several naps before heading to Denver for Asher's game. She wouldn't see him before he played, and she might be able to steal a few minutes with him after the game, but that would be the extent of face-to-face contact for almost another seven weeks.

New Year's Eve, when he played in Denver again.

Somehow she had to make that opportunity work to tell him how she felt. She refused to let another midnight roll over into another new year without telling him that she loved him.

But before then, she had to summon the courage to tell him about the University of Florida, because while she wasn't ready to admit it to her sister just yet, she was ready to take the next step in her career, which meant leaving Glenwood Falls right after the holidays.

CHAPTER 4

～∽⌒

*H*is body was getting used to the injections. The effect of the cortisone seemed to be weakening after months of abuse. Fully dressed in his hockey gear and ready to go, Asher opened his locker and retrieved the last of the prescription painkillers that he'd been resisting the urge to take all afternoon. He shook the four pills into his hand and popped them into his mouth, chasing them down his throat with a shot of Gatorade from his water bottle.

Hopefully it would be enough to reach the numbing sensation in his limbs to prevent him limping visibly onto the ice, but not too much to throw off his other senses. He still needed his razor-sharp focus and sensory awareness.

He wasn't sure when he'd become an expert on pill popping and the dosing effects on his body, but his heavy reliance on the meds was starting to bother him. Before the injury, he barely took anything at all. He rarely needed anything.

But he wasn't addicted to the shit. Not yet.

After Tuesday's game, it all ends.

Luckily, the electric energy in the stadium would be enough to get him through his twenty-six minutes of ice time.

Checking his phone a final time, he read a text from Emma, saying she'd arrived and wishing him luck. An emoji at the end of the text blew him a kiss and he grinned. He looked forward to her pregame text. Counted on it on his off days. He was glad she was there tonight. Having her in the stands somehow put him at ease.

Closing the locker, he reached for his helmet and swayed slightly off balance, his shoulder falling against his teammate, lacing up on the bench next to him.

"You drunk, Westmore?" Darius joked.

No. Just probably high as a kite. He felt sweat gather on his lower back beneath his jersey as he forced himself steady. "You're not?" he retorted.

Darius laughed. "We will be." He checked the clock on the wall of the locker room. "In two hours and forty-six minutes. Do not let your brother push this game to over-time," he added.

"Don't sweat it. Ben's got a girlfriend now waiting for him at home. He's not allowed to stay out past eleven," Asher said, only half joking. Since winning the cup for the Avalanche that spring, Ben had visibly relaxed on the ice. Asher didn't doubt for a second that his brother's new, laid-back "there's more to life than hockey" attitude had to do with the lawyer he was crazy about, the one who'd almost destroyed his life earlier that year. How easily love made his brothers blind to reality.

Sticks before chicks used to be the bro code between the three brothers…one the other two had forgotten. Not Asher. After hockey, when he retired his number, then he'd think about a lifelong commitment. Right now, his focus and heart were in the game.

It wasn't like his future was a complete mystery. Whenever he allowed himself to think about it, there was always one constant: Emma. He just wished she was still competing, still focused on a professional sporting career. It had made it easy to put off talks of where they were going…but lately it seemed to be playing on her mind.

And he just needed her to wait.

Ten minutes later, as he skated out onto the ice, it didn't matter that he wore the opposing team's colors: the fans and his friends and family and neighbors were all on their feet. There was Emma cheering and smiling at him from the seat reserved for her behind the players' box. Immediately, the tension in his shoulders eased as he winked at her.

The reception whenever he played in Denver was always positive, but that evening the significance of the game was felt throughout the arena. He swallowed hard, raising a quick hand to acknowledge the love, feeding off the energy of their support, but knowing he needed to temper his own excited nerves to get through this game.

Nine hundred and ninety-nine games weren't enough.

His blades cut across the ice, and he felt the painkillers taking effect. The throbbing sensation in his knee subsided as he made several warm-up laps around the rink.

Still slightly off-balance, he shook his head, hoping to knock his equilibrium back into place.

Taking his spot in line with his team as the lights dimmed, he barely heard the words of the anthem, desperate to get this game started.

Desperate to get it over with.

The first period, he played six minutes and was relieved to have to sit out a two-minute penalty for the team's goalie. Less time on the ice, less chance of injury. He hated his new chickenshit mentality, but he was too close to a professional career goal to throw it away on overeager cockiness.

He'd spent years proving himself in the sport. They could cut him some slack if he played at less than 110 percent tonight.

Coming back for the second period, there was still no score, and the pacing of the play was more intense. The Devils coach could be heard shouting the same sentiments as the Avalanche's: *steal the damn puck, head up—pay fucking attention to the play.* The two teams were neck and neck for points in the league so far that season, and the Devils had a very real shot of stealing the Stanley Cup away from the Avalanche. Not that his brother's team was letting the trophy leave Colorado without a good fight.

Asher's legs felt heavy as he pushed through his second shift, and his mind was foggy. Skating through a haze, he climbed back over the boards as the lines changed, grateful for the break.

But when the Avalanche sent Ben out on a double shift, his coach gave him the nod. "Westmore, get back out there."

Shit. He'd been hoping for a few minutes to calm his thundering heart rate and clear his head. Most games, he loved facing off with Ben. He knew his brother's few weaknesses on the ice better than anyone, and it made for exciting hockey for fans to watch the two of them square off, but tonight, he lacked enthusiasm…and energy. Damn, he was feeling drained, zapped of the adrenaline-induced drive he usually thrived on.

But grabbing his stick, he was back on the ice in seconds, skating toward the puck. A Colorado right wing took a shot and he stole the biscuit, skating back toward the blue line with it. The ice beneath his skates felt far away, and he shifted his gaze to the sidelines, but the advertisements blurred in a colorful psychedelic pattern that made him blink furiously. He struggled to focus and shifted his weight as his balance swayed left.

The puck left his stick and he switched directions, moving on instinct more than anything else, following the player in burgundy and steel blue back toward his net. When the offensive player passed, he intercepted and skated along the back of the net with the puck, looking for someone to pass it off to. A defensive player who longed to play offense, he was usually eager to score any chance he had, but not tonight. Right now, he wanted nothing to do with the puck. He was a liability with it.

He glanced at the time clock, desperate to hear a line change. His shift had to be coming to an end, and as soon as his ass was on the bench, he was heading into the locker room.

Something wasn't right. Dizziness was making him nauseous, and he could hear his heart beating in his ears, felt it pounding in his chest.

He scanned the ice. Where the hell was Ericksen? Or Taylor? Or any other fucking teammate. He was going to black out, and there was no one to safely take this puck.

The only person he did see was his brother skating at full speed toward him, where Asher still lingered too close to the boards.

Fuck.

The hit took him clean off his feet, and the pain in his knee almost stole his consciousness. The arena lights blinded him from above as the ice below his body spun uncontrollably before his eyes shut.

The last thing he saw was his brother's cocky grin replaced with a look of concern.

Asshole took me out.

*   *   *

I'm going to kill Ben.

That was just one of the thoughts racing through Emma's enraged mind as she paced the Denver hospital waiting room after midnight. Five freaking minutes left in the second period and Ben pulls that shit on his brother?

The Westmores were the closest family she'd ever known, but sometimes she wondered about Ben. He was a nice guy beneath the cocky hockey god attitude, and she knew he loved his family, but his rivalry with Asher was intense, and it seemed almost too convenient that he'd chosen to mess with Asher's upcoming achievement. He knew as well as she did Asher wasn't playing at a hundred percent. They'd both noticed and commented on Ash's apparent injury several times over the last year. Ben couldn't possibly claim not to have known that a hit that hard could do more serious damage.

One period, several line changes, less than five game-time minutes, and a few days away from the biggest individual achievement of Asher's career, one they all knew he was desperately striving for, even risking his health to reach.

He'd been so close.

Damn Ben!

She forced a steadying breath as she glanced at him now across the waiting room. Her hands made fists at her sides, and she felt her temper rise to an unhealthy level.

She didn't need to yell at him. His mother and fiancée were already giving him an earful, and he looked wrecked. He was sitting with his head in his hands, his knees bouncing, worry etched across his forehead as the lips of both women continued to fly. Jackson and Abigail sat across from him, silent, but sending him their own suitably annoyed looks. He was lucky Becky wasn't there as well; having a baby at home and a husband overseas, she hadn't been at the game.

The collective sentiment among the group obviously wasn't lost on the oldest Westmore brother as he continued to hang his head in shame. Everyone thought he was an asshole tonight. Including himself.

Sympathy for him almost crept in, but then the doctor appeared, shaking his head, as he removed a pair of plastic examining gloves.

Emma hurried forward, then stopped. She wasn't technically family. She had no right to charge ahead first.

"What's going on? How is he?" Beverly asked, jumping up from her seat and approaching the doctor.

"Surgery. We have him scheduled for tomorrow morning, and then there will be six to ten weeks of recovery," Dr. Fredrick said.

Emma's stomach fell to the floor. Asher must be devastated. The urge to push past the doctor and go see him was overwhelming. One game away. She felt like punching something on his behalf. Preferably Ben.

"It's that bad?" Olivia asked, moving closer, obviously the only one who could find a voice to speak.

The doctor nodded.

"No…it can't be," Ben said in typical pro athlete denial. "He was complaining about his knee for months and was still playing. Doc, when you say six to ten weeks of recovery, you really mean like two, right?"

"This isn't jail. You don't get a reduced sentence for good behavior." Dr. Fredrick shook his head, implying how he felt about pro athletes and their stubbornness. "Ten weeks is what he needs to fully recover. Six weeks is being optimistic that he will push himself to get better as soon as he can. And yes, he admits to playing on the injury." He paused, glancing around at the waiting room, obviously making sure no reporters had made it past the triage desk before continuing. "I pulled his records, and he's been self-medicating…a lot."

Emma's eyes widened. "Like addicted to painkillers a lot?"

The doctor glanced at her. "Who are you?" he asked, not rude, just matter-of-fact.

Who *was* she? Not his girlfriend, not part of the family…Just a woman so stupidly in love with him that the wind had been knocked from her lungs when she'd seen him go down in a crumpled heap on the ice. A woman who'd seen the hit coming seconds before it happened and who'd felt the impact almost as hard. A woman who wanted to yell and scream or break down in that moment as she understood far too well the feeling of defeat her best friend had to be feeling in a hospital bed just down the hall. "A friend," she said quietly, knowing a friend would get zero information.

The doctor shrugged. "Hopefully not, or recovery will be that much harder." He turned his attention back to Beverly, obviously not willing to say more about the sensitive subject in the waiting room. "Anyway, he's resting and in one hell of a shitty mood, so I'd save your visits for tomorrow after surgery."

Even Beverly reluctantly agreed that was probably for the best. "Thank you, doctor," she said, then waited until the doctor disappeared down the hall before turning to Ben. She slapped his arm. Hard. "What did I tell you boys about roughhousing?"

*   *   *

Every time Asher closed his eyes, the replay of the hit made his pulse race in his veins. Lying in the hospital room bed, well past midnight, too medicated to feel anything but numb, he fought the slumber threatening to take over.

Surgery for a torn ACL in six hours, then six to ten weeks of recovery.

Four hours ago, only twenty-five minutes of hockey and another few days stood between him and the one-thousandth-game milestone. Now there was a three-hour procedure and months of therapy.

He blinked and jumped, his heart rate monitor beeping loudly next to the bed as a sensation of falling made him clutch the bedsheets.

He'd nodded off.

He forced his drooping eyelids open. He didn't want to sleep. He wanted to lie there, alone in the dark, empty, hollow room, where the only light was a street light streaming through the window, and try to force emotions to the surface. Anger, despair, disappointment—all or any of the things he knew he should be feeling—would hit him like a freight train once the sedative meds wore off.

But they wouldn't come. Morphine dripping through his IV prevented anything but drowsiness. *Comfortably numb* was the saying.

He found no comfort in it at all.

CHAPTER 5

❧

"When you're done feeling sorry for yourself, slap on a smile and come on down for breakfast." His mother's voice drifted up the stairs to his bedroom in the family home.

Awake for hours already, Asher's stomach did grumble with the need for food as the smell of bacon followed the sound of his mother's voice. But a smile wasn't happening, and he knew he wouldn't be fed until he could produce a better mood, so he stayed where he was.

The surgery had gone well, but his leg hurt more now than ever, and the painkillers they'd given him were doing jack shit—the result of his overuse before.

His reliance on the drugs had made him a patient not to be trusted, and the hospital had only signed off on him going home if he was released into his family's care. His mother, of course, was thrilled to assume the role of nurse and warden, but the worried, sidelong looks he'd received from her and Jackson on the way to Glenwood Falls had put him severely on edge, and he'd lashed out.

It was not exactly the best way to convince them all that he wasn't an addict.

Back at the house, he'd gone straight to his old bedroom and tried to focus his mind on getting through the next six to ten weeks. Nope. Not six to ten. Six tops. Hopefully not that long. He couldn't put his career on hold until the New Year. He hadn't gone ten weeks without playing hockey since he was five years old. He didn't know what it felt like not to lace up almost every day, not to feel the cool stadium air against his face and the smooth surface gliding beneath his feet. Hockey was a part of who he was, the biggest part—it defined him. Without it, he was already lost.

Sleep the night before was impossible. Getting comfortable with the thick bandages around his knee and brace on his leg was something he'd given up on around midnight, and the image of his brother charging at him with four minutes and thirty seconds left in the second period was on repeat in his mind.

Unlike the night before the surgery, his emotions were a whirlwind now, competing for top spot. Anger, disappointment, despair all circled around him into the early hours of morning, and he longed for the numbness he hadn't fully appreciated.

It was hockey. Shit happened. But the fact that it was Ben…His jaw clenched. Out of everyone, his brother knew how important that milestone meant to him. He also knew that he wasn't at full capacity, so why choose *that* game, *that* moment to deliver the hardest hit of his career?

The sound of Christmas music drifting up the stairs to his room took his mood for an even deeper plunge.

It was November 19.

Being home for the holidays was going to drive him insane.

Glenwood Falls did Christmas in a big way, and he used to love the festivities when he was a kid. But since moving away to live with another hockey family at sixteen, he'd learned to treat holidays and special occasions as just another day. It helped keep any loneliness or longing at bay. His career had come first since the day he'd been drafted, and things like sleigh rides and ice-carving contests had become distant memories. And now he'd be here, surrounded by the festivities, still unable to enjoy them all with his mood like a BB gun taking out each and every last joyous twinkling light.

Hammering outside his bedroom window made him jump.

"Shit!" His teeth clenched as pain shot through his leg from his ankle to his thigh. Sudden movements felt like bones snapping at the knee joint, resulting in radiating pain in the connective muscles and ligaments.

He shut his eyes tight, but it didn't block the noise or the pain. Rolling carefully, slowly to his side a second later, he saw Jackson's blue ski jacket pressed against a ladder outside the frosted window. A string of multicolored Christmas lights dangled past him.

Bang, bang, bang went the nail gun. *Bang, bang, bang* echoed in his throbbing brain. He needed painkillers, but his mother had them on lockdown. Under strict orders from the doctor, she was releasing them every four hours as directed on the bottle, and not a minute earlier.

May as well flush them down the toilet for all the good they were doing anyway.

Jackson's face appeared in the window, and he waved when he saw Asher staring at him. "Hey, you're awake," he yelled through the glass. His breath melted the thin ice on the outside pane. "Come hold the ladder!"

Gesturing with his middle finger, Asher rolled over, intending to show his family he could block out everything they wanted to throw at him. They could *fa-la-la* their hearts out, but he wouldn't be swayed into embracing the season and this new shitty situation. He'd stay in his room for the next few days if he had to, and as soon as his leg didn't feel like hell, he was on the next plane back to New Jersey. Back to his own apartment, where he could wallow in self-pity in peace. Fuck the doctor's orders—he didn't need a babysitter or pain meds. He'd man up and deal with this shit on his own, his way, without anyone telling him what to do or expecting him to act or feel a certain way.

Though he wondered if Emma might come along to play nurse. It was the first positive thought he'd had in two days. She was the only one who wouldn't make him crazy. She was the only one who would truly get what he was feeling.

Funny how now he finally understood how she'd been feeling four years ago when her own life had changed. Of course, his setback wasn't nearly as crippling as her accident on the ski slope.

Watching her fall, going at breakneck speed, had caused the blood to leave his body. He'd been frozen in fear and helplessness as the ski resort's medic crew had rushed to her side, where she'd lay motionless near the

stunt pipe, and carried her away on a stretcher. Every second until he'd seen her had been torturously slow, and
seeing her defeated, terrified tears in the hospital room
as the doctor told her the news—broken bones, torn ligaments, and no Olympics—had shattered him as well.

It was the first time in his career that he'd taken time
off, to be with her while she recovered. He hadn't even
thought twice about it, and that had terrified him as well.
She was the only person who could potentially make him
lose focus or change his priorities, and he wasn't ready to
do that yet.

It had been years, and still she was determined not to
return to snowboarding. As much as he wanted to believe
it was her injuries and fear keeping her off the slopes, he
was starting to think she'd really moved on.

And now his recovery was forcing an unwanted extended holiday of his own.

Bang, bang, bang went the god damn hammer…

We wish you a merry freaking Christmas came from
the blaring CD player…

Then…raised voices? Arguing downstairs.

Fuck my life!

Tossing the sheets back, he pushed himself up and
onto his feet, taking a second to steady himself. Then,
grabbing one of the crutches they'd given him in the hospital, he headed downstairs, careful not to fall and break
his neck. He hadn't needed crutches since he was twelve
and had broken his ankle in a skateboarding accident. Of
course, he'd had them every summer before that, so he
was pretty good at using them.

The front door was open and his mother stood on the
front step, motioning wildly. "The maple tree is the cut-

off line," she was saying. "We've had the same discussion every winter for three years."

"Right. *After* the maple tree, not before," another voice said.

Asher groaned. Mr. Callaway. Emma's father had moved in next door to the family home after his wife died, and the man and his mother only spoke when there was something to argue about. Three years of constant bickering. Thank God he lived in New Jersey, though he often heard about the arguments from his mother…then got the actual story from Emma.

"What's going on?" he grumbled as he poked his head outside, leaning his weight on the crutch and shivering as a snowy blast of wind drifted inside. His bare chest and stomach were immediately covered in goose bumps.

"He shoveled too much," his mother said, pointing to the very straight line where the snow started on their property just a little ways past the maple tree on the lawn.

"Too much?"

"Yes. It's my responsibility to do that section in front of the tree," his mother said, pointing to it. "Right to the fire hydrant on the…"

Asher turned and went back inside, closing the door to their argument. They were both ridiculous. He wished Emma could see that, instead of getting so worked up over their silly disagreements. Since her mother's death and her father moving in next door to Beverly, Emma had taken on the role of referee for all of their senseless bickering. He wondered when she'd realize this small-town life with the normal job, normal lifestyle wasn't for her and get her ass back to the slopes where she belonged. He knew she still wanted that. Even if she pretended she didn't.

Turning the music down, but not off completely, because he didn't want to be next on his mother's shit list, he went into the kitchen. A plate of food sat covered on the table. Bacon, eggs over easy, four slices of buttered homemade toast, and three sausage links had his mouth watering on sight. One perk of being home was his mother's cooking. He may be ready to die by the end of his six- to ten-week recovery in his hometown, but it wouldn't be from starving to death.

He set the crutch against the wall and sat awkwardly, pushing out the chair next to him to prop the leg up. This wasn't the first time he'd had a leg in a brace, but it was by far the worst. At thirty, his body seemed to be attempting to resist time and failing miserably. Even without the injury, in recent years he'd noticed his muscles seizing more following game nights, and it took more training and working out to maintain his endurance on the ice. He saw the newer, younger players move faster, sleeker, taking hits far better, and it only fueled him to try harder. But at some point, his body would win the battle of wills with his mind...Just not anytime soon.

Folding a piece of bacon in half he shoved it into his mouth as Abby entered the kitchen. "Hey, you're out of bed," she said, pleasantly.

He glanced at the clock. It wasn't even eight o'clock. Why were *they* all out of bed? "Morning," he grumbled, stabbing a piece of egg.

"How's the leg feeling?" she asked, pouring coffee into Jackson's travel mug. The Colorado Eagles logo was still visible but fading into the past, like Jackson's own hockey career.

"Peachy." Another piece of bacon followed the sour reply.

She sat on the edge of the chair that held his leg and touched the brace.

He shot her a look, but she didn't appear fazed. "Look, I know this setback must be tough, but you're with family, it's the holidays. We'll all help you get through this, and in a few months, you'll be back on the ice."

"Weeks. Not months. And I'm not staying for the holidays," he said, pushing the plate away. Could he eat in peace? Alone?

His brother's fiancée's eyes widened, then she frowned. "Why not?"

"Not feeling festive, I guess."

"Since when does that matter?" She looked ready to deliver an earful about how he needed family right now and how they all had one another's back.

He could do without the afternoon special. He didn't expect anyone to understand what he was going through, but if they could all just leave him alone, that would be fantastic. "Abby, look…"

"No, *you* look. What happened the other night was crap. Bad timing, probably even bad decision making on Ben's part…"

His jaw clenched at Ben's name.

And her perceptive eyes must have caught it. "Ah, so you're blaming Ben."

"Can we not talk?" He liked his brother's fiancée well enough, but she was too meddling and too glass-half-full, too much like his mother. And one of those right now was more than enough.

Abby stood, picking up Jackson's coffee. "Fine. Just

don't read the paper," she said, sliding it away as she left the kitchen.

As soon as she was gone, he struggled to reach for it and swore under his breath once he'd flipped to the sports section. The headlining news of the day was all about him.

WESTMORE OUT ONE GAME SHY OF MILESTONE.

One game shy of milestone.

* * *

"You got him a puppy?"

Was her sister losing her mind? Their father was sixty-five years old and having a hard enough time taking care of himself. Their mother had done everything for him over the years. Emma couldn't remember ever seeing her dad cook a meal or do a load of laundry. In the four years since her death, he'd quickly learned just how much her mother used to do, but he hadn't picked up the new domestic skills all that fast—in part due to the fact that Jess insisted they pick up right where their mother had left off.

But there was more to it. In recent years her father's mind didn't seem as sharp as it once was. Little things, like confusing them with their mother or forgetting where he lived the week before when he'd gone out for a walk, were becoming common. Emma had found him a block away, sitting on a bus shelter bench. She was worried about her father, and she didn't think more responsibility was the answer.

"He's all alone here, and I thought it would be nice for him," Jessica said, carrying the brown cardboard box from the Glenwood Falls Animal Rescue Center up the cleared path toward the house.

"A puppy is a lot of work. Couldn't you have gotten him a stray adult dog from the pound?" An animal that was big enough to fend for itself.

"This is better. Trust me," she said in her best younger-but-wiser-sister voice.

"Fine," Emma mumbled, knowing she'd be the one picking up dog poop from the snow with one of those mechanical grasping things next week. Her sister continued to baby their father, insisting they take turns checking in on him every few days, dropping off premade meals and throwing in a load of laundry, but lately it was Emma running double duty as Jess claimed to be extra busy with work.

Which reminded her...She glanced next door toward the Westmore home as she followed her sister up the steps. She hadn't seen Asher since she'd watched him crumple on the ice. Jackson and his mother had insisted on picking him up from the hospital in Denver the day before, and she hadn't felt it her place to step in. After all, she was just a friend. She sighed.

"What's wrong?" her sister asked, laying the box on the step to unlock the door.

"Nothing."

Dark, perceptive eyes stared at her beneath a pale pink knitted hat and blond fringed bangs. "That's right, Asher's in town."

Emma nodded, her expression hardening a little. "Which you know full well. Seriously, Jess—did you have to pounce while he was down?" She'd seen her sister's article in the *Glenwood Times* about Asher's untimely injury. She just hoped Asher hadn't seen it yet.

"It's my job to report news, Emma. As much as I think it's insane just how much people around here idolize those guys…" She rolled her eyes. "It was newsworthy."

"But did you have to make the comment that his career may be over? We both know that's not true." She wondered how much of her sister's article had come from her journalist side and not her anti-Asher personal side.

Jess shrugged. "Could be true. Yours ended after *your* injury."

Kick delivered to the gut. "It's different for Asher. It's just a torn ACL—he's only out for six weeks," she said, knowing she couldn't be completely honest and tell her sister that it could be longer or about the doctor's fear that he could be addicted to pain meds. She never knew when things with Jess were off the record. Probably never. She almost felt bad for her sister's husband. She wondered if he always felt like he had to be on. Jess definitely put people on edge.

The puppy yipped from inside the box. A tiny brown and white paw appeared in one of the side holes.

"Let's get him inside, so he can begin trashing the place." Which she'd have to clean up.

But Jess blocked the door when she tried to sidestep her.

"What?"

"Asher's not staying *here* for six weeks, right? I mean, he's going back to New Jersey…to his own home to recover, right?"

Emma shrugged. "I'm not sure how long he plans to stay here, but with the holidays coming, I would think he would be staying for a few weeks at least." Trying to keep the excitement from her voice about that prospect was nearly impossible. She was devastated for him over the thousandth-game milestone being delayed, but it was just a delay. And while the injury sucked, it was probably the only way Ash would slow down a little, take the needed time off to heal properly. She hadn't talked to him about it yet, but she hoped he'd let her be his therapist for his recovery. She knew him better than anyone else and would know when to push him and when not to. When to kiss him, when to not to...

"Oh God—you're hoping to help him recover," Jess said.

The puppy yipped again. Louder this time.

"I am a therapist, Jess. One of the few in Glenwood Falls. Can we go in now?" She shivered as a gust of blowing snow crossed her boots.

"But you're leaving."

She had been, but now she didn't know if accepting the offer for January enrollment was the right thing. Ash needed her, whether he knew it or not. And her disappointment in having to put her graduate school plans on hold for a while was overshadowed by the opportunity to use this unfortunate turn of events to connect with him. For the first time, he was here for longer than a few fleeting hours. He was laid up, without hockey to distract him, and well, it was getting close to Christmas—a magical time of year. This was the opportunity she'd been waiting for. Of course, she wouldn't spring her feelings on him just yet, but as he started feeling better...

"You *are* leaving, right?" Jess asked when she was silent.

"The puppy is probably freezing." Emma danced from one foot to the other, casting another glance toward

Asher's old bedroom window. Was he awake yet? Was he naked? Her cheeks flushed from more than the cold. She couldn't wait to check in on her father and then get over there to see him.

Unfortunately, her sister was relentless. "I thought we talked about this."

Oh, here we go. "No. You talked. I listened." Then chose to disregard everything her sister had to say on the subject. Just because Jess was married to Mr. Perfection and had three beautiful kids and a great job at the local newspaper didn't mean she had everything figured out.

Okay, maybe it did, but what Emma wanted out of life was different from what her sister thought was ideal.

That was okay.

"Well, listen harder," Jess said, turning to face her, still blocking the front door. "You can't make decisions based on Asher. In fact, you have to stop wasting time with him. Hooking up when you were both professional athletes only focused on having fun was fine."

"That's how you saw my career?" Had her sister forgotten how much time and dedication went into making the Olympic team? Fun had often been pushed aside for months at a time while she trained, focused on becoming the best. It still annoyed her that her father and sister had obviously never been able to see that.

"Don't get defensive. That part of your life is over now, so let's not argue about something irrelevant." Jess wrapped her pale pink cashmere scarf closer around her neck as she continued, "All I'm saying is your life is different now. Don't you want something real?"

What she had with Ash *was* real. It was also really

confusing and complicated and not something she wanted to discuss with her sister.

Again.

"At least tell me you've decided to complete the PhD therapy program…even if it's not this upcoming semester."

She nodded. "Yes, of course. I'm just not sure the timing will work now."

"Because of Asher," Jess said, shaking her head.

Their father appearing in the doorway saved Emma from answering. He was still in his robe and pajama pants, and Emma knew that he'd be in them all day unless he had a reason to leave the house.

"Hi, Dad," she said.

"Why are you two standing out here?" Delaney Callaway asked, shivering as the cold wind blew inside the house. "If you're discussing putting me in a home just because I fell asleep and burnt my macaroni and cheese last night…"

Unfortunately, the burnt dinner was just the most recent in a long line of reasons why Emma thought a retirement home might be the best thing for him. Unfortunately, the one and only time she'd mentioned it to Jess, her sister had immediately shut the conversation down.

Jess shot her a look now that said *This current conversation is not over* before picking up the puppy box and turning to their father. "Of course not. In fact, we bought you a surprise."

We? Oh no. Her sister was not dragging her into this disaster. Her dad would take one look at that puppy and see all the trouble it was going to be.

And then she'd probably get stuck with a new four-legged houseguest.

"A dog?" he asked as they entered. He opened the box and the little brown mixed-breed pup gave a happy yelp. He lifted him out of the box and held him out at arms' length. His thick eyebrows joined and his lips pursed. He turned the puppy from one side to the other, scrutinizing it as the little thing continued to yelp in defiance of being restrained.

A spirited terror, no doubt. Her sister would never settle for anything else. "It was Jess's idea," Emma said quickly as her father continued his evaluation. Any second now, that puppy would be placed back in the box and Emma would be looking for a new pet-friendly place to live.

But then her dad surprised her by smiling. "This is perfect."

"It is?"

Even Jess was surprised by the reaction. No doubt she'd had the perfect speech prepared to give about why the puppy was a good idea.

Their father grinned as he cuddled the thing to his chest. The puppy's tail wagged wildly and he licked her father's scruffy face. "Yes. The little Terror will drive Beverly Westmore nuts."

Apparently that was a good thing.

*   *   *

As Asher climbed out of the shower and wrapped a towel around his waist, he heard Emma's voice downstairs. It was the first sound that hadn't annoyed him all day.

Heading down the hall, he went into his bedroom and closed the door partway. Sitting on the edge of his bed, he slowly put his jeans on, then the leg brace. This thing was a pain in the ass. Six to ten weeks—no freaking way. He'd have this off in two and be back on the ice in four. That morning, upon waking, he'd been depressed and angry still, but now, after coaxing a handful of pain meds from his mother, he was just determined. Determined and hell-bent on recovering as quickly as possible.

That's where his best friend came in. He was prepared to pay her whatever she needed to clear her patient schedule for the next few weeks to whip him back in shape.

She tapped on the door once before entering. "Hey…oh sorry, didn't realize you weren't dressed." Her gaze landed on his bare chest and her cheeks turned an adorable shade of pink.

"You've seen me a lot more naked than this," he said, standing and reaching for a T-shirt.

"Not in your old bedroom in your mother's house," she hissed, checking the hall before moving farther into the room, but still lingering hesitantly near the door.

He laughed. "Why are you so afraid of my mother?"

"She sees and knows everything. And I think she suspects that we are…"

He waited for her to define what they were, but she didn't.

She shifted feet and subjects. "Anyway, heads up—my dad has a puppy."

"*That* will piss Mom off," he said, wrapping his belt around his waist.

Growing up, they'd all begged for a pet—a dog, especially—but the answer had always been no. His mother claimed it was because their older sister, Becky, was allergic, but Ash called bullshit on that. Becky smothered every four-legged creature she saw in kisses and cuddles. If she were allergic, she'd be dead by now. He knew the real reason was that Beverly knew the boys all had far too much on their plates already with hockey and other extracurricular activities. She would have been the one in charge of taking care of the dog. Four kids was enough.

"That was the point. Partly at least." Emma sat on the corner of his bed, and he realized it was the first time she'd been in his room.

The first time *any* girl had been in his old room. When they were growing up, the rules in the Westmore house were few, but his mother was very clear about one: no girls in their rooms. He'd always been too busy to care. Ben had had issues with it and had broken it once. But only once.

"Jess thinks it will be good for Dad to have company. She thinks he's lonely in the house by himself."

He couldn't hide his disdain at the mention of Jessica. Miss Know-It-All was always sticking her nose where it didn't belong. He knew she was the one to encourage Emma to take a longer break from snowboarding than necessary after the accident. It was her idea for Emma to pursue physical therapy and not return to the slopes at all. And he wouldn't lie and say he wasn't the least bit peeved at her article in the *Glenwood Times*. He would have hoped his own hometown's paper would have printed a more encouraging article at least. "Doesn't your sister have her own life to worry about?"

Emma's face clouded slightly. "No. Hers is perfect already." She stood and scanned his display case near the window. Hockey trophies and medals covered the dustless shelves. It amazed him how his mother still kept up the room. Unlike Ben, he hadn't wanted to take the trinkets of all of his former successes with him when he moved out. But unlike Ben, he only had a small bachelor apartment in New Jersey, not a multimillion-dollar home in the city. "It's so great that your mom keeps your room intact with all your accomplishments displayed like this," Emma said, picking up his Triple A division win trophy and reading the inscription.

"It's a little odd, actually. Feels like walking through a time warp." His mother had dismantled the other boys' rooms and Becky's room years ago.

Of course Abby had a theory. She believed it was because Asher was the baby of the family and had left home so young, and he was the only child living too far away to visit often. She might be right, and if it gave his mom comfort to keep the room like this, then that's all that mattered.

"Where are your things?" he asked. Emma had her share of trophies and medals, yet they weren't displayed in her apartment. And he couldn't remember ever seeing them in her family home…the few times he'd been inside.

"In a box in Dad's attic, I guess."

"Why?"

She shrugged. "They used to be displayed in a cabinet in our living room, but Mom died and the accident happened, then Dad moved. We packed everything up, and keeping them packed up just seemed like the right thing to do. Keep the past in the past," she said with a sigh, tucking her blond hair behind her ears.

Crossing the room slowly and awkwardly he wrapped an arm around her waist, drawing her back into him. "That sounded like Jessica speaking," he whispered against her ear. He suspected boxing up her incredibly impressive past had been her sister's idea.

He felt her stiffen in his arms. "Jess isn't always wrong," she said, her voice sounding strange—faraway, almost.

"She's not always right, either. Don't forget that," he said, kissing her cheek before releasing her. He may be an adult now, but he knew the same rules of the home applied. He was surprised his mother had even sent Emma upstairs to find him. Though he suspected she lurked nearby, ears perked. His hard-on couldn't go any further...not while he was in his old bedroom. "Now, how much do you make an hour?"

She raised one eyebrow as she turned to face him. "That's quite rude."

He laughed. "It was, actually. Sorry. I'm only asking because I'll double it for your undivided attention for the next few weeks."

"You're not ready for therapy yet. The doctor said it would be at least a week or ten days before the swelling..."

He shook his head. "For a normal person, maybe... not me."

"Right. I forgot you're superhuman." Her sarcastic remark made him grin.

"I'm an athlete. We recover faster. You know that." Which is why it irritated the shit out of him that she hadn't tried. Sure, her injuries had been so much worse than his, but the woman who gave up on her dream wasn't the one he'd met years before, and it killed him to see that spark in her going out. He brushed the thought away. She'd made her choice. He would make his. Which was: "I want to start therapy tomorrow and introduce mild exercise in two to three weeks. I read online that that's okay." He grabbed a sweater and, balancing on his crutch, righted it and slid it over his head.

She rolled her eyes. "Oh, well, if WebMD says it…"

He reached for his boots. "You'll have to help me with this part."

Emma sighed as she knelt on the floor to help with the boot. "Where are you going? You're supposed to keep the foot elevated."

"You're driving me to the pharmacy. I need painkillers that aren't on lockdown."

She shot him a look.

"Come on. Not you, too. You know me—I'm not addicted." He slid his foot into the other boot and tied it himself.

"That's not what I was thinking. I was wondering if you were paying me to be your therapist or your slave," she said as she stood.

Despite the pain in his knee and the awkwardness of the high school throwback room, he felt himself start to harden again. He moved toward her and grabbed her hips, pulling her into him. "That depends on what kind of slave we're talking about."

She shook her head, but her attempts to push against him were futile. Maybe there were a few pros to staying in Glenwood Falls during his recovery. "No. Not in your old room with your mom downstairs. You know the rules. No girls."

"I'm not a kid anymore," he said, brushing her short blond hair aside and kissing her neck. She always smelled so good. He loved that she never wore perfume. The flowery scents or powerful vanilla fragrances that so many women wore made him gag. Emma just held the faintest smell of soft, gently scented body wash or moisturizing cream—a light peppermint scent that tempted him.

"That won't stop your mother from grounding you." She shoved against his shoulders, but her hundred-pound frame didn't even budge him. "Ash, seriously…" The note of desperation in her voice only made him harder. He gripped her tiny waist, holding her against his body, running his hands along her sides, upward to graze the sides of her breasts. All the blood rushed to his crotch, and the house rules were the last thing on his mind.

"I'll be quick," he whispered against her ear, the thought of taking her right there on his bed making his pulse race. His hands dipped lower to cup her ass, lifting her slightly off the floor. He squeezed the tight, tiny rear end he could stare at for days, and suddenly his teasing her was torturing him.

"You're supposed to be in pain," she said, reaching around to remove his hands from her body.

"This will make me feel better." A lot better. Already he hardly noticed the throbbing leg. He wrapped his arms around her again quickly when she tried to step back and lowered his mouth toward hers.

"Ash. No," she said firmly, placing a hand over his lips to push his mouth away. "This is not happening. Not right now, anyway," she said, her gaze looking longingly at his mouth.

He sighed, releasing her. "Fine. For now."

When he heard the sound of raised voices coming from downstairs, his hard-on immediately vanished.

What now?

Emma's eyes widened. "Shit. I'm guessing your mom just met Terror."

CHAPTER 6

Going into her office the next morning, Emma flicked the light switch and shivered in the cool reception area as she waited for the lights to illuminate the large, open-concept space. The office had been closed on the weekend, so it was freezing. The old heaters in the two-story historic downtown building took forever to warm the upstairs therapy offices, so she left her coat on as she adjusted the thermostat.

As usual, she was the first one in, just after seven. She dumped Friday's leftover coffee down the sink and washed and refilled the pot with water. Setting it to brew, she went into her therapy room and opened her blinds. The sun shining in would help warm the five-hundred-square-foot space.

The old building on Main Street had been a brewery in the early 1900s. She loved the history of the building and its preserved original décor—maple hardwood floors, rounded archways, and an open concept design with crafted metal ceilings. She'd been thrilled when Glenwood Therapy and Rehabilitation had moved in above the medical walk-in clinic.

Of course, she enjoyed it much better once the heaters kicked in.

Rubbing her hands together for warmth, she sat at her desk and opened her Outlook calendar. In a town of five thousand residents, she was surprised that she'd been able to establish a fairly busy client schedule. Most were seniors with mobility issues or teenagers with random and—for some of them—frequent recovery from fractures and breaks. With Dr. Masey and herself being the only two therapists in the town, she was definitely kept busy.

Contrary to what Asher wanted to believe, he wouldn't be able to train all day every day. Overtherapy would only make the leg worse and wouldn't speed his recovery, but she scanned her schedule for the weeks ahead and added his name to as many of her open appointment spaces as possible.

She'd get to see him more in the next few weeks than she had in years. The thought made her heart race. At some point she would tell him how she felt about him. He was home. There were no distractions. She planned on spending as much time with him as she could, showing him how she felt, proving to him that there was more to what they had than just the amazing physical chemistry that still sizzled between them, despite years of sex. With his lips on her neck yesterday and his hands gripping her ass, it had taken all of her strength to push away.

Remembering the way his hard-on had pressed against her, she folded one leg over the other and tried to dull the immediate throbbing between her thighs. Damn, he better be right—he better heal quickly. She wasn't sure how long she could take him being there and not being able to have sex with him.

Her cell phone chimed with a new text message. Seeing Jessica's name on her screen, she groaned. It was seven a.m.—too early for Jess.

Dinner at my place Friday night next week.

Why did everything with her sister feel more like a command than an invite?

She didn't respond, tucking the phone into the top drawer as she stood and gathered that day's patient charts, grabbing a blank one to start on Asher. His first session would be that afternoon, and she was actually a little nervous about it. She knew what she was doing, and the average person with an average injury didn't make her doubt her abilities, but this was an NHL pro athlete looking to recover as quickly as possible. Not to mention the man she was in love with.

No pressure.

* * *

The sound of the front door opening just after eight that morning had Asher hiding a handful of aspirin as he awkwardly descended the stairs.

"Hey," Ben said as he entered, shutting the door behind him and shaking snow from his dark brown hair.

The sight of his brother made him instantly annoyed. He grunted a response as he continued his way to the kitchen. Then he swung back. "Why aren't you in Tampa?" The Avalanche were scheduled to play the

Lightning that evening, and Ben was supposed to have flown out already. Annoyed, angry, or irritated, Asher's hockey brain still took over.

"I'm taking a later flight," Ben said, removing his winter coat and tossing it on the back of a chair in the living room. "I wanted to check in on you. See how you were doing."

Only took four days.

"That was unnecessary." Asher went to the kitchen and opened the fridge for a bottle of water. Twisting off the lid, he tossed the four pills into his mouth and washed them down. They weren't doing shit for the pain, which seemed worse today than it had the day after surgery. No doubt the good hospital meds were out of his system now. He'd yet to find where his mother had stashed the T3s, so the over-the-counter junk he'd bought the day before was his only hope. He chugged another mouthful of water, draining the contents, and tossed the empty bottle into the blue recycle bin near the kitchen door.

"How's the leg feeling?" Ben asked behind him.

"Perfect."

"Ash, look, I wanted to say that that check the other night probably wasn't the best decision I've made on the ice." Ben shoved his hands into his jeans pocket and stared at the floor.

"Is that an apology?"

"I guess, yeah."

"You guess. Wow." Asher shook his head. Opening a cupboard, he grabbed a mug, purposely selecting one with a New Jersey Devils logo on it, his annoyance rising when he had to reach far in the back, past three Avalanche mugs, to find one.

And the family said they didn't play favorites. Bull-shit.

"Is that what you need, an apology? Because the brother I know would have delivered the exact same hit if the roles had been reversed," Ben said, reaching for his own team mug.

"So you're not apologizing?" Asher poured the weak coffee into his mug, then set the pot back.

Ben reached for it and filled his own. "I am sorry…" He seemed to choke on the word. "But only that I made your injury worse. I'm not sorry that I played the game the way I always do. The way *you* always do. One hundred and ten, man—remember?"

"One night. One game away, Ben. You couldn't let your competitiveness slide for one night?" He hobbled toward the fridge, but his brother got there first.

"Me? *I'm* competitive?" Opening it, Ben reached inside for the cream and handed it to him.

"Yes," he said, adding it to his coffee, making it extra creamy, draining every last drop from the carton.

Ben shot him a look. "And you're not?" He blocked his access to the sugar and only an unwillingness to damage his leg further prevented Asher from physically moving his brother out of his way.

"I wouldn't have done this to you," he said, abandoning the sugar.

"Bullshit. Westmores win. Plain and simple," Ben said, his voice rising, but he handed him the sugar bowl. "I'd have delivered that body shot to Mom if she'd been protecting the puck."

"Excuse me?" Beverly asked, entering the kitchen.

Ben's eyes widened, then he shrugged. "Well, I would

have." Then he pointed at Asher. "And so would you. You're just butt-hurt because you have to wait a little longer for the milestone game."

"And that makes you happy, doesn't it?" Asher said, advancing toward him.

Ben scoffed, putting his coffee cup down. "Fuck off, man. You know that wasn't my intention."

"Language, Ben," Beverly said, stepping between them.

"No?" Asher leaned around his mother to stare at his brother. "Admit it, you hate that I'm hitting this milestone so much earlier in my career than you did."

Ben ran a hand through his hair. "Every milestone you reach, I've beaten you to it, little brother. Blame the birthing order, not me."

"Hey, don't drag me into this." Beverly held out an arm to each man.

Asher's hands clenched at his sides and he forced a breath. Their mother would knock both of them out, if things came to blows. "Look, you're not here to apologize, so why don't you just get your ass on a flight to Tampa."

"Fine." Ben shrugged.

"Fine."

"Boys, it's the holidays. Ben, just apologize to your brother, and Asher, accept that it's part of the game, and let's move on," Beverly said, looking back and forth between them expectantly.

Ben remained silent, his gaze burning into his above their mother's head.

Asher leaned on his crutch and waited.

"I've got a flight to catch." Ben kissed their mother on the head and turned to leave.

Beverly shot Asher a look.

"What? You heard him, he's got a flight to catch." And good riddance to him.

*   *   *

Limping into the arena without his crutch an hour later, Asher stopped to sign hockey sticks for several Bantam players leaving their early morning practice.

"When do you think you'll be back on the ice?" the tallest kid asked.

"Hopefully before the end of the year," Ash said, handing him back his stick. He had his first appointment with Emma that afternoon, and he hoped she could work some miracles on his leg. His argument with Ben that morning only fueled his fire to get back on the ice quickly. The next game against the Avalanche was on New Year's Eve in Denver, and that was his new goal, his new focus for his recovery.

"Sorry about the milestone game," the other boy said, readjusting the oversize hockey bag on his shoulder. "It totally sucks."

Asher forced a nonchalant shrug. "I agree, but I'll have it in a few weeks." These kids looked up to him, and part of the role of being an inspiration was to fake a positive attitude, even when he wasn't feeling it. Injuries were part of the sport.

"Well, if you're feeling up to playing sooner than that, let us know. We could use an extra player on the lake. It's finally frozen enough to play on," he said.

"You got it," he said, though Asher could barely remember the last time he'd actually played a game of hockey on an outdoor lake or for fun. Thirteen maybe? No. Even then, the drive to beat his older brothers had always dulled the joy of the game.

Seeing his brother Jackson entering the coach's bench near the ice, he waved goodbye to the kids and hobbled over. "Hey."

"How'd you get here?" Jackson looked surprised to see him.

"Walked." After the confrontation with Ben, he'd needed the forty-minute walk in the bone-chilling cold to clear his head and cool him down.

"What part of 'stay off the leg'…never mind," Jackson said. "Feeling any better?"

"I will soon. Going to see Emma today," he said, taking a seat on the cold wooden bench. He stared out toward the ice as Jackson's Atom team players skated out and did several warm-up laps. They were all so eager to get out there. He remembered that feeling well, though his determined drive was always to prove he was the best. The youngest in the family, he'd had a lot to live up to. His gaze landed on the HOME OF THE WEST-MORE BROTHERS sign hanging on the wall across the arena. *Westmore Brothers.* Not Ben. Not him. Both of them.

Why did sharing the town's pride with Ben irk him so much? Did Ben feel that way? Would Asher feel differently if *he* was the one always a step ahead?

"Did you talk to Ben?" Jackson broke into his thoughts.

"You knew he was coming to see me?" He stretched his leg out in front of him, feeling the error of his ways for having taken the walk. The muscles around the knee joint seized and throbbed.

"He stopped by here first to borrow my balls or for validation or something, I'm not entirely sure," Jackson said, checking his player lineup. "So you two are good?"

"No."

He glanced at him. "Why not?"

"Because the asshole's non-apology went from condescending to insulting in less than a minute."

Jackson muttered something under his breath as he sat. "Look, Ben can be a jerk, and you know he doesn't like to admit he was wrong."

"Understatement." He didn't know how his brother's fiancée put up with him. Though, as an attorney, Olivia was probably the only one who could effectively argue with Ben.

"But you're just like him," Jackson said, opening his coach's bag and grabbing a stack of pylons.

"More insults?" Was everyone forgetting he was the victim here? He should have gone to see Emma early. She wasn't a fan of Ben. She'd be on his side.

"Not insults. Truth. And here's more. Without the rivalry with Ben, you wouldn't be where you are." Jackson waved his team in closer.

"Wow." His family really wasn't concerned with his ego.

"Ben has always forced you to work harder, dig deeper, push yourself further…"

"I work my ass off. I always have." His jaw tightened. So, now they were giving credit for *his* success to Ben as well?

"Relax, man," Jackson said, sensing his growing frustration. "I'm not saying you wouldn't have done well on your own, but competing with Ben has always been a driving force in you. The competition between you two has made you *both* great. You feed off of one another's energy. You push each other."

Asher sighed, unable to argue with the words.

"Just think about it—if Ben didn't raise the bar so high, what would you measure your success with?" Jackson stood and skated out onto the ice, calling his junior league team in to the center of the rink.

Asher's gaze landed on the community pride banner once more. That was the problem. He thought about Jackson's question more than he cared to admit. And he wasn't sure of the answer.

CHAPTER 7

~∞~

$\mathcal{E}$mma stood in her therapy office doorway, saying goodbye to her previous patient as Asher entered the clinic's reception area. The receptionist had gone for her afternoon break, so he didn't stop to check in, just continued on toward her.

"That guy only comes in here to see you, you do realize that, right?" Asher asked as she led the way into the therapy room. Asher's gaze—or rather, glare—was still focused on Marcus Fields—a single dad who'd just moved to town with his daughter the month before—as he left the office.

She rolled her eyes. "Right. It has nothing to do with his dislocated rotator cuff," Emma said, placing a new sheet on the therapy table. She'd learned a long time ago not to get her hopes up about Ash being jealous. He was merely afraid of another guy interrupting their arrangement. "Besides, I only cause him pain."

"Maybe he likes that."

She sighed. "And maybe you're just trying to prolong the inevitable. Pants off."

Asher laughed. "See, I bet he likes it when you're bossy, too," he said, bending down and removing the brace.

She took it from him and set it aside as Jane, the receptionist, knocked and entered.

"Emma, I'm heading out. The snow's getting bad out there and I need to pick up Aiden from…" She stopped when she noticed Asher unbuttoning his jeans. "I, uh… sorry, I didn't realize you had another patient today…Hi, Asher, I mean Mr. Westmore, Ash…"

Oh geez. The three of them had gone to school together since kindergarten. And it was just Ash. Watching women get blubbery around him definitely ignited Emma's jealousy fuse. It was annoying enough knowing women fell at Asher's feet wherever he went, seeing it made her gag.

He smiled. "Hey, Janie. How are you?"

The receptionist blushed. "Janie—wow, haven't been called that in forever…"

Okay, that was enough. "No problem, you can head out. I'll lock up," Emma said, sounding sharper than she'd intended. The beautiful redhead with the curves of Jessica Rabbit made her feel inadequate on the best of days. She really didn't need Ash comparing the two of them.

Emma would lose.

"Right. I'm leaving," Jane said. "Sorry to hear about the knee and the game. My son cried watching it on television," she told Ash quickly.

"Tell him I almost cried living it. But Emma's going to get me back on the ice in a couple of weeks…"

"*Six* to *ten*." A couple? He was insane.

"A *couple*, and then I'll make everyone proud," he said.

"Oh, you already do…You *and* Ben," Jane gushed.

Emma noticed him twitch and his smile fade slightly at the mention of Ben, and she wondered if he'd spoken to his brother yet. "You better go," she told Jane, glancing out the office window. Thick, blowing snow blocked her visibility of the buildings across the street. "It looks nasty out there."

Jane nodded. "Yes. Right." Her gaze returned to Ash and she hesitated. "Unless you need me to stick around…"

Nope. Definitely not. "I can lock up," she said.

"Okay. Thanks, and be careful leaving. A lot of snow has accumulated already."

"Thanks. Drive safe," Emma said as the receptionist shot a final dreamy look at Asher, before shutting the door.

"She's still as cute as ever," he said.

Cute? Ha! The woman could be a playboy model. "You do realize I'm in control of how much pain you experience here today, right?" she snapped.

He laughed as he slowly removed his jeans and sat on the table in his boxer briefs. "Don't be jealous, Em. You're still my favorite."

She ignored the comment. "You're supposed to wear shorts to therapy." Her mouth was slightly dry at the sight of him in his underwear. Sure, it was a sight she saw often, but never in her workplace.

"It's November, Em. Where would I get shorts? Besides, I didn't think you'd object." He winked at her.

And damn, she wished it had zero effect on her, but even after years of friendship, years of add-on benefits, the simple, playful gesture had her heart in a mess. It wasn't fair that she'd moved to this unrequited love territory and he was still the same old oblivious, fun-loving Ash.

She sighed, pushing the thoughts aside for fear of actually taking her frustration out on him during the session.

Professional. Just keep it professional. "Okay, let's get started." Lifting his leg, she helped him rotate to lie on the table. "I'm just going to slowly start adding movement to the knee joint…"

As Asher lay on his back, she carefully lifted the leg and slowly started to bend the knee. "Let me know when the pain gets to a five or six…" Normally, she'd start slower on a patient, but Ash was an athlete, an athlete in top physical shape other than his knee, and his body could handle an extra push. While she'd insisted moments before that his recovery would take the full six to ten weeks, she knew it would be faster.

He winced as the leg approached a ninety-degree angle and she eased back on the pressure slightly. The surgery was less than a week ago; she wouldn't push him too far too soon.

"It's okay. I can handle the pain," he said, gripping the white sheet at his sides.

She straightened the leg slowly and the tension eased from his face. "Okay, take a breath. We're going to bend farther this time," she said.

He closed his eyes as she folded the leg at the joint,

taking him slightly farther than the first time. Several more back-and-forths and beads of sweat appeared on Asher's forehead.

She hated seeing him in pain. Working on strangers was tough enough; rehabilitating him would be a whole new challenge. He wanted to get better quickly and he could handle anything she threw at him, but she questioned her ability to get him where he wanted to be as fast as he wanted to get there.

And no part of that had to do with the fact that a speedy recovery meant less time with him in Glenwood Falls. None.

After several more slow bends, she straightened the leg and laid it on the table. "I'm going to hook you up to a CPM," she said, moving away to get it.

The continuous passive motion device would move the damaged joint through a small, continuous range of motion that she would increase each session.

"Does it hurt?" Asher asked as she placed the device around his knee.

"It might, a little, but we'll start slow and work our way up to complete range of motion." She touched his arm. "You're not going to heal overnight, Ash." Patience in his recovery would be his biggest challenge. She knew exactly how it felt to want to heal faster, how frustrating it could be when the simplest actions required so much effort and had often resulted in pain in the first few months following her own injuries.

He nodded, touching her hand. "Just don't go easy on me, okay?"

She couldn't make any promises, so she ignored the question, turning her attention to the machine. Setting the range, she turned it on and watched his expression for signs of pain.

He took a deep breath, but relaxed against the pillow.

"It feels okay?"

"It feels like shit, but that's okay."

She sat in the chair next to the bed and jotted a few notes on his file, then, setting it aside, she said, "So, have you talked to Ben?"

His expression hardened slightly. "He stopped by this morning."

"I assume it wasn't the apology you were hoping for?"

He sighed. "Not exactly." He shifted on the table, and she saw his hands clench at his sides. From pain or the mention of Ben she wasn't sure.

She hesitated. "You know Ben's not my favorite person, right? But he was really a mess that night at the hospital. I don't think he knew how injured you were going into that game." No one had really known, because Ash had kept the extent of the injury to himself. Examining his knee now, she saw the markings of the multiple injection sites.

Obviously, *someone* had known. The team's doctor, most likely.

She knew it was useless to ask him who'd been providing the cortisone injections and meds.

He nodded. "The only person I have to blame is myself," he said, but she wasn't sure he fully believed it.

He rotated slightly and closed his eyes as his forehead wrinkled. She watched his chest rise and fall as he took several deep breaths. She remembered her own recovery—the intensity of the pain, the back and forth between determination to get better and a lack of will to push through.

Removing the machine a few minutes later, she gently touched the red, swollen joint. "How does this feel?" she asked, her fingers applying a little pressure as she massaged.

"A lot better than the machine," he said, releasing another slow, deep breath.

She increased the pressure as she continued to massage, careful to avoid the area around the surgery incision. Her fingers roamed over the bruises from the needle injections he'd been administering himself and she swallowed hard. "You should have told me how bad this was," she said.

"You would have convinced me to stop."

"Exactly." Her hands circled the knee joint, her fingers caressing the soft, tender flesh. She couldn't believe he'd done this to himself. "I know the timing sucked, but I'm actually glad this happened now. You don't know how much more damage you could have caused if you'd kept going." Or how bad of an addiction to the pain meds he could have developed. That thought haunted her most. Asher was a strong, capable man. His heavy reliance on the drugs was out of character for him, and she hated to think that if this hadn't happened, he might have spiraled into a situation that would be even harder to climb out of.

He reached out and touched her arm. "I'm not happy that this happened when it did, but you're right. I messed up," he said, sliding his fingers down her bare arm and back up again. Down and up. A shiver danced along her spine and her knees felt slightly unsteady. The simplest, slightest touch from him and she nearly came undone. The gentle way his rough fingers stroked her skin caused goose bumps to surface.

Suddenly, she was aware that they were completely alone. The office was quiet and empty. Everyone else had left for the day. The sound of the old baseboard radiator kicking in echoed in the hallway and the wind howling outside the old, thin-paned windows were the only noises shattering the silence of the building.

She swallowed hard and focused her attention on his knee. This was her office. Her place of work.

Professional. Keep it professional.

Taking her right hand, he slid it farther up his thigh, away from his knee. "You know, it kind of hurts here as well."

She shot him a look, but proceeded to massage the thick, sexy muscle just inches from his crotch.

Not professional. And just the thought was turning her on. *Not professional at all.*

What was she doing? He was her patient in that moment. Not her best friend with benefits that she was desperate to climb on top of. She tried to return her hand to the knee, but he held it at his thigh. "That feels good, and it's taking my mind off of the pain in my knee," he said, sliding her hand even higher.

She sighed. The point of therapy was to make him feel better, right?

No. Not like this!

Still, with her left hand, she continued to massage the knee, while she allowed him to move her right hand higher and higher, until she could feel his erection beneath it.

She swallowed hard as she slid the hand inside the underwear and around his cock, squeezing slightly. He moaned, closing his eyes as he rested his head back against the pillow. "See…much better," he said. "I can hardly feel the pain anymore."

She stroked the length of him slowly, rolling her thumb over the tip, as she continued her therapeutic massage on his knee. "I'm pretty sure I could lose my license for this," she said, feeling her body tingle with desire for him. Her own aching throb between her legs matched the pulsating throb she felt beneath her hand.

"Only if I file a complaint, which I almost certainly won't," Asher said, reaching down to cover her hand with his own, forcing her to apply more pressure and quicken the pace.

Damn, he was far too sexy to be injured and out of commission.

Her patience would be tested as well while he recovered.

She tightened her grip around him, abandoning the knee to move her other hand inside the underwear to cup his balls, applying pressure where she knew he liked it most.

He moaned, opening his eyes and reaching for her. Grabbing her shoulders, he dragged her body down toward him, then, cupping her face between his hands, he brought her mouth to his and kissed her.

She savored the taste of his lips, deepening the kiss as his breathing increased. Both hands working to make him harder, she parted his lips with her tongue and started an exploration of his mouth. She could feel her own ache grow and the need to have him inside of her intensified with each second that passed.

He ran his hands down her body, slipping them down the back of her pants, inside her underwear to cup her ass, his fingers digging into her flesh. Her breath caught as he separated her cheeks and slid his fingers along the folds of her pussy.

"Do you always get this wet while massaging your patients?" he murmured against her lips.

"Just the crazy hot ones," she teased, rubbing her thumb along the tip of his cock where pre-cum had moistened it.

Removing her hands from inside his underwear, she moved the fabric aside, freeing the hard erection. Then, her gaze locked with his, she lowered her mouth to it, flicking her tongue around the head.

Asher's grip tightened on her ass as he moaned.

She continued to lick and tease him, sliding her tongue all the way to the base of his cock and back up. Watching him watch her, the desire and need reflected in his icy blue eyes made her body surge with heat.

"Emma, I need to feel your mouth around me," he said.

"Like this?" she asked, before taking his full length into her mouth, allowing her lips and tongue to connect with every inch. Slowly, in and out. She grabbed the base of his cock and followed the up and down motion with her hand as she went.

He removed his hands from her pants and tangled his fingers in her hair as he guided her head over him. "Fuck, that feels so good. I can't feel my knee at all anymore," he said.

She paused, letting him slide slowly out of her mouth. "So, should I stop?"

"Hell, no…Actually, on second thought—yes." Sitting

up, he grabbed her by the waist and lifted her effortlessly to set her on top of him.

Her legs on either side, straddling him, she prayed the table could hold their combined weight. "I think maybe me being your therapist is not the best idea." Though the idea of anyone else touching him, healing him, didn't appeal. She wanted to be the one taking care of him. The one he needed.

"I think it's a perfect idea. You are very good at your job. I feel better already," he said, taking her hands and sliding them up under his shirt. "I want to feel those hands everywhere."

Oh God, he was impossibly sexy and impossible to say no to…But as she scanned their surroundings, remembering where they were, she put on the brakes. "I can't do this. This is my therapy room. We can't do this here."

"Why not? We've done it almost everywhere else." He removed the shirt and as always the sight of his body sent common sense packing. "Besides, you just had me in your mouth, this can't be any worse."

He had a point. But…"If my boss walked in, I would be fired." And more than likely have her practice license revoked…And she could say goodbye to the PhD program at the University of Florida. The one she'd yet to tell him about. That thought, too, made her hesitate.

"No one's here. Everyone's gone for the day. It's just you and me." He kissed her neck, sliding his hands under her shirt and around her back, unclasping her bra, making her forget her reservations. "Besides, if you got fired, I'd hire you to be my own personal therapist. Fly you everywhere with me."

Her breath caught at the thought. Be with him on the road while he traveled with the team. Be with him in New Jersey. Just be with him…They'd never ever talked about anything close, though in recent months, they had been talking about the future. But was he just messing with her again or would he actually like having her with him? And would it be just a therapist and sex partner he'd want, or something more? She had to get answers to that.

Soon.

Later.

Right now, his hands were moving upward over her ribs, higher to cover her breasts. He squeezed, massaging gently at first, then harder, his thumbs rolling over her hardened nipples.

Fuck, it felt so good. Almost worth kissing her career goodbye. Almost. "Asher, we have to stop…" What if someone came back? What if Jane forgot something or Dr. Masey had a late client booked? Though the weather outside suggested no one was venturing back to the clinic that day.

Asher ignored her anyway, lifting her shirt over her head and tossing it along with the bra onto the floor. His head fell into her chest, and he took a deep breath before letting his lips drag across her skin, over to her right breast. He licked her nipple, before taking it into his mouth to suck hard.

She gasped as his teeth brushed over it and he bit gently.

She clung to his shoulders, feeling his erection pressing into her leg.

Moving to the other nipple, he repeated the lick, suck,

and bite—harder this time. The mix of pleasure and pain sent shock waves through her core and she felt her panties get wetter between her legs.

"Take your pants off," he whispered against her ear.

She hesitated slightly. They were really going to do this? Here?

Could she really take that risk? She glanced toward the door…They'd hear someone coming in…

"I want you, Emma," Ash whispered, sliding his tongue along her neck.

Screw it.

Climbing off of him, she quickly removed her pants and underwear, then, naked, she climbed back onto the table to straddle him once more. "You're the worst-behaved patient I've ever had." She pressed her pelvis against his straining erection and rocked her hips back and forth, allowing her wet folds to moisten every inch of his cock.

"I'll settle for the best sex you've ever had," he said.

There was no competition there.

He gripped her waist, his hands holding her firmly in place as he lay back against the pillow. Then his fingers trailed the length of her thighs and back up over her stomach and ribs and breasts. The sensation caused ripples of pleasure to dance down her spine. The tickling torture of the soft touch making her body come alive.

One hand slid between her legs and his fingers found the wetness there. He grinned. "Okay, so I wasn't the only one turned on by that massage?" he asked, pushing his body up so his gaze met hers.

She swallowed hard as his fingers traveled along her folds and one slipped inside.

"So wet," he said, his voice hoarse as she slid her body up and down over his finger, clenching tight, needing to feel him fill her completely.

"Asher, I want you inside of me," she said, lowering her body to his. Now that she'd made up her mind to break every one of the rules of her code of ethics, she was desperate to have him.

He needed little prompting. Sliding the finger out, he immediately replaced it with his cock. The feel of him entering her nearly brought her over the edge and she pressed her mouth to his. She loved kissing him while he was inside of her. It made the physical connection between them feel that much stronger. Having sex with him was one of the best sensations she could ever wish for, but kissing him filled her heart with the foolish hope that maybe it was more than just sex. And she needed that foolish hope. She clung to it, just as she clung to him now as he pushed deeper into her body.

Moving faster, desperate for release, Emma rocked her hips back and forth, feeling him slide out all the way to the tip, then plunging back in before he could leave her completely.

He broke the kiss, burying his head into her shoulder as he grabbed her ass and pumped her harder. "Jesus, Emma…it gets better every time."

Closing her eyes, she arched her back to bring her breasts against his chest, rubbing her nipples against his pecs, her mouth watering over the intense sensations happening everywhere all at once.

"I'm coming." Asher's warning was right on time as she felt her own orgasm topple over the brink of pleasure, creating waves of release and a feeling so good, she tried to hold on as long as possible, before collapsing against him on the therapy table.

"Damn," he muttered, gripping her shoulders. His eyes rolled back slightly and she frowned.

"You okay?" she asked, immediately shifting her weight off of him, remembering her patient's leg.

He nodded, grabbing her hands and pulling her back into him. Kissing one palm, then the other, his gaze never leaving hers, he said, "You're the best drug I've ever found."

CHAPTER 8

∽◦∾

E leven days and six therapy sessions later, Asher was already making progress. Emma hadn't been lying when she said she was a fantastic therapist. She knew when to push him and when to ease off, and she was letting his body dictate the treatment. At the end of all of this, he would owe her.

She was locking the clinic door as his phone chimed with a text message from Becky.

His heart fell to the floor as he read, *Emergency. Get over here, quick!*

"What's wrong? You look like you saw a ghost," Emma said, turning to face him.

"Something's going on at Becky's house. Can you drive me there?"

"Of course," she said, as they hurried to her car.

Less than six minutes later, they pulled into his sister's cul-de-sac right behind Jackson's truck.

"Anyone know what this is about?" Jackson asked as he jumped out, just as Emma and Ash reached Becky's front door first.

Behind Jackson, Abby and her daughter, Dani, wore similar worried expressions.

"No. Just got the text and we got here as quick as we could." Asher tried the door handle, his heart still pounding in his chest.

The sound of loud music blaring reached them before Ben's minivan appeared in the otherwise quiet neighborhood. His brother had sold his flashy Hummer that summer, but he drove the minivan like it was the coolest vehicle on earth.

Asher knocked on the door and Jackson hit the doorbell twice.

"What the hell is going on?" Ben asked, sprinting across the driveway, as Olivia climbed out of the passenger side.

"Don't know," Emma told him.

Becky opened the door, a surprised expression on her face. Wearing a snowman apron covered in flour and Ugg boot-type slippers, she didn't look injured…just frazzled, like usual at this time of year. "You *all* came?" she asked in disbelief.

Jackson immediately moved her aside, rushing into the house as the others followed. "What's wrong? Is Taylor okay? The baby?" He looked around frantically.

Becky held up a hand as Emma and Abby approached, checking her for signs of injury. "I'm fine, everything's fine." She laughed. "Can't believe you're all here."

Asher held up his phone. "Emergency. Get over here."

He should have known this was a setup. He felt his heart rate finally returning to normal.

"We were on the highway heading back to Denver, I nearly went off the road taking the exit. What's going on, Becky?" Ben asked, his own annoyance evident as he, too, realized his sister's "emergency" probably wasn't as life-threatening as she'd made it sound.

Becky looked sheepish as she grinned. "Sorry to get all of you worked up. But, actually, it's probably good that you all did show…Follow me." She led the way to her kitchen.

Emma glanced at him and her expression was clear— they'd given up going back to her place where they could be naked for this?

"As soon as we find out what this is about, we are out of here," he whispered as he followed her down the hall. They hadn't had sex in a few days, and he was craving her.

"I offered to make the Christmas candy for Taylor's class," Becky told the group. "I followed the recipe, and Kim Marshall mentioned there was a lot of stirring involved…" She shook her head, motioning them all over to a large pot on the stove where the smell of peppermint escaped on the steam.

They all glanced inside and saw the hardening liquid, the metal spoon she'd been stirring with stuck, standing straight up in the thickening goo.

Unbelievable. They needed to give their sister a list of things that constituted an emergency text.

"My arm is dead and this shit's not even close to being ready," Becky said, yanking out the spoon and handing it to Jackson. "You're up first. Switch off once you lose circulation in your arm," she said.

Jackson shot her a look, but started stirring. "I can't believe this." He struggled to move the spoon in a circle. "This is like tar."

"Right?" Becky said.

"Well, since it was nothing even close to an emergency, we're going to go," Asher said.

"No way, if anyone's leaving, it's us." Ben blocked his exit from the kitchen. "We need to be back in Denver...I have a game to play."

His hands clenched at his sides as he met his taller brother's staredown. "Against Arizona, right? Didn't they beat you guys twice this season already?"

Ben's eyes narrowed slightly, but he grinned. "Yeah, our record against them is almost as bad as the Devils'. What was that last game score? Five to nothing, Coyotes win?"

Asher took a step closer, and Ben answered with a step closer of his own. His nose was almost touching Ben's chin.

"You two are not doing this in my kitchen," Becky said, moving between the two men. Turning to Ben, she motioned toward the door. "You're free to go."

"Yeah, let the real men handle this," Asher called after him.

Ben swung back, unzipping his winter coat. "Jackson, give me the spoon."

From the corner of his eye, he saw Emma and Olivia exchange looks.

"Ben, we need to go. You're playing in three hours," Olivia said.

"I'll make it," he said, rolling the sleeve of his sweater as he started to stir.

"Harder than it looks, right?" Jackson said, massaging his forearm.

Ben shook his head no, but within seconds, his pace slowed and beads of sweat were visible on his forehead.

"Give it to me," Asher said, taking the spoon next and pushing Ben aside. Damn, this shit was like tar. His arm burned from his shoulder to his wrist within minutes, but he refused to show any sign of discomfort. The strong scent of peppermint wafting from the pot made his eyes water. What the hell was this supposed to be, anyway? His sister said it was candy, but how this lump of goo was getting transformed into anything other than a big chunk of white and red rock, he didn't even want to know. He wiped his forehead against the sleeve of his sweater as he continued to stir. It must be eighty degrees in the kitchen.

"Want me to take over?" Jackson asked.

"Nope, I got this."

"You're injured, baby brother," Ben said.

"I said I got this," he said through clenched teeth. He could kill Becky. At that moment, he was supposed to be taking Emma's clothes off at her place, not competing in this macho man competition with his brothers.

The sound of the baby crying down the hall had the women making a beeline out of the kitchen. Becky, Olivia, Abby, Dani, and Emma disappeared, leaving the three brothers alone.

"Why do we fall for this still?" Asher asked, finally handing the spoon over to Jackson. Emma wasn't watching anymore. He grabbed a gingerbread cookie from a tray on the stove and bit the head off. One thing about his sister's place—there were always delicious homemade treats to eat. Though his lack of exercise these past two weeks was already taking its toll, he still put the rest of the cookie into his mouth.

"Because Neil's overseas until next month, and if there was a real emergency we'd never forgive ourselves for not being here," Jackson said, continuing to stir, his forearms straining. "Shit, this stuff keeps getting thicker."

Ben rolled his eyes. "Move aside," he said, taking the spoon. But his eyes widened as the thing almost refused to budge. "Jesus."

Hearing the women approach, Ben gripped the spoon with two hands and stirred as fast as his arms could go.

"How's it going?" Becky said, poking her head in.

"Nothing to it." Ben's words were said through clenched teeth.

Asher grinned. It was actually nice to watch his brother struggle at something for once.

The timer chimed and she grabbed a set of oven mitts.

"Is it done?" Ben asked, slightly out of breath.

"Not even close. It just needs to be removed from the heat. We'll take it into the living room. Grab a towel and those pot holders," she told Asher.

"When did we become your elves?" he muttered, but grabbed the stuff she asked for before following everyone into the living room.

Emma was holding his baby niece, Lily, and Abby and Olivia were *oohhh*-ing and *ahhh*-ing over the precious one-year-old.

Asher's mouth went dry. The one thing he and Em

almost never talked about was kids. When she'd been pursuing her pro athlete career, it hadn't even occurred to him that children were something she'd want for herself.

Now, things were different. She was living the small-town life, with a normal career—would she want a family of her own?

Watching her with his niece made his gut twist in a million different uncomfortable ways. Hockey and family didn't mix well. He'd had to learn from a young age how to separate the two and not allow himself to miss home when he was away. Hockey first…until he no longer could, *then* family.

That was *his* goal at least.

One Emma had once shared.

Did she now? Or was she looking for more out of her new life path? Things he wasn't sure he could give her yet?

She glanced his way and the look in her eyes was unreadable—giving him no answers at all.

"Don't kid yourself, man. She wants one of them, too," Jackson said, answering for her.

* * *

"What is that?" Beverly asked, squinting as she peered past him out the kitchen window later that evening.

"What is what?" Asher asked. He'd been barely listening to his mother, his mind still on the sight of Emma with Lily. It had confused him so much, he'd made up an excuse about needing to help his mother with something to avoid going back to her place. Getting a hard-on while thinking about the possibility that she might actually want children would have been near impossible. He'd needed some distance, but he felt guilty when she'd looked so disappointed.

"That blinding light coming from next door," she said, standing and going to the window.

He carefully bent and straightened his leg the way Emma insisted he do at home. He was probably going overboard with the exercises, but the more he worked the muscles surrounding the injury before they weakened completely, the less rebuilding it would take to get them back once his ACL healed. Also, working out was always his go-to when he needed to clear his head, and this was about as much physical exertion as he could do. He'd work on his upper body by lifting his old set of weights...as soon as he could feel his damn arms again.

"Oh, you've got to be kidding me. Has the man completely lost his mind?" his mother asked.

Asher pushed himself up to join her at the window. The snow had finally stopped, but now, after seven p.m., it looked dark and frigid outside. In contrast, Mr. Callaway's house was lit up like the Fourth of July with red, blue, and white string lights covering nearly every inch of the peaked roof. A construction crew truck was parked in front with a hand-painted sign on the side that read WE HANG CHRISTMAS LIGHTS.

The construction business in Glenwood Falls was slow in winter.

"It's festive," he said.

"It's tacky...and an eyesore...and..." His mother's voice trailed off as she grabbed her sweater from the back of her chair. "First that damn noisy adorable dog and now this…" she mumbled.

"Mom, where are you going?" he asked, attempting to block her escape from the kitchen.

She shot him a look that suggested even if he was *uninjured* she could take him.

He sighed and moved out of the way. Sitting in the chair, he quickly refastened his leg brace and followed his mother to the front door. He waved to Mike Miller, the owner of Miller Construction.

Still on the roof were two teenage boys…Mike's kids, he assumed.

"Hey, man. Tough break about the leg," Mike said.

"Yeah. Literally," he said, wrapping his arms around his body. The temperature drop at night was nut-numbing. "Was this your idea or his?" he asked, nodding toward Mr. Callaway, who stood on the snow-covered lawn in a pair of sweatpants and robe, pointing to the only section of roof not yet covered.

"His." Mike rolled his eyes. "But I get paid by the hour, so I don't care."

"I'll pay you double to stay and take them all down," Asher muttered, seeing his mother's arms flail as she reamed out Mr. Callaway.

Terror danced from one paw to the other on the snow around them.

The older man had obviously mastered the art of the smile and nod as he ignored Beverly's complaining and continued to instruct the kid about where he could locate the extra set of lights. His ability to tune out was the product of forty years of marriage, no doubt.

Mike shook his head. "As tempting as that offer is, it's

twenty degrees out here and my wife has already texted twice that dinner will not be waiting for me anymore if I'm late again."

Another blissfully wedded man.

Why did these guys torture themselves by putting a ring on it? He wasn't opposed to marriage, but if more couples focused on having the kind of relationship that he and Em had—great sex and great friendship—the world would be a much more peaceful place.

A memory of her expression when Lily giggled and kissed her cheek that afternoon made his stomach knot. Was his best friend developing a maternal instinct and a ticking biological clock now that her professional snow-boarding days were over?

Man, what he wouldn't give to get her back on the slopes.

"Boys, come on," Mike called to the kids on the roof, then turning to Mr. Callaway, he said, "We'll be back first thing in the morning. Can't do much more in the dark."

"Okay. I'll pick up more lights," Mr. Callaway said.

"Don't you dare," he heard his mother say, as the kids and their father hurried to their truck.

Asher groaned. The lights were an eyesore, but they were just lights. "Mom! It's freezing. Come back inside."

She ignored him.

"Mom! Leave the man alone, it's his house."

She shot him a look, and he shrugged and slipped back inside.

He tried.

But this arguing between his mother and Mr. Callaway

had to end, otherwise they were both in for a real shitty rest of their lives, bickering over every little thing. Three years was long enough.

He couldn't remember ever fighting with Emma. They had a live-and-let-live philosophy to life. She didn't expect anything from him. He expected nothing from her. Their friendship was based on trust and a mutual understanding that they had no claims to one another.

Would that always be the case?

Returning to the kitchen, he took advantage of Mr. Callaway's misfortune and hunted down his painkillers. His leg ached and his head wasn't much better. Finding the bottle hidden behind a box of puffed no-name-brand cereal, he shook several into his hand and two directly into his mouth. He swallowed them, put the others in his pocket, and tucked the bottle away just as his mother reentered.

"That man is impossible."

"He refuses to take some of the lights down?"

"Yep. And he insists he's not done," she grumbled, peering out the window at the house next door.

"Well, you tried, right?"

Her eyebrow rose. "Oh, I'm just getting started. If he wants a war, he'll get one."

"I doubt he wants a war. I think he's just trying to get into the spirit of the holidays."

She wasn't listening, she was already scheming. He could actually see wheels turning in her mind.

"Mom, what are you going to do?"

"Nothing crazy."

Yeah, right.

"Just a little extra holiday decorating of my own," she said, leaving the kitchen.

"Mom…" But she was gone.

Asher sighed as his cell phone rang on the kitchen table. Checking the caller ID, he saw his coach's New Jersey number. He'd been away from the league as well the last two weeks, dealing with a death in his family. "Hey, Coach Hamilton. How are you?"

"I'm good, Ash. Shitty time of year to be burying someone, but then, there really isn't a good time, is there?" he asked, ever unsentimental.

"No, sir."

"How's the knee?" Straight to business.

No doubt by now the team and the NHL officials had received all of his hospital records, so there was no point sugarcoating things. "Surgery went well, but the doctor says six to ten."

"Almost two weeks ago…You've started working with a therapist?"

"Yes, sir." Emma would send his coach updates as well throughout his progress. The league left nothing to chance, and they were all about full disclosure.

"And everything else is good…"

Shit. He knew what his coach was alluding to. "Yes, sir. There's no overreliance on meds."

"Good. Glad to hear it. An injury we can work through. An addiction is a little tougher to overcome, but we have resources…if you need anything, we're supporting you."

Ash swallowed hard. "I appreciate that. I assure you, the knee injury is the extent of my issues."

"Great, son. Take care of yourself. We need you back for that milestone game."

"Yes, sir." Disconnecting the call, Asher tossed the

phone onto the table. They needed him back for his milestone game. It didn't escape his notice that his coach hadn't said "rest of the season." His pending contract renegotiation suddenly weighed heavy on his mind. Even before the injury, his game had been off, and he'd been stressing over whether the team would re-sign him. Now he was really sweating. And he hated the feeling.

Pushing himself up, he went to the pantry, took the bottle of pills, and tossed them into the trash.

Mental toughness and determination would get him through this, not drugs.

* * *

"Did Christmas elves puke all over the neighborhood?" Emma asked, entering her father's house the next morning through the front door, which was wide open…for who knew how long? The chill inside suggested her dad had forgotten to close it a long time ago.

Terror ran up to greet her and immediately started licking the snow from her boots. She bent to pick him up and a wave of doggy breath hit her. "Whoa…you stink really bad for such a small thing," she said as her father appeared slowly behind him. "What are you feeding him?"

He shrugged. "Whatever I eat. Turns out he likes whiskey."

"Dad!"

"I'm kidding. He's eating whatever that mushed-up crap is from the cans of food your sister brought over."

Emma put the dog down and followed her dad into the kitchen, debating whether or not to mention the front door…Better to focus on the bigger issue. For now. "So, seriously, what's with the lights?" Between her father's house and Beverly's, there was enough electricity to light a small village.

"Just a little neighborly competition," he said, filling an old teakettle with water and setting it on the stove. He preferred the battered old kettle to any of the new electrical ones she and Jess had bought him over the years. At least the thing whistled when it was ready, and her father wasn't able to completely forget about it.

"Can't the two of you get along? Or at least ignore one another like normal neighbors do?" she asked, leaving on her coat and scarf. She'd stopped by to walk Terror before heading to work.

"She started it."

Right.

"Oh my God, Dad—the house looks amazing!" Jess's voice in the hallway made Emma sigh. Her sister hadn't mentioned she was stopping by that morning. Otherwise Emma would have let *her* walk Terror.

"See—Jess likes it," her dad said with a wink as she entered the kitchen.

As usual her sister was the picture of perfection, wearing knee-high tan boots over a pair of dark brown leggings and an off-white cashmere coat that hugged her body. With its military-style collar and big brown buttons down the front, the coat was obviously a result of a shopping spree in Denver.

Her sister had inherited their mother's fashion sense—all of it, apparently. If Emma's thermal coat and practical winter boots were any indication, she'd inherited her father's sense of practicality. She just didn't see the need of dressing up in the small town. There was no one here she was trying to impress. And the one person she'd ever been concerned with impressing was usually only seeing her head and shoulders through a Skype connection.

And he didn't care what she wore. In fact, his favorite outfit of hers was no outfit at all. Which never used to bother her before. But lately, the idea that the only thing he wanted from her was sex was plaguing her.

Which was ridiculous. They'd been best friends long before sex had worked its way into the equation, and besides, she wanted it just as much as he did.

Unfortunately, she also wanted so much more. And it had disappointed her on various levels when he'd called it an early night the evening before.

"Oh, was it your day to walk Terror?" Jess asked, interrupting her thoughts.

Emma wasn't fooled. Jess had an internal scheduling system that outranked any online calendar. "Yes. But since you're here, maybe I'll head to the office early."

"No. Wait!"

Emma stopped.

"Why don't we walk him together?" Jess suggested.

Emma sighed. Her sister obviously had an agenda that morning. "Okay." She grabbed the dog's leash and, after hooking it to the dog's sequined collar, followed her sister outside. Once out of earshot, she said, "When I got here the door was wide open."

Jess waved a hand. "He probably just forgot."

That was the problem. Their dad was forgetting a lot lately. Her sister didn't seem to get it. Or she was choosing to not get it.

"So, you're coming to dinner tonight, right?" she said, changing the subject. "You never actually answered my text."

Emma shivered in the early morning wind and zipped her coat higher around her neck. "Yes, I'll be there." She hadn't seen her nephews in weeks, and she needed to get the inside scoop on what they wanted for Christmas. If she asked Jess, she'd only insist that Emma buy an educational savings bond or some other gift that would launch her straight into lame-aunt territory. She wanted to get the boys something they really wanted. Preferably something messy and impractical…something Jess would never buy them.

"Great," her sister said a little too enthusiastically.

Yep, she definitely had an agenda. Emma suspected it had to do with the University of Florida. Her sister hadn't brought it up since the week before, and her silence was unusual and a little unnerving. But she was happy to delay the conversation until that evening.

"Turn left here. I didn't check the mail yesterday," Jess said as they reached the corner.

"You know, at some point Dad needs to learn where the mailbox is," Emma said. Her sister's babying of their father had to come to an end. Their dad needed to become more self-sufficient. Or they needed to discuss other options.

"Let's just get him through the holidays without Mom, and then we can start pushing him to be more independent."

Fourth holiday without their mother. While Emma suspected the holidays would always be tough, time did ease the pain. She wondered if maybe her sister was using their dad as an excuse to hold on to some of the hurt herself.

Reaching the mailbox, she shoved her hands into her pockets as she waited for her sister to retrieve the mail. Terror danced in slush puddles, getting the insanely expensive doggy boots Jess had bought him—insisting his paws were too fragile for snow and ice—covered in salt and dirt.

Heading back toward the house, she said, "And what are we going to do about the Christmas light situation?"

Jess shrugged. "Help Dad win his battle against Mrs. Westmore."

Emma laughed before realizing her sister was actually serious. "Come on, Jess. There are already six hundred lights on the roof. I counted seven plastic Santas throughout the property, and he's talking about adding a sleigh and reindeer to the roof…"

Her sister didn't seem fazed. "People like it. Dad said cars drove by last night and stopped to admire it."

Admire? Probably not.

"Look, he's happy. It's giving him something to focus on this season, instead of moping around, missing Mom."

"Okay, fine." She sighed as they reached the house. "Anyway, I have to go. I have a full schedule today." Though there was only one patient she was excited to see. As usual, Asher had booked himself as her last appointment of the day, and she wondered if he'd consider going to dinner at Jess's tonight. Probably not.

Her stomach turned slightly. Beverly and her father didn't get along. Asher and Jess had never warmed to one another. How could a real relationship ever fare well in that situation? Did it matter? She was willing to try to make one work…if she ever got the nerve to tell Ash that she wanted one. "Anyway, tell Dad I'll stop by to walk Terror tomorrow at lunch." How the dog had become her problem, she'd never know.

Jess wasn't listening, nor was she accepting the dog's leash. Her gaze was on an envelope in her hand and her eyes were glistening.

"Everything okay?" Emma asked, moving closer to see what it was.

Jess nodded. "It's a final reminder that there are a few tickets left for the University Hospital's holiday luncheon and fashion show in Denver on Sunday. Mom and I used to go every year."

Right, the tradition they'd started years ago. One Emma had never been around to participate in. Not that the high-end holiday event had been of any interest to her.

"The last few years Dad must have tossed the invites out before I could see them."

Huh. Maybe her father recognized who was having trouble moving on as well.

"Well, you should go again," Emma suggested. Her sister was friends with just about everyone under forty in town. No doubt she could organize a fun girls' day out and start a whole new tradition while still holding on to the memory of the times with their mother.

Jess shook her head. "It would be too hard without her." She wiped the corner of one eye.

"I'm sure she'd want you to continue going…remember the times you went together."

Jess sniffed as she shook her head. "I don't know…"

"Okay, well, it's your choice…"

"Would you go with me?" Jess surprised her by asking.

Crap. "Uh…" Fashion was not her thing, and if Jess's current state at just the sight of the invite was any indication, it wouldn't be a fun event. "Why don't you invite a bunch of girlfriends and book an entire table? Start a whole new tradition." Two hundred dollars a ticket for an event she really had no interest in attending didn't appeal to her, either.

"You don't want to go…that's fine." She slid the invite back into the envelope. "I'll let Dad know you'll be by tomorrow." She took Terror's leash and opened the front door.

Emma released a deep breath. As much of a pain in the ass as her sister was, she hated to see her upset and disappointed. Jess had been close to their mom, and if she needed this to help with the healing process, Emma could be there for her. "Okay, fine, I'll go."

Jess shook her head, sniffing once more as she removed Terror's boots and hung them to dry. "No, it's okay. It's not your thing. I won't insist on dragging you to something you'll hate."

Since when? Her sister had passive aggression down to a science. "Jess. I'll go," she said again, already regretting it.

"Really?"

Emma nodded.

Her sister stepped back outside and hugged her tight. "Thanks, Em. I'll make the reservation as soon as I get to work."

* * *

Had his mother been up all night?

With the aid of his crutch, Asher made his way down-stairs, where boxes of Christmas decorations—lights, inflatables, and an old wooden practically life-sized na-tivity set—sat at the bottom of the stairs. Half of this stuff he hadn't seen in years. She'd had it all this time still collecting dust in the attic? His mother didn't get rid of anything.

She opened the front door and stomped snow from her boots as she reached for another box of lights.

"How long have you been up?" he asked. He'd gone to bed sometime after midnight, and she'd been in the attic then.

"I haven't been to bed yet," she said, though she looked anything but tired. Obviously running on compet-itive holiday fuel and pumpkin spice lattes, judging from the smell coming from the kitchen. "You should come out and see what I have done so far."

"Maybe later," he said as his cell phone rang in his pocket.

"Great. I'll let you know when it's done so you can get the full effect," she said, heaving the box of lights outside.

"Can't wait," he mumbled, heading into the kitchen. At least she wasn't expecting him to help.

He glanced at the caller ID and contemplated letting it go to voice mail. "Hey, Juliette, what's up?" He answered the call on the last ring.

"You haven't RSVP'd to the award ceremony next weekend. I'm sure it was an oversight, but I need a con-firmation," the assistant to the head of NHL corporate events said, sounding as though there were a million other calls she needed to make and she just needed a quick response.

Unfortunately, he hadn't decided if he would attend. Had he played his milestone game the week before, he would have been recognized at the annual holiday event that celebrated achievements throughout the year. Now, attending would feel like rubbing salt in a wound, knowing the award had slipped through his fingers.

"Asher…"

"Yeah, I'm here. With the injury, I'm just not sure I'll be able to make it." He poured himself a cup of his mother's homemade pumpkin spice latte and took a sip, his eyes widening at the strong taste of amaretto. Spiked homemade pumpkin spice latte. He poured it down the sink—too early.

"You're recovering back in your hometown right? In Colorado?" Juliette asked.

"Yeah…"

"So there's no excuse. It's not like you'd have to fly from Jersey," she said. "I'm putting you down as confirmed."

She wasn't an easy woman to argue with. He shouldn't have answered the call. "Fine…sure." He didn't have to stay long. Just make a quick appearance and get out of there. With his contract renegotiation coming up, it was probably best that he at least show up.

"Great, because your brother is nominated for the NHL Man of the Year award."

Asher clenched his teeth. Yes, he knew all about it. Ben had been nominated for the prestigious award in September, due to his leading the Avalanche to a Stanley Cup win and the fundraising he'd done for his children's charities. It had been irritating enough to know that the year Asher was going to be honored with an award, Ben was potentially in the running for one as well. And now it was *only* Ben.

"And…we were hoping you'd present him the award," Juliette continued.

His grip tightened on the phone. Ben had won? Fuck Ben. Was there anything his brother wanted that he didn't get? Asher couldn't name a single, solitary thing.

And now his brother would be accepting an award and he wouldn't be.

"Asher—so you'll do it?"

Of course they assumed he would. They were brothers and co-athletes and professionals who could put aside grievances on the ice…He sighed. "Yes, yeah, I can do it. I'll be there."

"Plus one?"

Damn right. He wasn't doing this alone. "Yes, plus one."

"Great. Also, I need the addresses for your parents and siblings…and anyone else you think should be there to see Ben being honored. Their invites will remind them to keep the secret, and they will be held in a private dinner area until the award is presented."

She continued to ramble on with more details about his role, but he tuned out. After giving her the information she needed, he disconnected the call and tossed the phone onto the counter.

He ran a hand over his scruffy chin and then rested his palms against the counter, his head falling forward.

Unbelievable. Now, not only did he have to go to the event, knowing he wouldn't be honored that year, but he had to award another honor to the guy responsible?

Reaching for the coffee pot, he poured another cup of the spiked pumpkin spice latte.

* * *

Staring at her acceptance letter in her office, Emma sighed. Even at the best-case scenario and Ash fully recovered in four more weeks, that would bring them up to January 1. There was no way she could get everything organized and arranged to be in Florida to start the semester by the following week.

The disappointment she felt at the idea of turning down the early enrollment opportunity reconfirmed her desire to pursue her PhD. She wanted this. Giving up snowboarding might have been premature at the time and something that had been partially out of her control, but she'd gone out at the top of her career. Ultimately, the forced retirement had been a good thing.

If only there was a way to make this work.

But Ash needed her, and this was where she needed to be. September wasn't that far away, and it had been the original plan anyway, right?

Jane knocked on the therapy room door, and Emma folded the letter and tucked it away. "Is my eleven o'clock here already?" she asked, glancing at the time on her computer.

"No. I, uh…just wanted to ask you something."

Emma waited.

"Do you know if Asher is seeing anyone? He keeps his

personal life out of the media so well…" She gave a nervous laugh.

Emma's mouth went dry. The gorgeous redhead was interested in Ash? Of course she was. Who wasn't?

"Em?"

She blinked. "Oh, right…um, no. I mean, I don't think so. He doesn't always tell me everything," she said, hoping to dismiss the conversation with a wave. She stood. "I better get everything set up for my next appointment." She walked toward the table, but instead of leaving, Jane followed.

"But as far as you know, he's single?"

Emma's throat felt like it was closing off. "Yep." She ripped the old sheet from the table and balled it, tossing it into the hamper.

Jane released a deep breath. "Well, do you think he'd go for someone like me?"

Someone drop-dead gorgeous with a full figure and amazing hair? Probably. "I really don't know Asher's type…" She shrugged, opening a cabinet and taking out a clean sheet.

"Come on, Em…give me something. I'm a single mom who hasn't been on a date in almost three years."

Emma sighed. "He'd be crazy not to be interested in you," she said, flicking the sheet into the air and securing the corners as it fell.

Jane smiled. "Well, I know this will sound completely lame, but do you think you could set us up?"

"No!" The word slipped out before she could stop it.

Jane frowned. "Okay…"

Emma forced a laugh. "It's just, I think he'd respond better to you asking him yourself." This entire conversation was killing her. She wanted Asher, and she needed to do something about it before she lost him. His leg was starting to feel better, his mood was better…Soon, she'd tell him how she felt.

"Is he coming in to see you today?" Jane asked.

Emma turned to glance at her, hoping for a miracle and that the woman had forgotten to put on makeup that day…or at least was sporting a sloppy ponytail. Nope. Jane was as put-together and gorgeous as ever, pulling off a dark charcoal pencil skirt that accentuated her waist and full hips in a way Emma would have to get butt implants to pull off. "Yes. He is."

Jane smiled. "Okay. I'll do it. I'll ask him out."

"Fantastic. Hey, can you close the door behind you?" she asked as Jane headed toward it.

Once it shut, Emma slumped in her chair, glancing at her sensible black dress pants and pale blue polo shirt with the therapy logo in the corner.

Given the choice between her—his flat-chested, no-ass friend whom he'd seen naked a million times already—and the mysterious sex bomb, who would Ash choose?

*   *   *

His brother Jackson turned in to the therapy office parking lot. He had made the mistake of stopping by that morning, and immediately their mother had put him to work on the decorations for the yard. Driving Asher to his therapy session had been Jackson's escape. "Can't catch a break, huh?" he asked him.

Asher had spilled the beans about the Man of the Year Award, unable to keep the frustrating, ironic turn of events to himself. "Look, you know I'm happy for Ben...for everything he's achieved, but this is just a kick to the nuts." He didn't begrudge his brother the award; he just wished it were happening under different circumstances. Delivering a speech the following weekend that praised Ben for all of his accomplishments wouldn't be so damn hard if he wasn't still pissed at the guy.

"I don't envy you, man," Jackson said. "The only advice I can give you is to just think of him as Ben, your brother, and not Ben, your competition, for once."

"Probably the only way I'll be able to get through a speech honoring him," he agreed, knowing Jackson was right.

"And you know Mom's going to expect you two to put this fighting behind you before the holidays."

Asher reached for the door handle. "The only thing on her mind is beating Mr. Callaway for the tackiest house on the block."

Jackson's cell chimed. "Speak of the devil." He read the text. "I've been gone too long." He sighed. "Do you need a ride back?"

Asher climbed out of the car. "Nah. I'll hang out with Em tonight. I'm her last patient of the day," he said, suddenly feeling a little better and eager to get this appointment finished so they could go back to her place for the evening. Without the meds he was suffering a little more, and she was the only thing that eased his pain.

"All right, man. Take it easy," Jackson said as he closed the door.

Entering the clinic, he tugged the big, heavy old door closed behind him.

"Hey, Asher," Jane said, standing as she saw him.

"Hi, Jane. How are you?" he asked, approaching the desk and leaning over it. If he sat again, getting up would be a struggle.

"I'm great. Um, actually, I wanted to ask you…if maybe you wanted to grab a drink at the Grumpy Stump tonight?"

Caught slightly off guard, he laughed. "You don't hang out there, do you? You're far too pretty to be slobbered on by all the local single men."

She blushed. "Thanks. Actually, I don't hang out anywhere. Single-mom life doesn't lend itself to many dates. Not that this would be a date…"

Oh damn. He felt like an ass saying no to the woman who was obviously putting herself out there…but he wasn't interested in dating. In fact, since his last semi-permanent situation ended a while ago, he'd been enjoying how things were going with Emma. Right now, she was certainly the only one he wanted to be with. "I…uh…"

Emma appeared in the reception area, an unreadable expression on her face as she glanced back and forth between the two of them.

"Well, the thing is…I promised Emma I'd do that… thing with her tonight," he said, looking at her to save him.

Her expression softened slightly as she slowly nodded. "Right, you did promise me you would do that…thing tonight."

He smiled. Saved. Now he could resume getting excited about a full evening with her, naked, with no pressure of a flight out the next day or having to be anywhere at all. The idea excited him beyond the sexy thoughts coming to mind. He looked forward to just being with her, holding her, kissing her, and talking. He'd been so caught up in his own problems the last few weeks, he had no idea what was going on with her.

"Okay, yeah, no problem," Jane said, busying herself with the papers on her desk.

He felt like a jerk. He turned to Emma for help.

"Um…maybe Asher could get you and Aiden tickets for a game in Denver," she said.

Perfect. Right there—that's why he loved her so much. The thought made him pause. Love? Of course, love. She was his best friend.

"Right, Ash?" she said when he'd yet to confirm her suggestion.

"Oh, yeah…no problem."

Jane smiled. "Aiden would love that. Thank you," she said, sitting back down at her desk as the phone rang.

Emma's eyes held a hint of amusement as he followed her into her therapy room.

"What?" he asked.

She closed the door behind them and grinned. "You just turned down a hot date to suffer through dinner at my sister's house tonight."

Oh shit.

CHAPTER 9

◆

S o, you're sure it's okay that I come along?"

Emma nodded as they got out of her car in her sister's driveway.

Asher glanced toward the two-story home. Unlike most neighborhoods in Glenwood Falls, where the houses were all different shapes and sizes, with full backyards and lawns, these homes were mirror images of one another, with so little space between them that he suspected the neighbors could hear one another sneeze…among other things. He liked his privacy far too much. A home like this would make him claustrophobic. Even his bachelor pad in New Jersey was a top unit, corner suite, giving him the illusion of privacy at least. "Like 'she invited me' okay? Or 'she'll give you pointed looks all night' okay?" he asked, struggling to get out of her low-riding vehicle and reaching into the backseat for his crutch. Two weeks into therapy, he'd removed the brace, but still relied on the crutch for support.

"Does it matter?" she asked, a look of anxiety on her face.

She'd been slightly on edge since picking him up, but she was always that way whenever she was seeing her sister. "Yes."

"Fine. The second one."

"Emma!" he growled, contemplating getting back in the car, but it was too late.

The front door opened and the first of the many looks appeared, before Jess hid it behind a forced smile. "Asher, nice to see you."

"Oh, you don't mean that, Jess," he said with a wide, fake smile of his own as he leaned in to accept her awkward-as-shit hug. "But something smells delicious," he said as she closed the front door behind them.

"Hey, Jess," Emma said, handing her sister the expensive bottle of wine Jess had asked her to pick up on the way over.

Jess frowned, looking at the bottle. "This is a ninety-six. I wanted the ninety-seven."

"This was the only one they had," Emma said.

"Did you ask Cliff? He usually puts it away for me."

"No, I did not ask Cliff." Emma's voice was tight. He could almost see the knots of tension forming in her neck and shoulders. Being around her family always had this effect on her. Why she insisted on putting herself—and him—through it, he didn't know.

"Ninety-six, ninety-seven, either way, it's old grapes, right?" Asher said with a shrug.

"Its fine," Jess said—look number two, the one that

said, *You're even dumber than you look,* appearing on her thin features.

Body-wise, the two sisters couldn't be more different. Jess was tall and slightly curvy, not at all athletic-looking like Em, but their features were identical. The same small nose and brilliant brown eyes, framed by long blond lashes, full pouty lips, and high cheekbones. Their beauty came from their mother, who'd always been mistaken for a third sister.

Emma removed her coat and took his, hanging them on a hook near the door.

"Dinner's almost ready," Jess said, glancing through the side window near the door. "We're just waiting for one other guest."

"Is Dad coming?" Emma unwrapped her pale pink cashmere scarf from around her neck, but leaving it on, letting the ends dangle.

The way they framed the swell of her breasts, visible beneath her V-neck sweater, tempted him to reach out and grab the ends and pull her into him, but he knew they had to keep things PG around Jess.

"Jess, are we waiting for Dad? I could have picked him up," Emma said when Jess didn't answer.

Jess actually looked slightly nervous. "No, we're not waiting for Dad."

"Then who else is coming?" Emma asked.

A parade of kids interrupted the answer. "Aunt Emma!" the littlest one—whose name he could never remember—said as he ran to hug her.

"Hey, Brayden," she said, scooping him up.

Right. Brayden the brat, Emma had affectionately labeled this one. The youngest of her nephews, he was

the spirited troublemaker. She always had stories about
him whenever they Skyped. Hearing her talk about her
family and the kids left him feeling slightly home-
sick for his own nieces, and he usually changed the
subject.

"You three are supposed to be washing up for dinner,"
Jess said, but her voice and expression actually softened
at the sight of her kids.

Okay, but even Darth Vader had a soft side for his own
kid.

"We heard Aunt Em's car pull up…and then we saw
Asher," said the older boy…he was going to go with
Baxter…no, Baxton. Damn, Jess and all her B names.

Asher noticed he held a small hockey stick. "You want
me to sign that?"

The kid nodded eagerly.

"Sure, man. Got a pen?" he asked, taking the stick.

He handed him a marker. "It's Braxton," he said.

So close.

"Can you sign my puck?…I found it under the bleach-
ers at the arena, and your brother…I mean, Coach Westmore said I could keep it," the middle kid—Asher had no
clue whatsoever what his name was—said shyly.

"No problem," he said, grateful there was only
enough space for his spirally signature and no room to
personalize.

"Sorry, we don't get many visits from athletic royalty
around here," Jess said with an eye roll.

Right. Only her own sister. The way the family de-
valued Emma's Olympic career drove him crazy. There
was nothing like family to keep you humble. His own had
never given him a big head, but the Callaways took it to

a whole new level when it came to Emma. One he didn't like. To them, it was as if her career had been a joke…or something to be ashamed of. He didn't get it, and Em could say it didn't bother her, but he knew her better than that.

Though, to her credit, she refused to let any hurt or disappointment show as she continued to tickle the little boy in her arms.

His gut twisted at the sight of her with the kid, the same way it had the other day at his sister's house. She was wonderful with children, and she obviously adored the little rugrats…Did she want one someday?

Tearing his eyes from her, he turned back to the boys. "Hey, next time I play in Denver, I'll get you tickets to the game, okay?"

Jess was shaking her head behind the kids, but he ignored it.

"Your Aunt Emma can take you," he said.

"That would be so cool," Braxton said.

"Yeah, thanks, Ash," the other kid said, then blushed. "Can I call you Ash?…Aunt Em does…"

"Yes, you can call me Ash, and the tickets are my pleasure," he said, winking at Jess over their heads. According to Emma, Jess didn't allow the boys to play competitive sports, and the family rarely attended any sporting events. That was something else he didn't understand. Sports taught kids so much. It was a shame the boys weren't allowed to benefit from the camaraderie and life skills gained from the ice or on a field.

Jess sighed. "Okay. Now go wash up, you three."

Going into the kitchen, they found Trey up to his elbows in buttercream. Emma's brother-in-law was a closet pastry chef, according to Em. He hated his corporate law job and would quit to pursue his real passion—baking—but the legal career paid for the family's lifestyle.

Asher could never do a job he hated every day. Luckily his dream job also paid a ridiculous salary, but he knew even if he'd only made it as far as the East Coast Hockey League like Jackson had for years, he'd be happy making the five-figure salary, if it meant he got to play for a living.

"Hey, you two," the man greeted him, spreading the icing onto a three-layer chocolate cake.

Asher's stomach growled as the scents of cocoa and coffee and vanilla cream reached him. They could skip dinner and go straight to dessert. He needed to get back to his clean eating and workouts, and he would…after this cake.

"Trey, that looks amazing," Emma said, running her finger along the edge of the bowl to collect a generous dollop of vanilla-flavored buttercream.

Reaching out, Asher caught her hand before she could bring it to her mouth. Redirecting the buttercream, he licked her finger clean, immediately regretting the impulse as her wide-eyed gaze fell to her finger between his lips—regretting it only because they had an audience and he couldn't grab the bowl and frost her entire body with it to lick every inch clean.

Her gaze flew to his, and the hint of a smile on her lips revealed she'd had a similar thought.

"Good?"

"Heaven," he muttered, savoring the taste on his tongue as he released Emma's finger, but still held her gaze.

Trey broke the moment between them by handing Emma the spatula-like thing he was using to spread the icing. "Enjoy," he said, before turning away to put the cake in the fridge.

Oh, how Asher would like to.

* * *

There were so many other things Emma would rather be doing with Asher that evening, and the images that had just sprung to mind at the sight of him licking buttercream from her finger had leaped to top of the list.

Maybe Trey could whip her up a batch of buttercream to go.

Asher raised his eyebrows, and she had to resist the temptation to grab his hand and ditch out on dinner with her sister. She'd been so relieved when he'd turned down Jane's invitation.

She needed to talk to him. She couldn't continue to put off telling him how she felt for fear that he didn't feel the same. She could feel the same intensity from him, the same attraction, the mutual respect and admiration they shared through their friendship, which brought them closer on a deeper level. She couldn't go on like this, pretending she was okay with the idea of him dating anyone else. She wanted a commitment from him.

Hearing voices in the hallway, she turned on the stool as Jess approached the kitchen. Their mystery dinner guest had arrived.

"Make yourself comfortable. We'll just be a second. Can I get you a glass of wine?" Emma heard Jess say.

"Yes, red if you have it," a male voice answered.

Emma's chest tightened and she saw Asher's expression change to a look of slight annoyance as Jess entered the kitchen.

Emma stood and gave her sister a gentle shove back to the privacy of the hallway. "Who's that?" she whispered.

Jess looked squirmy.

"Jess! Tell me you did not invite a guy here to set me up. Ash is here," she hissed.

"I didn't invite Ash. You sprung him on me," Jess said. "Anyway, it's not a setup."

Emma released a breath. Thank God. Talk about awkward. "Oh, so who is it?"

"Don't be mad," Jess said, holding her shoulders.

"What did you do, Jess?" Her eyes widened and the momentary relief she'd felt dissipated.

"It's Sean Whitney."

Sean Whitney…Emma's eyes widened. "You invited the head of the University of Florida's physical therapy department?" Her heart raced. The man awaiting her response to his acceptance letter was in the living room?

"No. I invited an old friend," Jess said calmly.

"So this *was* a setup." Just a different kind. "I haven't responded to the offer of early enrollment yet, and I totally dodged the man's call earlier this week," she said, frantically pacing. Now she had to meet him in person for the first time…with Asher there? This was not the way she'd wanted to tell Ash about the program. She was going to strangle her sister.

Jess stopped Emma's pacing. "Look, it's nothing. He was going to be in Denver for the holidays, so I thought it was the perfect opportunity for you two to have a face-to-face, that's all. Relax."

Relax. Sure. Because her future decisions were suddenly demanding an answer. One she hadn't fully worked out yet…in front of the man she hadn't even told about the opportunity. Damn. She knew this anxiety was worse because she didn't know how Asher was going to react, and while her mind told her she shouldn't be even considering making decisions about her future based on him, her heart already was.

Her commitment to his recovery and the fact that she'd always put him first were the reasons she'd decided not to accept the early enrollment.

Asher and Trey came from the kitchen, and she resisted the urge to push Ash back in and give him the Cliffs Notes version of everything.

"Here's the wine," Trey said, handing the glass to Jess.

Her sister forced a smile and shot Emma a look suggesting she do the same. "Shall we?" she asked, leading the way to the living room.

Where the youngest head of anything stood.

Youngest and hottest.

Emma blinked.

Weren't university professors old? Didn't they wear sports jackets with patches on the elbows? Not this one. Dressed in a pair of charcoal dress pants and a red-and-black-checkered sweater over a body that made him look more like a *GQ* model than an educational professional, he certainly didn't fit the stereotype. His hair was long in the front and gelled to the side, and he wore a pair of dark-rimmed glasses that made him look sexy-smart. Suddenly Emma couldn't feel her tongue as she stared.

"Hey, man."

Emma jumped. It was Asher who'd spoken behind her, extending his hand to Dr. Whitney. Not her. Nope, she just continued to stare.

"Asher, this is an old friend of mine from college, Sean Whitney. He's the head of the physical therapy department at the University of Florida. Sean, this is Emma's *friend*." Jess stepped forward to do the introductions. "And you know Trey," Jess continued as the two men shook hands. "And this is my sister, Emma," she said, shoving her not so gently forward.

Emma swallowed hard, ignoring the questioning look on Asher's face as she accepted Sean's outstretched hand. "Hi. Nice to meet you."

His hand was firm, solid, yet soft and smooth. Desk job hands. So different than Ash's sports, calloused, rough hands...

"I feel like I know you already," Sean said.

Yep, the smile was definitely straight from the pages of *GQ*. "Yeah...um...yeah." What did she say to that? The comment felt far too personal, intimate almost, and awkward in the small living room, filled with too many people.

Filled with too much Asher and his questioning looks.

Asher cleared his throat and she realized she was still holding Sean's hand. She pulled back quickly, but not before catching another smile from the professor.

Shit. Where were her legs?

"Jess didn't mention we had a hockey superstar coming to dinner," Sean said, addressing Asher. His words were casual, but the steely gaze he offered was not.

Emma shifted uncomfortably as Asher nodded. "A Devils fan?" he asked.

"No. I'm not really into sports."

"There must be some impressive athletes at the University of Florida, though, right?"

"I can't say I've noticed. I prefer spending time with the graduate students in my program who are attending university for the education, not as a stepping stone or back-up plan to their professional sports career," he said.

Again his tone was far too casual for such a debate, revealing an underlying tension.

Emma removed her scarf from around her neck, suddenly feeling much too hot.

Asher raised his hands. "Hey, you can't peg me as one of those students. I skipped college hockey and went straight to the pros," he said.

Emma spun to look at him. Oh, come on. Where was that arrogance coming from? Manly pride? Really? She shot him a look, but he wasn't looking at her. His gaze was locked with Sean's.

"Now, you're benched though, right? A knee injury?" Sean asked. "Can't play forever, I guess."

Asher's jaw locked and Emma's eyes widened. Shit, this discussion had escalated quickly, and she wasn't completely sure why. She opened her mouth, desperate to say something to cool the tension, but she had nothing.

Trey thankfully saved her. "Dinner's ready. Why don't we head into the dining room?" he said, leading the way.

Good. Eating would prevent more talking.

She hurried after Trey, but Asher grabbed her elbow, forcing her to hang back as the group left the living room. "Head of physical therapy at the University of Florida?"

"Yeah, an old friend of Jess's." She shrugged. A young, sexy old friend of Jess's who wanted her to attend his graduate PhD program. Somehow the clarification she knew he was expecting refused to surface from her lips.

"So his profession is a coincidence?" Then his eyes narrowed. "Or a perfect match for you?"

Damn. "Look, I wanted to tell you, but you've had other things to worry about." She paused, studying her hands. "I was accepted into their PhD program."

He released a slow, deep breath. "I didn't know you'd applied." He looked hurt, and she wished she'd told him sooner.

"I didn't want to tell you until I got in." It was the truth, but it didn't make it any better. They were best friends. They told each other everything. They got advice from each other about big decisions—and this had been big. She knew why she hadn't asked him his opinion—he would have brought up her snowboarding career and tried once again to convince her to give it another shot before moving on with her new life path.

"And you did."

He didn't sound happy about it.

She nodded, suddenly wishing he could at least pretend to be supportive. Yes, she should have told him, but this was the exact reason she hadn't. She hadn't wanted to be influenced by him, knowing that he was still hoping she'd go back to the slopes.

"Guys. Dinner," Jess said, the look on her face when she poked her head around the corner clearly stating *Don't embarrass me in front of guests.*

Asher sent Emma a searching look, obviously not done with the conversation.

"We'll talk later, okay?" she said. Now was not the time. No, the time had been months ago…or two weeks ago when she'd gotten the early acceptance letter. She couldn't blame all of this on Jess.

Not waiting for a response, she followed her sister into the dining room.

* * *

Leave it to Jess to know how to turn a bad situation worse.

"I'm sorry, Ash, I hadn't expected you," she said as she pointed to where he'd be dining that evening.

The children's table.

It was about two feet off of the ground, with little blue stools around it. The adults' table had four place settings set, and conveniently enough the round table could only comfortably accommodate four. "No problem," he said casually as the kids took their spots at the table. At least he would have more stimulating conversation than with the dull, academic sweater, and at least Jess had been kind enough to give him an Avengers-themed plate.

"Jess, can't we all just move a little?" Emma asked.

"I can add the extra leaf to the table…" Trey said, earning him daggers from Jess, who obviously had zero intentions of making him feel like he was welcome there that evening. Her agenda was perfectly clear.

Any other man would probably have the sense to leave, but the idea of giving Jess any sort of satisfaction was absurd. Besides, he would rather be annoyed watching the interaction between Dr. Harvard and Emma than be imagining what was happening. "It's cool. I love the Avengers," he said, struggling to lower himself onto the tiny stool and praying it could support his weight.

"Ash, your leg won't be comfortable stretched out like

that. You can have my spot, I'll sit there with the boys," Emma said.

He gently shoved her toward her place at the table. "I'm great. You go ahead."

"Jess sucks," she muttered under her breath.

No argument there. "I'm an uninvited guest," he whispered, shooting her a look that said *You're not the innocent one this time.* He set his crutch against the wall next to him and moved his seat until his leg was positioned as comfortably as possible.

"This is awesome. I can't believe Asher Westmore is sitting at my table," Braxton said.

That made two of them.

"I thought Ben was your favorite player, Brax," Jess said with a smirk as she unfolded her grown-up cloth napkin and placed it on her lap.

"Jess!" Emma said, her cheeks reddening and her guilty look, full of sympathy, getting worse by the second.

Asher just smiled. "Ben is everyone's favorite. The kid knows greatness when he sees it."

Jess ignored him, instead uncovering the serving dishes on the table. "Help yourselves," she told the adults.

In the center of the kid's table, he removed the lid on the casserole dish to reveal a veggie lasagna. Jess's insistence that her kids share her vegetarian lifestyle was ludicrous. Kids needed meat.

He needed meat. Which of course was on the table.

Fantastic. He'd have to struggle to stand and reach past Dr. Genius to fill his own plate, unless he wanted to eat this gluten-free, meat-free, taste-free lasagna with the kids.

His appetite vanished.

"When can you play again?" Brayden asked.

"Hopefully in two or three weeks," he said, reaching for the orange juice on the table. "Juice, boys?"

They nodded. He poured.

"At least four weeks," Emma corrected from her spot next to Dr. GPA.

"Two to three," he repeated to the boys. "Your aunt is a wonderful therapist. She's whipping me back into shape." As soon as the words escaped him, he wished he could pull them back.

Dr. High IQ looked impressed, and Jess sent him a smile that said, *Perfect lead-in, thank you.*

Damn.

"That's right, Emma is a fantastic therapist. And I agree with Asher. In two to three weeks he will be good as new and on a plane right back to where he belongs… ahem…lives," Jess said, biting into a broccoli spear.

If Dr. Textbook observed the tension between them, he ignored it as he turned to Emma. "So, tell me about the kinds of injuries you're treating here in Glenwood Falls."

She took a sip of the ninety-six-not-ninety-seven wine and looked slightly uncomfortable as she answered. "Well, anything from shoulder dislocations to knee injuries like Ash's. I work with all ages, as the office here is small, only one part-time and two full-time therapists on staff."

"So you have your certification to work with children?"

She nodded.

"That's wonderful. Already ahead of the game." He cut into a thick piece of honey-glazed ham, and Asher's mouth watered. He reached for the spoon and dished the casserole onto his plate.

"What specialization were you thinking of pursuing?" Dr. Smartypants asked Emma.

"Sports injury I think would be most interesting. As a former athlete, I can understand that world a little better."

He nodded. "Yes. You had an impressive sports career of your own. I Googled you," he said.

Emma blushed. "Thank you."

"That was another lifetime ago," Jess said.

Asher shoveled a forkful of lasagna into his mouth and resisted the urge to gag. What the hell was this anyway?

"Sean's area of expertise is sports injuries as well, isn't that right?" Jess said.

The youngest-looking professor on the planet nodded, taking a second to swallow his food before saying, "Yes. You would be working directly with me should you choose to join our program."

"Of course she will," Jess said.

Emma shot her a look.

"Sorry, I'll stop talking for you," Jess said, not sounding the least bit sorry.

Asher couldn't decide if Jess's intent was to secure for Emma a place in the school or a place in this guy's bed. And he hated that it seemed Emma wasn't fighting against either one. In fact, as she asked Dr. Diploma questions about the program and the course load, she became more relaxed and confident, and within minutes, she seemed to have completely forgotten he was there.

The head of the department seemed more and more impressed, the more she talked.

And Asher felt more and more ill.

"It sounds like you're perfect for the program. We've offered you early enrollment. I think you and I could work well together, and you seem interested in pursuing the opportunity, so what's holding you back?" he asked, setting his fork aside and leaning on his elbows on the table.

Jess and Trey sat quietly, waiting for Emma's response.

Her gaze met Asher's, and he silently asked the same question. He hoped it was the fact that she hadn't completely walked away from her snowboarding career just yet. That some part of her still wanted that life. That this four-year break was just that, and she didn't want the everyday normal life that small town Glenwood Falls would have to offer. He almost needed that to be true. Otherwise, it meant he wasn't as clued in about his best friend as the other people sitting around the table, and that made his chest tighten.

While they'd never officially had the conversation, he'd assumed they were on the same page—sporting careers as long as they could ride it out, and then a future…together. But if hers was really over already, could she wait for him?

The look in her eyes didn't give him any comfort. His mouth went dry, and he took a sip of the orange juice, but the liquid felt stuck in his throat.

"I'm just not sure the timing will work," she said finally, her gaze still locked on his.

Timing? Because she was helping him recover? She was putting this opportunity on hold, not because she wasn't sure she wanted it, but because she was committed to helping him heal?

And yet he wasn't entirely sure he could put her first above his own career…not yet at least.

He broke the hold on their gazes and could sense her disappointment from across the dining room as she said, "But don't worry, Sean. This program is what I want."

Shit.

*   *   *

Neither of them spoke as Emma climbed behind the wheel later that evening, and the unusual tension between them in the car was unbearable, forcing her to roll down her window for a little air, despite the freezing temperatures.

She was suffocating on unsaid words and conflicting emotions.

Meeting Sean had been unexpected, but she couldn't deny that he'd definitely intrigued her more with his information about the program. But the entire evening, doubt had dampened her enthusiasm. Doubt over whether the early admission date was something she could pull off. Asher's recovery was her main priority right now. She wouldn't leave him while he still needed her.

Though he was healing faster than expected.

Pulling out of the driveway, she waited for Asher to speak first, to call her out on the Jess thing or to ask why she hadn't told him about the PhD program, but he was excruciatingly silent as he stared through the front window at the quickly accumulating snow.

A long silence fell between them as she drove out of the cul-de-sac. The sound of the windshield wipers swishing back and forth grew louder as the only noise.

Her hands tightened on the steering wheel and she cleared her throat. She had to say something.

"I'm sorry about the kids' table." Seemed the easiest place to start. "Jess is…Jess."

Asher nodded.

He was obviously pissed. "And I'm really sorry I didn't tell you about the program at the University of Florida. I just knew you'd have a very definite opinion, and honestly, I didn't want to hear it." The truth came out in a rush.

"Pull over," he said.

She glanced at him but he stared straight ahead. "What?"

"Pull the car over." He pointed to the side of the street and undid his seat belt as she slowed the vehicle.

Where was he going? Was he *that* upset that he was walking home? He couldn't walk that far in this weather on his leg. "Ash, don't."

But instead of getting out, he turned in the seat and reached for her.

She went willingly into his arms, breathing in the scent of his soft cologne, enjoying the feel of his arms around her as she released a sigh of relief. The evening had been awkward and tense and a little overwhelming with the feeling that she was on an impromptu interview she hadn't prepared for—all in front of the man she loved. Right now she just wanted to sink into him and stay there. Avoid making any big decisions. Avoid any arguments. Just be there. In his arms. The only place she ever truly felt like herself. "I would have told you." At least about the school. That part would have been easy in comparison to the other secret she was hiding.

There was so much more she needed to say. So much he should know.

He pulled back slightly and tucked her hair behind her ears. He cleared his throat, and his blue eyes looked troubled, like he was struggling with something. The only thing she'd ever seen Asher look conflicted about was hockey. And this new, serious, pensive expression that she knew had nothing to do with his career made her hold her breath as she waited.

And waited.

And waited.

He continued to shift his gaze from one of her eyes to the other, and his palms felt slightly damp against her cheeks.

"Ash?" she said finally when the sound of the wipers once again started echoing in her brain. He needed to say something. Anything.

He took a breath. "Okay, the thing is, I don't do relationships well."

Or at all, really. She nodded slowly. Where was he going with this? And did she want to know? Her own hands felt clammy as she stared at him, trying to read his mind.

"The only thing I've ever really placed any importance on was hockey."

Again, not breaking-news information.

"That is, besides you."

Her mouth gaped. She hadn't exactly expected that. Not even close. His words were slow to register, but her heart pounded in her chest.

"You are the only other thing in my life I need."

Mind. Blown. All coherent thoughts vanished.

"I mean, not need...just want...a lot...Okay, maybe

need. I'm not sure. I've never had to test that theory." He frowned, looking frustrated by the emotions he was revealing.

"Where are you going with this, Ash?" Her chest was about to explode if he didn't get to the point soon.

"What I'm saying is, I don't want to test that theory. I don't want you to not be here."

"In Glenwood Falls?" This was about Florida? He was worried about her moving?

"In my life," he said.

Oh.

He took another breath. "I want to go on a date with you," he said quickly, his hands sliding down her cheeks to cup the back of her head. His fingers tangled in her hair as his gaze searched hers.

A nervous laugh escaped her, easing the tension. Just slightly. "A date?"

"Yes. A real date. Not a hookup or all-night sex… Okay, maybe that, too. But this time, start with a date that we both acknowledge is a date and see if we—you and I—work together that way."

She hesitated, wondering where this was coming from. She suspected it had everything to do with Sean's blatant interest in her that evening. And she wasn't sure if Asher's asking out of jealousy or a sense of desperation was the way she wanted to accept this rare opportunity…

But she'd be an idiot to tell the man she loved she didn't want to date him, so she nodded. "Okay. We can go on a date."

CHAPTER 10

⋐∾⋑

$\mathcal{T}$he décor inside the Denver event center ballroom nearly took Emma's breath away. The annual fashion show and luncheon featured a Nutcracker theme, and unlike the overwhelming tackiness of the décor on her father's house, this event was so elegantly styled, her Grinch-like heart almost grew in size.

Live models, dressed as soldiers and ballerinas, stood posed on platforms, rotating and shifting positions every thirty seconds, the painted-on expressions on their porcelain-looking faces never faltering. Their movements were smooth and elegant as they changed from one stance to the next. Their costumes alone were breathtaking, and the vibrant colors and attention to detail were surprising. Never having attended the event before, Emma was impressed by the level of planning that had obviously gone into one of the University Hospital's biggest annual charity fundraisers.

"Last time I attended, the models were dressed like snow angels for the snow globe theme," Jess said excitedly, taking in their surroundings.

Emma was happy to see that her sister was in a good mood and not at all depressed as Emma thought she might be, attending that year without their mother.

It was the main reason she hadn't brought up the fiasco of Friday night's dinner. Yet. She would though. Jess wasn't off the hook for that.

Though it was harder to remain upset with her sister when Jess had unknowingly done Emma a favor. That evening two nights before had certainly gotten to Ash, made him start to sweat a little about losing her. It had obviously put the idea in his head that he could.

A real date, he'd said.

He'd invited her to the NHL award ceremony the following weekend. Not as his best friend, but as his date. It was a step in the right direction and had given her hope. She knew not to expect big gestures from Ash. Baby steps.

She smiled as she and Jess entered the main dining area for the event.

The catwalk in the center of the room had a castle backdrop, and the runway was covered with glistening white felt that looked like a winter wonderland. The walls were bathed in projected images of a toy shop, and it felt as though they really were stepping inside a kid's sugarplum dream. Around the runway were round tables of ten with numbers in the center.

"Every year gets better," Jess said, accepting two glasses of Champagne with cranberries floating in them from a waiter's tray and handing her one.

"I'll admit, it's a lot more impressive than I'd thought it would be."

Jess beamed, and suddenly Emma was glad she'd agreed to go. With her travel and training schedule over the years, the two hadn't gotten a chance to become close, like other siblings did. She'd left home to train in Breckenridge when Jess was twelve. And their vast differences in interests kept them from connecting…but maybe it was time they found something to connect on.

Maybe this yearly event could be a start. She felt a sharp pang in her chest as she thought of the previous events she'd never gotten to experience with their mom. And suddenly, *she* was the nostalgic mess for something she'd never even experienced.

"We're seated near the left side of the stage," Jess said, checking the table numbers. "This way."

Emma followed and smiled in greeting to the other ladies already sitting at the table. On her seat was a gift bag full of expensive items from the event's organizers and sponsors. The bag alone was worth the two-hundred-dollar ticket, which her sister had insisted on paying.

"Hi," Jess said, setting her purse down under the table and removing her winter coat. "I'm Jess, and this is my sister, Emma."

Introductions were made, and an event official approached the table with an envelope. "Hi, everyone. Here is your donation envelope. Feel free to slide in anything you'd like and pass it along. We'll draw names for the centerpieces from these envelopes once the fashion show is over."

"The centerpieces are donated from a local artist for

the event. Each year, I tried to win and I never did. Maybe this will be my year," Jess said.

The centerpiece was a beautiful tall statue of a ballerina and the Nutcracker soldier, missing one of his wooden legs. The soldier was holding the ballerina in one arm, and touching her face with his other hand, his tender gaze staring deep into hers. The dancer's right leg was lifted and her head was titled delicately to the side as she returned the lovestruck expression. Emma swallowed an unexpected lump in her throat. An injured hero and the woman who loved him. The sentiment struck her at her core as she saw herself and Asher in the beautifully sculpted art piece.

Next to her, Jess slid her tiny envelope of cash into the bigger envelope and handed it to her. "Could you pass it along?"

Emma hesitated, then opened her purse and removed a twenty-dollar bill, slid it inside her own tiny envelope, and wrote her name on the outside, ignoring Jess's look of surprise. "What? The money goes to charity, right?" In truth, she was shocked at how much she wanted to win that centerpiece. It was inspiring in the oddest of ways.

"Okay, we'll go with that," Jess said with a knowing look that made Emma shift her attention to the runway stage.

The fashion show started as the delicious three-course lunch was served by waiters who drifted through the room like ghosts, and Emma couldn't believe how much she was enjoying both. The chocolate raspberry mousse for dessert melted on her tongue, and she closed her eyes to savor the taste. She could admit when Jess was right, and she'd been right about how wonderful the event was.

Definitely the way to start the holiday season. Her festive mood had finally arrived, and she was certain they'd just started their own holiday tradition.

"Oh my God—that winter coat is gorgeous," Jess whispered excitedly next to her as a new song started and a single model appeared on the runway in a red wool coat that reached the floor, with a big fur-trimmed hood and brass buttons along the front. Jess jotted down the store name on her napkin and tucked it into her purse.

Guess they were making a trip to LaDeserie in downtown Denver after they left here.

But then the model removed the coat to reveal a dark green, strapless evening gown. Emma's eyes widened. It was beautiful. Floor length and form-fitting with the slightest flare at the bottom, it was breathtaking. Tiny flecks throughout the fabric caught in the overhead runway lights and created a shimmering, glistening effect.

"That dress would look amazing on you, dear," the older woman next to her whispered.

Emma shook her head. She hardly had the same lines and curvy figure as the model wearing it. She'd need two padded bras to pull off the cleavage pouring over the top and an extra three inches of height to accommodate the length…Could she walk in six-inch heels?

The broken ankle was tempting.

"I agree, Em," Jess said. "It's the perfect color for you and you're so tiny…It's too bad there isn't an event in Glenwood Falls you could wear it to."

Maybe not one in Glenwood Falls…She discreetly wrote the name of the store on her napkin as well and stashed it in her purse. Not buying it later that day with Jess might be a challenge, but she didn't want to ruin their day of bonding with talk of Asher. But that dress was suddenly the only thing she wanted to wear to the NHL award ceremony. For their date.

What would he think if he saw her in that dress? Would he finally see her in a different light?

As the last model left the runway, the event organizer took to the stage with their donation envelopes. "Okay, it's time to announce the winners of the centerpieces. Thank you to everyone who donated."

Emma sat straighter as the table numbers were called and a winner was announced. Her hands clenched in her lap as their table number was called. There were only ten of them at the table. Her chances weren't terrible…

"The winner for table forty-two is…Jessica Callaway," the announcer said, with a smile in their general direction.

"Yay!" Jess said, clapping her hands along with everyone else.

Disappointment filled Emma's chest, but she forced a smile. Great. Now she'd have to see the centerpiece at her sister's house. Each one was designed by the local artist exclusively for the event, so any hope of getting one for herself was nonexistent. She was happy her sister finally won, but it would be easier if the beautiful, hauntingly symbolic statuette that had her emotions raging were in someone else's home for the holidays.

They are just statues.

"Congrats, Jess."

Her sister reached forward to collect her prize, carefully picking up the wooden statuette and accepting the congratulations of the other ladies around the table. Then, sitting back down, she placed it in the oversized gift bag the organizers had provided and handed it to her.

Emma's mouth gaped.

"For coming with me today," Jess said, touching her hand.

"Oh no…You won it…" Her protests were half-hearted.

"I want you to have it." She collected her purse and coat and stood. "Now, let's get out of here and go get that winter coat for me and that stunning dress for you…so you can wear it for a man I totally think it's wasted on."

* * *

Not being able to pick Emma up for their first real date wasn't exactly getting the evening off to a fantastic start, but unfortunately Asher was in Denver already, getting briefed by the ceremony committee about tonight's events. Sixteen players were being honored that evening, and Ben's award was the last one.

So much for calling it an early evening to be alone with Emma. She would be driving into Denver later that day, and he couldn't wait to see her.

Though he was admittedly nervous as shit.

Since suggesting that they try a real relationship, he had only seen her at his daily hour-long therapy sessions, not wanting them to end up in bed together. Now that they were going to try dating, he figured they should cool it in the sheets. Though how he was justifying that idea to himself he didn't know.

He paced the back of the event hall, his speech in his hand. He'd written it in the car, on the way, while Jackson drove and his mother and Abby insisted on putting in their two cents on what he should say. No matter how many times he read it, it still sounded lame.

Not an easy task.

"Hey, Ash…you ready?" Juliette asked, coming up behind him. Wearing a headset and carrying a clipboard, she looked organized and in control, as always. "We're going to quickly run through the order of things to make sure everything goes smoothly at the ceremony."

"Yeah, I'm good to go." The speech would have to do. There was no time to write anything new, and he'd captured what he'd wanted to say, anyway. Following Jackson's advice, he was only thinking of Ben as a brother that evening. One he really was proud of.

He followed Juliette inside the hotel ballroom, and his heart rate increased at the sight of the setup. The three-thousand-square-foot space was decorated in black and silver with white rose centerpieces and thousands of white lights draped from the ceiling. A stage was set up in the front of the room, a big projection screen to play game highlights behind it. Several wine and dessert bars were ready to serve the VIP attendees, and soon Emma would be there. As his date. In a few hours he'd be standing up on the stage presenting his brother with an award, and that was the thing about the evening he was suddenly the least nervous about.

CHAPTER 11

❦

$\mathcal{E}$ mma took a deep breath and stole a glance at her re-
flection in the mirrored walls of the Ritz-Carlton
Hotel foyer as she abandoned her winter coat—a bor-
rowed formal coat of Jess's—at the coat check.

Oh God, what had she been thinking with the elaborate
gown? Sure, the event was formal, but her go-to sensible
stylish black pant suit blinged up with a pair of heels and
jewelry would have sufficed.

The glimmering emerald fabric clung to every curve
of her body, except where it flared slightly at the bottom,
making it possible to walk. She was relieved that Asher
hadn't picked her up, because if he'd laughed or made any
sort of discouraging face when he'd seen her, she'd have
changed into the practical, fade-into-the-background outfit she was famous for.

This night she didn't want to fade. She wanted to
shine. For one man only. She hoped the slight sparkle

dancing throughout the shimmering fabric might be enough to open his eyes a little. The jealousy he'd displayed at her sister's dinner party was definitely a start, and his wanting to take her on a real date had given her something to grasp onto.

As she approached the ballroom doors, her four-inch heels clicking against the tiles drowned out her thundering heartbeat. She opened her clutch and retrieved her driver's license. Ash had added her name to the guest list, but she still felt uncertain about arriving without him. "Hi, I'm Emma Callaway, a guest of Asher Westmore's," she told the woman holding a clipboard and wearing a headset, standing between two event security guards. She offered them a weak smile, but neither cracked the slightest of grins as they continued to stare straight ahead, the big, bulky bodies making sure no one crashed the party inside the ballroom.

The woman continued to flip through her will-call stack and frowned. "I'm not seeing your name here... Another name, perhaps?"

She only had one. "No. It should be under Emma Callaway." Her face turned a shade pinker as several other people lined up behind her. Great. She was going to be the crazy woman who thought she was Asher Westmore's date for the evening. The security guards looked ready to bounce her. "I'll have to text him," she muttered. Which meant she'd have to walk back across the hotel lobby to the coat check. The clutch hadn't been big enough to store her iPhone, and against her better judgment, she'd abandoned the strapless padded bra at the last minute and gone braless, so there had been nowhere else to put the phone.

"I'm sorry," the woman said. "I can't let anyone in unless their name is on the list."

"I understand. Excuse me," Emma said, turning and moving past the next couple in line.

"Emma, wait," she heard behind her and turned gratefully.

"She's with me," Asher said, appearing at the door. But when his gaze took her in, his jaw dropped. "I think," he muttered, not taking his eyes from her as he handed the woman with the clipboard her ticket from inside his suit jacket.

Her cheeks flamed, and she couldn't decide if his open-mouthed stare was a good thing or a bad thing. Heat crept across her bare chest and shoulders, and her mouth was dry as she stepped closer to the door, praying she didn't wipe out on the heels.

His eyes still glued to hers, Ash moved toward her. Taking her arm, he led her inside.

Pulling her to a private corner of the ballroom, he held her at arms' length and shook his head. "Wow. What…where…Wow."

She smiled. "Thank you," she said, feeling her confidence returning. "You look pretty wow yourself."

Dressed in a dark charcoal suit that stretched across his chest and shoulders, a dark green dress shirt, and black tie, it looked like they'd coordinated their outfits. His hair was combed to one side and gelled back away from his face, and he'd shaved. She couldn't remember the last time he didn't have at least a little scruff, and while she loved his facial hair, he looked absolutely gorgeous clean-shaven. The smell of his soft yet manly cologne filled her senses as he pulled her closer, and she wished they were completely alone that evening, instead of surrounded by a bunch of NHL bigwigs and their families.

His resolution to not see her outside his therapy appointments had been frustrating, to say the least. Touching him during the sessions, watching the reaction her touch had on him, and thinking about the amazing sex they'd had in that very room only a few weeks before had driven her crazy. But nothing she'd tried had worked—not the sensual way she'd massaged his leg, not the way she'd whispered in his ear—he was adamant about taking a step back and taking things slower. While she appreciated the effort he was making to show her that it was no longer just about sex, she wanted him. Craved him. Especially when he looked so smoking hot and smelled so wonderful. She snuggled closer, enjoying the feeling of being near him. All day she'd been nervous as hell, but here with him now, she felt the tension ease away, replaced with an intense desire to be even closer.

"Do you have a hot date after this or something?" he whispered against her ear as he wrapped his arms around her waist, holding her tight.

His warm breath against her exposed neck made her shiver with anticipation and excitement to be there with him. Together. With him. But she shrugged casually. "You never know where the night could lead." She pressed her body closer, her hands sliding up over his pecs, then higher to encircle his neck.

His gaze dropped lower to the view of her cleavage visible above the fabric of the dress, and his expression was pure longing when his eyes lifted back to hers. "Yes, I do," he said, reluctantly releasing her, but keeping one arm around her. His hand firm on her waist, as he led the way toward his reserved VIP table at the front near the stage. "Your place. That dress better be easy to slip out of."

* * *

He couldn't stop looking at Emma. No matter how hard he stared, he couldn't quite believe that the amazingly beautiful woman sitting next to him was his jeans-loving, casual best friend…girlfriend? Had they moved into that territory yet? God, as breathtaking as she looked tonight, he suddenly wanted her to be much more than that.

Funny how he could know someone so long, love them, even, and then like lightning a realization could hit. The jealousy he'd experienced the week before combined with the irresistible urge to announce to everyone in the room right now that she was with him, that she was his, was overwhelming.

Seeing her standing outside the ballroom in that dress had nearly knocked him on his ass. The way the fabric clung to her sexy, athletic yet feminine build had him practically drooling, and the way her short blond hair was slicked back made her cheekbones look even more pronounced, and elongated her slim, delicious-looking neck.

He couldn't wait to mess her up.

Watching her laugh now as the general manager of the Devils flirted with her, his heart pounded in his chest. He'd asked her here to help put him at ease over the speech and Ben and being around his fellow athletes after the injury, the way she normally did, but she was having the complete opposite effect.

His palms were damp, his mouth felt like sandpaper,

and a pool of sweat gathered at his lower back beneath his suit jacket. She was gorgeous, she was smart, and she was funny. She was the one person in the world he always knew he could count on and the only one he wanted to be with.

"You didn't mention your girl was a former Olympic athlete," Coach Hamilton said next to him.

She hadn't exactly been *his girl* until tonight.

Though he knew deep down she'd always been his girl. Man, he'd been so blind…or maybe he just hadn't wanted to see, hadn't been ready to acknowledge what she really meant to him. There was no denying it now.

His gaze locked with hers as he nodded. "Yes. She was—*is*—an amazing snowboarder."

Across from him, he could hear his GM praising her as well. He'd always known his best friend was universally known and admired for her talent, but he'd never had the privilege of watching her bask in the compliments as she was now.

She was beaming as she talked about her time on the slopes and the opportunity of being in the Olympics. And everyone around the table was taken by her enthusiasm and passion.

"So, I assume you two will be heading to Breckenridge next weekend?" his coach said.

Asher paused. Right. The snowboarding Winter Tour competition was next weekend in Breckenridge. Only a short drive from Glenwood Falls. Could he convince Emma to go? "Yeah, maybe we will," he said.

Asher sat back and drank his beer as he thought about it. Would she go? Not to compete, but just to watch the competitions. She'd avoided the slopes and attending the events for the last three winters. He hadn't pushed, knowing it was probably too painful at first to watch, not being able to compete. But it had been four years...

All eyes at the table were on her. She had his coach, GM, and several other players and their dates mesmerized as she spoke.

And Asher's emotions whirled into an even bigger tornado. She was planning on going to Florida and moving on with her new future. But right now, talking about her past, her real passion was lighting her up like the Christmas lights decorating the room.

Was she as ready to put her past career behind her as she claimed?

The glimmer of excitement in her eyes and her flushed cheeks as she recounted the training leading up to the Olympics made him think otherwise. Breckenridge might be the way to find out.

She glanced his way. "Sorry, I'm talking too much," she said as she sipped her wine.

He shook his head. "Not at all," he said. No. Now she was finally talking. He leaned closer, torturing himself with the scent of peppermint coming from her bare skin and whispered, "You have a captive audience."

He was certainly captured.

CHAPTER 12

❧

*A*sher paced near the back of the stage, hidden by a red velvet curtain. Onstage they were announcing the award for GM of the Year, and next would be Man of the Year. He could see Ben sitting with Olivia at a table with several of his teammates, but he'd yet to talk to him. His stomach was in knots. They hadn't really spoken since their argument, and now he had to acknowledge him onstage, in front of everyone who was anyone in the NHL, along with their family, who was waiting until Ben took the stage to appear.

Glancing toward his own table, his gaze fell on Emma, and his heart pounded even more. He couldn't wait to get the hell out of there. He had so much he wanted to do with her, and removing that sexy-as-hell dress was the beginning...but only the beginning. The urge to move forward with a relationship caught him completely off guard, and he had no idea what that really entailed, but he was excited.

Maybe the injury hadn't been as untimely as he'd thought. Being unable to play hockey was making him realize that there was more to life than his sport. The last few weeks had put things into perspective a whole hell of a lot quicker than he'd expected. Putting off a life with Emma until he was done with hockey had once been the only thing he could see. Now, things were shining in a different light.

He wanted both. Needed both. He just had no idea how to have both.

"Next, we will be presenting the NHL Man of the Year award, an award that recognizes a player who demonstrates great sportsmanship on the ice and off, contributing and giving back to their community…And we think this year's recipient embodies the true spirit of this award." The presenter's voice broke into his thoughts. "His work with the local children's hospital and his latest teaming with the burn victims unit at the Denver Burn Institute has made this player's personal charity contribution exceed any of the athletes in this year's category. He donates not only his money, but also his time, making appearances throughout the year, offering support and hope, and enriching the lives of others."

Asher swallowed hard and wiped his sweaty palms on his pants. Ben was all of those things, if not also an arrogant pain in his ass their entire lives. He sighed as the presenter continued.

"Here tonight, along with his family, is Asher Westmore to present the award to his brother. Ben Westmore, congratulations on being this year's NHL Man of the Year."

The crowd was on its feet, and a chorus of applause rang through the ballroom as Asher limped slightly to the podium. "Thank you," he said, taking the award in one hand and the mic in the other. "Maybe I'll just keep this one," he said, gaining some laughs as Ben climbed the steps to the stage.

His gaze met his brother's and he saw a look of surprise and apprehension flicker across his face.

He grinned and Ben's shoulders relaxed as he leaned in to hug him. "Congrats, bro."

"Thanks for being here, man," Ben whispered then pulled back to mess up his hair.

Right. Onstage he was being schooled by his bigger, better brother. In front of his family, his teammates, coach, industry bigwigs…and the woman he was in love with.

But for that evening, he was okay with it.

Ben grinned as he accepted the award.

"I want to congratulate my brother on this achievement," Asher started and the crowd sat. A silence fell over the room and all eyes were on him. The heat of the lights on the stage made him sweat even more as he unfolded his prepared speech with shaky hands.

He saw his mother, Jackson, and Abby now seated in the formerly empty seats at the table near the stage, and his confidence faltered slightly, so he looked at Emma. "Growing up with one of hockey's greatest heroes wasn't easy…Hell, it's still not easy," he said, glancing down at his feet and taking a steadying breath.

The spotlight was on him, and he was nervous as shit.

Next to him, his brother looked cool, calm, and relaxed. Ben reveled in the attention. Asher didn't.

But this was his brother's night. This was about Ben. For no one else would he be standing up there tonight.

"Hockey was like religion in the Westmore house. It was the only thing that we collectively agreed was the one thing that mattered. When Jackson started getting serious about playing, Ben and I quickly realized we couldn't let him have all the fun. Then the competitive spirit between the three of us came alive. We played, we practiced, we played some more. We pushed one another, and we supported one another."

His mother winked at him through her tears and again his gaze returned to Emma.

His rock.

He glanced at his paper before continuing. "Ben's accomplishments throughout his entire career, not just this year, are why he is awarded this honor tonight. His athletic ability is second to none, and his determination to succeed knows no bounds." He gestured to his leg, and a ripple of laughter went through the crowd.

"Sorry about that," Ben muttered behind him.

The first real, sincere apology—though Asher no longer needed one. "My brother is everything this award encompasses." He paused. A memory returning, he folded the speech, no longer needing it. "I remember as kids—I might have been five or six—playing on the frozen lake behind our house as long as daylight would let us and being so exhausted on the walk home hours later. The muscles in my legs would be aching and my feet would be sore from the skates and Ben here…" He stopped, the memory wrapping around him so vividly he could once again feel the chill in the air and the tired achiness of his young muscles as they'd trudge home through the snow after dark.

"Ben would take my gear and say 'hop on,' and I'd jump onto his back and he'd carry my tired ass the rest of the way."

Ben cleared his throat next to him, and Asher didn't dare glance at him. His older brother getting emotional would be the end of him. He avoided the women at the family table as well. And also Emma, knowing his feelings for her might prevent him from holding back his emotions.

He locked his gaze on the waiters, ready to serve dessert in the back of the room as he continued. "That was Ben. He was always looking out for me…looking out for all of us, and he still has that altruistic, giving spirit. No amount of fame or money or awards like this one has changed my brother. He's still looking out for those who need him, and I'm proud of what he has achieved." Swallowing hard, he finally turned to Ben again and extended a hand. "Congratulations, Ben. You deserve this."

Ben pulled him in for another hug, then wiped his eye as he pulled away. "Can't believe you remember that."

"You don't forget kindness, Ben." He tapped his shoulder and stepped away as Ben took the mic. Heading down the stairs, his heart felt lighter as he rejoined Emma at their table.

"That was nice," she whispered, tucking a tissue in her hand, her eyes still glistening.

He took her hand under the table. "This is Ben's night…until we get to your place, then I'm getting my reward for being a good brother." With his free hand, he ran a trail along her thigh, feeling the soft fabric and the curves of her legs beneath. Sexy, muscular legs that he wanted to have around him all night. A week without her had been a dumb idea. He felt himself harden as she leaned closer and whispered in his ear.

"How long do we have to stay?"

His grip on her thigh tightened. The delicious smell of her skin made him want to ditch out on the rest of the evening immediately. "As soon as Ben stops talking, we are out of here."

* * *

The idea of a date after their shared history had seemed silly at first, but as Emma opened her apartment door and led the way inside, the butterflies in her stomach and the slight intoxicating dizziness she felt had nothing to do with the Champagne she'd consumed.

The evening had been magical. The event itself had reminded her of what it was like to be a part of the pro athlete world. Watching some of hockey's greatest players being recognized for their accomplishments gave a nostalgia for events and nights like these of her own.

She'd been surprised that the people at their table had even known who she was, yet they'd been so flattering about her past career.

It had been wonderful to be seen in that light again. And yet, as she talked about her past, she realized further that while she'd loved her career on the slopes, she was okay with it being over. She'd always have those memories, those accomplishments, those stories, and now she was ready to achieve new ones.

And being there with Ash, on full display on his arm as his date—not a friend, not a casual acquaintance, but his date—in front of his family, his teammates, and the paparazzi had been the first step in that direction.

Her usually reserved, private best friend hadn't cared who'd seen them together, and that had made her feel like the luckiest woman in the room.

Asher followed her inside and locked the door, and his arms went immediately to her waist, drawing her closer to unbutton her coat.

She laughed. "Do you really think I'm going to put out on the first date?"

"Hoping," he said, sliding the coat over her bare shoulders and slowly down her arms.

Turning, she stepped out of it, and he placed it on the back of a chair in the living room before removing his overcoat and tossing it on top. His gaze took in the length of her in the dress and he let out a low whistle. "To say you are breathtaking this evening would be a lie," he said. "My breath has been coming hard and fast since seeing you in this dress."

She smiled. "Really? You like it that much?" She glanced at the fabric clinging to her slim frame. She'd been hoping it would have this effect on him.

"Me and every other guy in the room," he said.

He smelled so good. His cologne filled her senses and she closed her eyes, breathing him in. Being in his big arms made her feel so safe, so wanted. He tightened his hold around her and kissed the bare skin at her shoulder, his lips cool against her warm flesh and the light late evening stubble on his chin tickling her. She could already feel his erection, and the thought that she was the cause made her confidence soar.

"And it's not just the dress," he murmured against her

ear. "It's this tempting-as-hell body, and this amazing perfume you're wearing…The way those heels make your
legs look like they go on forever, all the way to these
sexy hips…" His hands gripped them tight and her breath
caught as his lips moved to the base of her neck. "And
seeing you smile and laugh, your face lighting up when
you talked about your career…"

"Past career," she corrected, though who the hell cared
when his hands were climbing higher over her rib cage
and his mouth was pressed against her soft skin.

He ignored her as he reached around to unhook and
unzip the dress.

She swallowed hard and held her breath as the fabric
fell away, leaving her completely naked in front of him.

"Holy shit. If I'd known you were naked under there,
we would have left a whole hell of a lot sooner," Asher
said, bending to pick up the dress, carefully laying it on
top of their coats. Then he loosened his tie, yanking it
off over his head before unbuttoning his dress shirt and
pulling the fabric free of his pants.

Emma kicked off her heels and immediately felt like
her old self, like Cinderella at the stroke of midnight…but
it didn't matter, because her prince was standing in front
of her, his bare chest and stomach and arms making her
mouth water as he unbuttoned his pants and let them fall
to the floor.

He wasted no time collecting his own clothing, simply
leaving it on the floor. Taking her hand, he led the way
to her bedroom and eased her down onto the bed. "You
were amazing tonight," he said as he lay next to her, trailing his hand along her chest, between her breasts, down
her stomach, and back up again.

She shivered beneath his soft, delicate caress. Sex was always passionate with Ash, always intense and full of desire, but she couldn't remember it being gentle and soft, the way it was starting tonight.

His want of her was evident in his cock straining against the confines of his boxer briefs, but he was taking his time.

"*You* were amazing. That tribute to Ben was really nice. There wasn't a dry female eye in the room." She knew because she'd been watching the women watching Asher. But for the first time she hadn't felt insecure. She hadn't been questioning who he'd rather be taking home. His eyes, his attention, and his desire had all been aimed at her and only her.

Reaching for him, she pulled him down on top of her and spread her legs as he lay between them. "How's your leg?" The therapist in her just couldn't be still.

"Perfect," he said, raising his upper body to stare down at her. "Emma, being with you tonight was…"

"Perfect," she said. She leaned up to kiss him, soft at first, then more desperate as his mouth crushed hers.

He rested his weight on his forearms as her head fell back against the pillow and his tongue separated her lips. His kiss was the one she was used to. Demanding, passionate, desperate. She lifted her hands overhead to lock fingers with him, and he squeezed her hands as he deepened the kiss even more. His tongue explored her mouth, his lips warm and wet.

She couldn't breathe under his weight and his mouth on hers, but she didn't care.

He pushed his hips into hers and the feel of his hard cock against her pelvis had her arching her back and aching with need.

She rocked her hips against him and he moaned against her mouth. "Emma, you are driving me insane. I want you so fucking bad."

"Then take me, Ash. I'm all yours." *I've always been all yours.*

He removed his underwear, then, rejoining their hands, he slid himself between her legs. Along her wet folds, the tip of his cock pressing against her opening.

She swallowed hard as she reconnected their mouths, her breath labored as he pushed a little deeper, so just the tip teased the rim of her.

Jesus, she was so close. Having him inside of her, but not fulfilling the burning ache, was torture, and just the thought of his long cock on the verge of entering her body had her pulsating. "Ash, please fuck me," she begged, breaking the contact with his mouth. Her nails dug into his shoulders as she clung to him, trying to force him deeper.

He remained on the edge, sliding the tip in and out in a torturously slow rhythm. He grinned at her as he stared into her eyes. "Anxious, Em?"

She wanted to hit him for the way he was killing her, but he had her hands pinned overhead. She was at his mercy. And he was showing none. Dipping his head to her neck, he began to suck gently at first, then harder as if he couldn't get enough of the taste of her. All the while, his cock hovered on the edge, refusing to give her the release she craved.

She moaned and forced her hips higher and he raised his mouth to her ear. "Patience, Emma…"

Damn it. She'd had patience. For too long. Waiting for this moment. When the sex wasn't just sex but a connection that solidified taking their relationship a step further. A step toward a future together. A real one. One she'd been wanting for so long. She'd had patience. Now she wanted him.

With all her strength she pushed her hips upward and felt his cock slide inside. He groaned as every inch of him plunged deeper, connecting with every inch of her warm, ready body.

She released a sigh of relief and immediately began rocking against him. The friction in her frantic pace provided some of the relief she sought, but not enough. "Harder, Ash. Faster," she begged, clinging to his hips now, forcing his body in and out of her.

"Emma, you're killing me. I was trying to make this last," he said, moving his hips in rhythm with hers, his head burrowed in the pillow next to her head.

"We can do it again. All night. Over and over," she said, feeling the length of him sliding faster, harder in and out.

She struggled for breath as the pace quickened and the pressure of his pelvis against her clit had her body screaming for release as she edged closer and closer. "Yes, Asher, Ash…" She closed her eyes and arched her back as the ripples of pleasure coursed through her. The intensity of her orgasm was almost painful as she clung to him, holding him still while she clenched and throbbed around him. "Oh my God…" she whispered.

"My turn," he said, picking up her legs beneath her thighs and wrapping them higher around his body. He pinned her shoulders against the bed as he plunged deeper at this new angle, making her cry out at the sensation.

Three fast and hard thrusts before his eyes closed and

his head fell forward. His fingers gripped her shoulders and he moaned his own release. He forced several deep breaths and she hugged his body with her legs, until she felt him slide out of her slowly.

As he rolled off of her, he pulled her into him, spooning her as he held her close. "So, pretty girl," he whispered against her ear, moving her hair away from her neck. "Do you think you'd like to date me again?"

Date him. Marry him. Grow old with him. "This one would be hard to beat." She snuggled closer, loving the feel of his body against hers, legs tangled together, hands folded against her chest, his stomach pressed to her back. Loved it so hard. It was the one thing in that moment that she was sure was right.

"Leave that up to me," he said, kissing her as her eyes closed in pure blissful exhaustion.

CHAPTER 13

⁓◌⁓

*H*e couldn't mess this up.

If Emma went to Florida, she'd never consider snowboarding again, and he didn't even want to think about what long nights of studying and the stress of the curriculum and working so closely with Dr. Model-Scholar would do to them.

The new them. *Together* them.

He may not know exactly how to make this work, but he knew he didn't want to lose her, and the way she'd looked at him the night before revealed that his friend may be hiding a lot more than just this PhD program.

Love was a strong word. And while he knew he did love Emma, he was starting to think that he was also falling in love with her, and he suspected that she may already be there.

Which made his promise of an even better second date that much more pressure filled.

Knocking on his sister's door, he turned the knob and entered. "Hello?"

He couldn't talk to his brothers, because he'd never hear the end of the teasing. His teammates spoke one language only: hockey. The players who were in relationships weren't the best at dealing with the pressure of both family and career commitment, and they certainly weren't winning awards for romantic guy of the year.

So Becky was his only hope. He had to do things right, and he was running out of time. "Hey, Becky," he called again.

"In the living room," Becky answered as he heard several other voices as well. Female voices. Reaching the living room entryway, he saw Abby and Olivia sitting on the sofa.

Nope. He turned to leave. "You're busy, I'll come back."

"No, get back here. When you texted that you were coming over, I suspected it had to do with Emma and you needing my advice on how not to screw this up, so I called in reinforcements," Becky said, dragging him back into the living room.

He shot her a look. How the hell had his sister figured that out by his "I'm stopping by" text?

"That's right. You need all the help you can get. This is a big deal. This is *Emma*." Olivia sipped her coffee and typed furiously on her iPhone with one hand.

"Finally," Abby added, with a told-you-all smile.

His brother's fiancées were pains in the ass. They were the perfect example of why he avoided relationships. One brother had walked away from hockey for the woman he loved, and the other was so lovesick it was resulting in a lack of focus on the ice.

Until it had come to taking him out on the ice. Now that honoring his big brother was over, his irritation had returned…a little. Though not enough to continue holding a grudge. He wondered how much of his forgiving attitude was a result of this new thing with Emma. If it hadn't been for the hit, he'd have continued playing throughout the season, not getting a chance to enjoy the holiday with her. And he may not have had this chance to secure what they had before she accepted the enrollment at the University of Florida.

The mere idea that his being out for weeks was somehow a good thing made him shake his head. Geez, was he getting soft, too?

He surveyed the eager expressions on the three women's faces, and his nerves over the whole thing returned. "No. This really isn't a big deal. *Because* it's Emma. She's not like you three."

Raised eyebrows and daggers. Ready to pounce. Damn. He'd almost need to go seek advice on seeking advice.

"What I mean is, she doesn't need a big, extravagant, elaborate gesture with flowers and dinner and all that shit." He wasn't there for date ideas. Emma was easygoing, and they enjoyed their time together wherever they went or whatever they did. He was just hoping Becky might have some advice on how to continue moving forward in a new way with a woman he already knew better than anyone. A woman whose body he knew every inch of…How did they go backward from amazing sex and a fantastic friendship to building a foundation for a more committed relationship? That's what he needed help with.

But right now, the three of them were staring at him as though he should run. Fast.

"We will ignore that anti-feminist generalization because you're injured, and it wouldn't be a fair fight," Becky said, motioning for the other two to keep the lectures they were about to deliver to themselves. "Sit," she told him.

"I should go." He'd already pissed them off in three seconds.

"Sit," all three said.

Nope. Relationships and being bossed around all the time were definitely not his thing. His brothers were whipped. Not him. Not yet, anyway. An image of Emma in the emerald-green gown the night before, immediately followed by an image of the fabric falling to the ground, had him questioning his vow.

Damn.

He sat. "I don't need dating ideas." Hell, he could afford to fly her to Paris for the next date if he wanted, and he knew how to charm a woman. That wasn't his dilemma. "I just want to know where we go from here when we've already..." He felt his cheeks grow red.

"Made love?" Abby supplied.

"Had lots of sex," he corrected. The term *made love* had always made him antsy.

"Can I hit him?" Olivia asked Becky.

"Not yet," his sister said. Turning to him, she looked as though she was struggling to keep her own annoyance at bay. "What is it that you're hoping for? Are you two ready to take things to another level?"

Another level. His mouth went dry. He didn't freaking know. All he knew was that he could feel himself losing the only person he could depend on, the only person he could ever see himself settling down with, and he had to do whatever it took to make sure it didn't happen. "I don't know."

"Well, do you love her?"

Whoa. It was hot in his sister's house.

Three sets of eyes stared at him, just waiting for him to give the wrong answer.

He pushed the sleeves of his sweater up and tugged at the collar. "Um…I mean…"

"*Now* can I hit him?" Olivia asked.

"It's tempting," Becky said.

"Look, stop judging. What Emma and I have is… complicated." It hadn't been a few weeks ago. Now all of a sudden, it felt like a big uncertain mess. "We are not making any wedding plans or anything, but I want to give this…thing…between us a real shot." He'd figure out his feelings and hers later.

The women softened a little.

"Okay, well, I think you need to take advantage of your time here, away from hockey. Focus on her. Make this holiday a memorable one, quiet and romantic…"

He was nodding. Focus on her. Quiet and romantic… Use this time to see if their connection was strong enough to go the distance. He already knew the answer to that. As long as she didn't get swallowed up in her new future plans, her new life goals…

Olivia nodded. "Right. Enjoy the town's Christmas fair this weekend. They have a dance and sleigh rides… Really make the next few weeks special."

"And you need to get a better answer to the love question," Abby said.

He sighed. He *had* a better answer. The truth was, it terrified him.

"Okay. You three were tons of help, but I should go." Standing, he noticed the local paper on the coffee table. An ad on the front page caught his eye. Breckenridge Ski Resorts Winter Tour…the snowboard and ski event that his coach had mentioned. In his stress that morning, he'd almost forgotten about it.

Picking the paper up, he smiled. The tournament was that weekend. It was the perfect thing to show Emma how much she missed life on the slopes. The past three years he hadn't been available to drag her butt up there for the Winter Tour, but this year he had nowhere else he'd rather be. Four days of ski and snowboard competitions, live outdoor concerts, and athlete meet-and-greets were the perfect Christmas getaway.

The perfect opportunity to get *her* away. Away from Jess and her father. Away from this boring small-town existence she pretended to be content with. He'd watched his brother Jackson struggle with the same disillusionment for years before Abby came back to Glenwood Falls. The difference was, Jackson had been truly done with hockey, and at least he'd made the last attempt at it to know for sure. Emma had been carried off the slopes on a stretcher and had never gone back. She needed to at least get back out there to be sure she was done.

Things would be so much easier if she wasn't. If she returned to snowboarding, their relationship could go back to the way it had been, with both of them focused on chasing and living a dream, meeting in the middle with a mutual unspoken understanding that someday they would settle down together. If he could get her back to the same page, he'd be free to concentrate on hockey for a little while longer.

"Can I take this?" he asked, noticing the website address. He had a lot of planning to do and a few strings to pull.

Becky shrugged. "Sure. Let us know if you need more help…"

He leaned forward and kissed her forehead. "I've got this."

* * *

Well, this second date was definitely starting off a lot differently than any other she'd been on, and it seemed Asher was striving to deliver on his promise of an even better one than the weekend before. The text from him earlier that day saying to pack an overnight bag with enough clothes for a few days had surprised her.

In a good way. In a fantastic way. The connection between them the other night had changed. She hadn't thought that simply relabeling their relationship could have such an effect on the way it felt to be with him, but it did.

Just the thought that he wanted to pursue something more with her had warmed her heart. Confessing her feelings for him now would be a lot easier. She'd wanted to the other night, but she'd hesitated and decided to wait. Now more than ever, when they were moving forward together, she didn't want to ruin things by rushing it.

Rushing *him*. She knew this was a big step for him.

She'd wait until the right time to tell him she loved him. Maybe on this secret trip.

His refusal to tell her where they were headed was actually kind of exciting. Other than a few camping and hiking trips as friends, they'd never gone away together before.

When her doorbell rang a moment later, she checked the clock. An hour early? Someone was eager.

Her smile faded as she peeked through the frosted-glass window next to her door. Jess. Crap. Despite their connection at the fashion show, she knew her sister was the only thing that could destroy her good mood right now. She'd probably have to tell her sister she was going to be out of town for a few days, especially since she wouldn't be around to help out with their father, but she'd been hoping to send a quick text when she was already on the way to their secret destination, then ignore incoming texts from her sister.

Standing at the door, she contemplated not answering, but it was too late. Jess could see her shape through the frosted glass.

"What are you waiting for? Open up," Jess yelled through the door.

Emma sighed, hoping she wouldn't stay long or inquire about her weekend plans. She was a terrible liar, and telling Jess she was going away with Ash face-to-face—no way. "Hey, Jess," she said, opening the door.

Her three nephews bum-rushed her from their hiding place behind the door.

Shit. So much for a short visit. "Hey, guys, why are you not in school today?" It was Friday and school wasn't out for Christmas break for another week.

"Teacher development day," Brayden said, removing his hat and mittens.

No, please don't get undressed. "Another one?" They seemed to be out of school more than they were in.

"Tell me about it," Jess said with a sigh as she removed her own coat.

An unexpected visit from the kids would normally be a pleasant surprise, but Emma was eager to get back to packing. She also wanted to take a shower, shave her legs…maybe other places, seeing as how this last-minute trip hadn't left her a whole lot of time to *prepare*. "What are you guys doing here?" she asked.

"The kids were driving me crazy at home," Jess said. "And I knew you had taken the day off…"

Last time she revealed that info.

"So, I suggested a visit with Aunt Emma. Also, I have a few errands to run this afternoon, so I thought maybe they could hang out here for a bit?"

Babysitting her nephews was something she enjoyed, but her sister's assumption that she was always available was annoying. What if she'd taken the day off to get her own shit done? And as a matter of fact, she wasn't available. She forced her tone to sound normal as she led the way into the kitchen. "Well, I would, but I'm actually heading out soon…" She opened the fridge and took out the milk, then she grabbed plastic Disney-themed glasses from the cupboard.

"Where are you going?" Jess asked.

Ignoring her sister's question, she called to the boys above the noise of her PlayStation starting up. Jess didn't let them own or play video games at home, so her place was their fun zone. "Do you guys want chocolate chip cookies or brownies?"

"Both!" all three yelled.

Jess shook her head. "They are monsters today. One chocolate chip cookie each," she said.

Emma slid a few extra on the plate and carried everything on a tray into the living room. After all, she wouldn't be babysitting.

"So, you didn't answer my question. Where are you going?" Jess asked again.

Emma hesitated, but she had to pack, which meant Jess had to either leave or join her in the bedroom so she could continue. She released a breath. "Away for the weekend. Follow me. I'm just packing."

Jess frowned as she followed. "Away? Away where?"

"I'm not sure," she said honestly.

"You're going away but you don't know where?" Jess stared at her.

"Right."

"Asher's idea, I assume?" Her irritation was immediate.

Buzzkill. "Yes. I'm going away with Ash. It's a surprise. For fun." *Hint hint. Don't ruin this for me.*

"Are you going on a plane?" she asked, noticing the half-filled suitcase open on the bed.

"Road trip, I think." He hadn't mentioned her needing her passport or anything. And he'd said warm clothes, so she suspected they were heading to the mountains.

"Breckenridge?" Jess guessed, giving voice to what Emma had been thinking.

Emma shrugged. "I don't know." There were other mountains in Colorado.

"I do. Guaranteed he's taking you there. But why?" Jess said, removing the low-cut black cashmere sweater Emma had just placed into a suitcase back into the open dresser drawer. "Too sexy," she said.

Emma rolled her eyes, repacking the sweater. "*If* that's where he is taking me, it's probably because it's a beautiful ski lodge during the holidays." Anywhere they went would be decorated for the season and would enhance the romantic mood. She couldn't wait to get on the road and away from Jess's scowl.

"So, it has nothing to do with the Winter Tour?"

Her sister would make a fantastic investigator. She really should give up the small-town editing desk and become an investigative reporter in a big city. Of course she'd know that the tour was that weekend.

The mention of it made Emma shift uncomfortably as she retrieved several pairs of skinny jeans and leggings from a drawer. When she'd thought their destination could be Breckenridge, the Winter Tour had occurred to her as well, but she hoped it wasn't the reason. She needed him to finally get the fact that she was done. "No," she said simply, hoping it was true, but her gut was telling her it probably wasn't.

If he was taking her to Breckenridge, then the tour was probably the reason behind it. And as long as Ash was okay with her experiencing it from the sidelines, they didn't have a problem. Experiencing the slopes from the bottom, they were good. The moment he tried to strap a snowboard to her boots, they were going to have an issue.

She'd gone to Breckenridge the winter after her accident.

She hadn't told anyone—not her family, her co-workers, or Ash. Only the contest organizers knew she was registered to attend and compete, and it was only in the freestyle division and not at the level she'd once dominated. But she was planning to get back on the slopes.

With no agenda or future plans, she'd simply wanted to be back on her board, back on the mountain, back in the game. She needed to prove to herself that she could. That was the first step back to the career that had been her life for so long and a big step forward in her recovery.

So, she'd gone to Breckenridge for the Winter Tour.

The day of the freestyle competition, she'd geared up and sweated the entire chairlift ride to the top of the mountain hours before the first competitor was scheduled to hit the slopes. The first two days she'd observed from the sidelines, still unsure about being there. So many familiar faces were there that week. So many surprised expressions.

And not *happy* surprised expressions. More like the expressions of people who felt they were in the presence of a bad omen.

That's what she'd become. The snowboarder who'd ended her career in tragedy, with a bad judgment call, a terrible accident, was back to bring bad luck on the competition.

She'd been determined to show them she *was* back. As a competitor. Maybe not one who could win or even place, but one who wasn't afraid to try.

Her palms had sweated and her mouth had felt like sandpaper as she'd climbed off the lift and stood at the top. Surrounded by the familiar open air, the fresh powder beneath her board, her adrenaline soaring, for a second she'd forgotten the past year, the accident, all the reasons she'd walked away, and she'd pushed off.

She moved slowly at first, gaining confidence as her legs moved by muscle memory. The wind whipping across her face helped to ease her anxiety. She'd been a professional snowboarder for so long, her body naturally knew how to bend and twist its way down the slope. She'd picked up speed, and the tension and apprehension tore away as the snowboard cut through the snow.

But her courage soon faded as she approached the part of the hill where she'd lost control before. As she neared the stunt ramps that she hadn't practiced on for a year, panic set in. What the hell was she doing? She hadn't ridden those rails in so long. She hadn't worked out or practiced the stunts she'd perfected in almost a year. What the hell made her think she could strap on a board and be able to do them now?

Like riding a bike, her coach's voice in her head reminded her.

Yeah, a bike that had nearly killed her, broken her spirit, and taken away the opportunity of a lifetime.

She'd slowed her pace and forced several deep breaths as fear made her muscles seize. The wind whipping against her face now felt like stinging needles against her flesh, and the speed was now terrifying as she continued down the mountain, away from the stunt ramps, simply praying to make it to the end of the hill without wiping out, before her panic attack could take hold.

And she had. Then she'd removed the board, removed herself from the competition lineup, and returned to

Glenwood Falls, knowing her snowboarding career was a thing of the past. She no longer had what it took to be the best. Her courage and confidence weren't there anymore. Oddly enough, the realization hadn't hit her as hard as she'd thought it would. She'd had a great career and retired on top.

So maybe heading back there with Ash as a spectator would be okay. Or maybe she could even convince him not to leave the lodge room.

On that note, she opened her top drawer and took out several matching lace bra and underwear sets.

"Oh my God, Emma! I don't want to see those." Jess looked away.

"Then leave. I'm trying to pack." She folded the sets and placed them on top of the sweaters, hoping her sister actually would. Five minutes ago, she'd been looking forward to this getaway, and in less than a minute her sister had her on edge about it.

"This really isn't healthy, you know," Jess said, staying in the room.

"What isn't?"

"Your pathetic one-sided relationship." Jess shot her an exasperated look as she folded her arms across her chest.

Emma clenched her teeth. "I'm hoping this trip might change that, okay?" Maybe she *was* pathetic for keeping her feelings to herself all these years, but hopefully that was going to change. Things already *had* started to change. Not that she owed Jess an explanation. It was none of her sister's business what was happening between Ash and her.

"He's going to break your heart, Emma."

She tossed more lingerie on top of the clothes in the

suitcase and swung around to face her. "How do you know that?" Her sister had no idea the strength of their connection. She had never made any effort to get to know him before making up her mind about who and what he was. Emma was tired of the judgment and criticism of the man she was in love with.

"I know because the only thing he cares about is hockey," Jess said as though it should be obvious.

"That's not true." She tucked a bikini into the suitcase. "And besides, so what if hockey is important to him? I get that. I understand that. And more importantly, I support it. His career is important to me, too."

Her sister's eyes blazed. "At the expense of your own happiness?"

"Asher makes me happy." And crazy and confused and conflicted. But happier than anything else, making all of the other feelings just things they needed to figure out.

"So, you've decided not to go to Florida."

She knew this conversation was coming. "Not in January." She'd made up her mind the weekend before. Asher still had weeks of therapy, and she wouldn't leave him. She would go forward with the doctorate program in the fall, after helping Ash recover and putting some time and effort into where this relationship was going. She couldn't focus on building something with him and concentrate on the intensive study program. But after the summer, which they would hopefully spend together, she'd be in a better place. Her heart would be settled, and she knew he'd support her with her new life plans.

They'd figure it out. But right now and for the next little while, the focus was on him—getting him back on the ice, and moving forward together.

"You're making a mistake," Jess said.

Anger simmered in her chest. "Well, it's my mistake to make, Jess. I don't know who died and made you queen."

"Mom," Jess said, tears springing immediately to her eyes. "*Mom* died."

Damn. Emma sighed. Bad choice of words. "Jess, I didn't mean it literally."

"Either way, it's true. Mom died and *I* was left to take care of things. You were off with the Olympic training team again three days after the funeral."

Emma swallowed hard. She'd needed to get away. The grief had been so overwhelming that staying in Glenwood Falls any longer would have suffocated her. For years, she'd traveled so much, and from a young age, she'd learned how to distance herself from family while going after her dreams. Losing her mother—her biggest supporter—had crushed her, and her desire to flee had made her leave even sooner. She'd needed to get back to where she'd had some control…and then she'd lost it all. "I'm sorry I wasn't here," she said quietly.

"I understood," Jess said. "But you have to understand how hard it was watching you compete, especially after Mom died. I was always afraid you'd get hurt. Then you did." She paused. "And I feel that same sense of foreboding when I see you with Asher."

She understood her sister's concerns, but Jess wasn't giving her any credit. She may have been right about snowboarding, but she was wrong about Asher. "Jess, I'm not going to get hurt." She prayed it was true, that putting her trust in Asher wouldn't give her sister another reason to say "I told you so."

Jess stared at her in silence for a long, excruciating moment, before she stood and walked to the bedroom door. "Do what you're going to do, Emma," she said, turning back to face her, looking defeated. "You always have." She left the room and Emma could hear her tell the boys they were leaving.

She resisted the urge to go out there, knowing there was nothing she could say to change Jess's mind and knowing there was nothing Jess could say to change hers.

And a moment later, she heard the front door slam.

CHAPTER 14

❦

Oh my God, this place is amazing," Emma said, admiring the luxury five-star accommodations of the Chateau Royale Lodge. The four-poster king-sized bed in the center of the room looked warm and inviting with its dark brown fleece duvet and oversized pillows, a direct contrast to the cold, snowy mountain peaks visible through the open curtains at the window. The interior, with its light mocha-colored walls and hardwood flooring, the stonework fireplace in the corner, and the four-person Jacuzzi tub, helped Emma forget about her argument with her sister and any reservations she'd had about coming.

After Asher had picked her up, her anxiety had increased as they'd made their way onto the highway and he'd taken the exit heading toward the mountains, but it had eased bit by bit as they'd traveled beyond the main lodge area, past the main slopes, and continued driving until they'd reached a secluded little valley, surrounded by the mountains, away from the ski and snowboarding competitions in Breckenridge.

The entire drive, signs and advertisements for the Winter Tour displayed everywhere had toyed with her emotions as memories resurfaced, but here, away from it all, she relaxed.

"It's pretty impressive. Their website barely did it justice," Asher said, opening the floor-to-ceiling curtains to the patio doors.

Emma gasped. Outside on their large private deck was a hot tub already filled with bubbling water, steam escaping and swirling as it tangled with the cold air. White Christmas lights hung above and a small evergreen tree sat decorated in the corner of the deck, near a small two-seater table. A bottle of wine sat in an ice bucket and two wine glasses were perched on the edge of the tub.

Any lingering hesitation she'd had about being in the mountains with him that weekend vanished. "Did you arrange this?" she asked, wrapping her arms around his waist.

He laughed as he turned in her arms and kissed her. "I'll pretend I did."

Taking her hand, he walked toward the bed and picked up a white terrycloth robe draped across it. "Shall we take advantage of whoever did?"

She nodded, already removing her cardigan. That hot tub looked like it could solve all of life's problems, and it would certainly help to melt away the stress of her morning.

Asher walked toward her, his eyes taking in her body. She knew the body-hugging tank top with lace at the top was his kryptonite. He practically drooled each time she wore it. The simple white cotton fabric clinging to her braless breasts and the hint of sexy with the lace was her favorite combination as well. It somehow made her feel confident, though it was more likely Asher's reaction to the sight that did it. "Remind me to leave a really big tip for whoever it was," he said, grabbing her waist and pulling her into him.

After another week of therapy sessions only, he hadn't kept his hands off of her from the moment he'd picked her up in his rented SUV. And she hadn't minded one little bit. Holding his hand as he drove through the beautiful rugged landscape on the way up the mountain had felt so right.

She wrapped her arms around his neck and pressed her body into him now. He smelled so good, like the outdoor mountain air combined with a soft masculine aftershave, and her body immediately responded to the kisses he was placing at the base of her neck. "Mmmm," she said, standing on tiptoes and taking his face in her hands to kiss him.

His lips were demanding as they met hers, and his hands gripped her tighter. She closed her eyes, savoring the taste of him...

But he abruptly released her and moved away. "Nope. This was not the point. Get dressed. Let's go to dinner."

She frowned. *Dinner?* Who gave a shit about food when they had this amazingly romantic setup right here in the room? "I thought we were doing the hot tub?"

She moved closer again and reached for the button on his jeans.

He stopped her hand and took several steps away from her. "Don't make it harder. My resolve is weakening by the second." He ran a hand through his hair, before placing both on his hips and forcing a breath. "But I promised you more than just sex, and if we get in that tub…"

He looked to be struggling with each word, contradicting what she knew he really wanted to do. She walked toward him, unbuttoning her jeans as she went. Stopping an inch from him, she wiggled free of the denim and stepped out. The desire in his eyes as he stared at her in only the tank top and a pale pink silk thong made it clear that she would be getting her way.

Still, he protested. Weakly. "Emma, I'm serious. I want to do this right."

She wrapped her arms around his neck and immediately his went around her. "And I want hot tub, Champagne, and room service…later," she whispered against his lips. "Much later."

* * *

So much for good intentions.

No one could say he hadn't tried. But it would take a much stronger man than him to continue saying no to Emma when she was shimmying out of her thong and lifting her tank top over her head. Standing right in front of him naked, looking so beautifully tempting and impossible to argue with. On the way to the mountains, she'd seemed a little nervous, on edge, but now she was

completely relaxed and killing him with her insistence.
"Are you sure?" One last half-hearted attempt to clear any
residual guilt on his conscience for diving right into sex
when they were supposed to be deepening their relationship in other ways. This was her idea. He'd made a valiant
effort.

"Take your clothes off, Asher."

Unlike his sister's and future sister-in-laws', Emma's
kind of bossy he could handle.

Removing his sweater and T-shirt together, he tossed
them onto a chair near the window. Unzipping and unbuttoning his jeans, he dropped them to the floor, feeling
only the slightest bit bad about messing up the gorgeous
room. Picking up one of the robes again, he held it open
for her.

She stopped in front of him and turned slowly. His
gaze slid the length of her sexy back, down her thin waist
to her round, perfect little ass, and it took every ounce of
strength not to toss the robe aside and bend her over the
big, inviting plush duvet on the king-sized bed.

The intensity of his insatiable want for her always
surprised him. In every other relationship he knew of,
the passion and sparks faded over time. He knew some
of the married men on his team longed to be single
whenever they were on the road. Hookups were common, and they always said they were envious of the
single guys who could have a different woman in every
city they visited. Ash never had that desire. The fire between him and Emma only blazed even more each time
he was with her.

When they'd first started having sex, it had been
slightly awkward, neither of them knowing where the

other really stood, but once they'd established things for what they were, they were free to be together, to enjoy one another without the limitations of labels and overanalyzing things. No strings or complications. Just mutual trust and respect and an unyielding need to be close to one another.

And damn if he didn't want her right now as much as he had the first time.

The longest, and arguably, most meaningful, relationship for both of them had been a nonrelationship.

His gut twisted slightly. He hoped this new attempt to turn what they had into something more didn't destroy everything.

"Asher, I'm getting a little cold," she said.

"Sorry. I was enjoying the view." He wrapped the robe around her shoulders and, taking the belt, reached around her waist to tie it. The smell of her peppermint body lotion making him want to lick her skin. Christmas had never been a reason to celebrate for him—being away from home, without someone to fully enjoy it with—but this year, he was enjoying every scent, taste, and sight the holidays had to offer…on Emma.

She turned and handed him a robe and he put it on quickly, but not before her gaze caught sight of his semi hard-on and she grinned.

"Your fault. I was cool with going to dinner," he said.

"Tell that to your penis," she said with a laugh, then ducked out of reach as he went to grab her.

"You're going to get it," he growled, sliding his feet into a pair of resort slippers and following her to the door.

"I hope so," she said with that wicked little grin of hers that drove him wild. Who had he been kidding to think he could resist her long enough to eat? There was only one thing he was hungry for.

Opening the patio doors, Emma shivered as the cold mountain wind blew mini snowdrifts inside the room. "It's so cold." She hesitated as she slid her feet into the other pair of slippers at the door.

"It's going to feel amazing once you're in there," Asher said, stepping outside. "Come on." Taking her hand, he led the way to the edge of the tub. Steam rose in misty spirals from the water. He removed his robe quickly, climbed the three steps, and lowered himself into the water. The contrast of hot and cold awakened every inch of his skin.

Sitting along the side bench, his shoulders the only thing above the water, he watched as Emma removed her robe at the top of the stairs and hurried in. Too soon her too perfect body was immersed beneath the hot water and steam blocked his view of her face for a second as she moved closer. "Ahhhh, you were right. This is amazing."

He reached for her and pulled her to cradle his lap, taking her legs and placing them on either side of his. His fingers massaged the muscles there, sliding higher to where her legs joined her hips and squeezing not so gently.

He was so fucking hard already. "So you're completely sure that it's okay that we do this date out of order?" he asked.

She wrapped her arms around his neck and slid her body farther onto his lap, pressing her pelvis against his erection. "You have me naked, so I'm pretty sure this 'date' idea of yours has evaporated."

He slid his hands up her waist, holding her in place, his grip tight on her rib cage. "I'm sorry…you're too sexy."

She laughed. "You just haven't had any in a week."

Since the night of their first date—the award ceremony. The night everything seemed to change. So far, for the better…but he was still nervous as shit that they were destroying a good thing. "Is that what you think? That I want you just because I'm sexually deprived?"

She nodded, running her wet hands through her short hair, slicking it back away from her face. "Yes."

He lowered his lips to her collarbone, placing gentle little kisses there. "So you think I'm a sex addict?"

"I think we both are," she said, massaging his shoulders as she rocked her body slowly back and forth over his thickening length.

"*You* might be, but I'd have to be having a lot more sex to qualify," he murmured against her neck, just below her ear. He slowed her motions even more. He was already too close to the edge and he wanted this to last. Surrounded by the mountains, breathing in the fresh, cold air with the contradicting heat of the water warming him, made for an intoxicatingly arousing setting.

"What are you saying? That you save yourself for me?" she asked, sliding a hand beneath the water and gripping him. Her gaze was full of teasing and torment, but he had news for her.

"Yes."

Her mouth gaped slightly and she studied him, looking unsure whether or not to believe him.

"It's true." He tucked several strands of wet hair behind her ear and let his fingers trail along her cheek. "The only person I've been with in a very long time…" Almost six years in fact. "Is you."

"But you could have any woman you want, any night of the week." Her surprise was evident in her voice.

He didn't know about that, but he couldn't deny that women were all over him whenever he traveled with the team. But since his friendship with Emma had turned into a benefits situation, he hadn't been able to bring himself to go there with another woman. He'd never told Emma before because it was his own decision, and he didn't want her to feel as though she had to adopt that choice for herself. They'd been very clear from the start that they were far from exclusive to one another, but… "I don't want just any woman, any day of the week," he said, his lips meeting hers before he could say any more, before he gave in to the seduction of the winter paradise all around him.

* * *

Emma's mind was racing at the same speed as her pulse. Asher wasn't sleeping with anyone when he traveled with the team? She'd always just assumed…never asking for fear of the answer. She tried to remember the last time he'd mentioned anyone he was dating. No one recent came to mind. The last few times there had been someone in the picture to interrupt what they had, it had been on her side. Men she'd casually dated. But even those had been more than a year ago, a last-ditch attempt to try to find someone who made her feel even half of what Asher did.

Her heart thundered in her chest as she kissed him,

their lips moving in sync, fast and hard. Air didn't matter. Kissing him was all that mattered. And touching him. Her grip tightened on his shoulders, and her pace quickened as she tried to turn off her head and not read too much into his revelation.

Asher put hockey first. Before everything. Maybe sex fell to the bottom of his priority list as well...until they were together.

I don't want just any woman...

Did she dare hope that things were really starting to change? Had their extended time together helped him see, helped him realize something? Was this attempt at a date really a sincere gesture to let her know that they could be something more? That he was ready? She'd had her doubts, thinking his recent actions were out of a desperation as he'd felt her slipping away slightly. Of course it had only been in his mind. Despite her consideration to pursue her doctorate, she was only more invested in him as time went on. Nothing would have changed that. Nothing could ever change that.

But maybe it was more than desperation fueling his interest in the possibility of a new form of relationship.

Her conflicted mind was torture.

Just stop thinking and enjoy this.

She fought for a breath and pushed all thoughts away as she savored the taste of him, enjoying the feel of his mouth against hers, the cool flesh at his neck and shoulders against her hot skin. She was in a mountain paradise getaway with the man she loved, that was all that mattered.

He lifted her and a second later he was sliding into her body. Her breath caught at the surprise, then she moaned as her forehead fell forward onto his. The pleasurable sensation of having him inside of her outweighed any pain from the tightness of his full erection plunging deep. Her fingernails dug into the flesh at his shoulders as he continued to guide her body up and down the length of him.

"Damn, Asher, I can't get enough of you."

Moving slowly, he stood, lifting her slightly out of the water. The cold air hitting her breasts and stomach made her gasp, before he quickly switched position with her and eased her back down into the water. "Spread your arms out against the edge," he said, bending to his knees in front of her.

She did and he lifted her ass up until she was floating in the tub, her body supported by her arms out along the edge and his hands gripping her ass cheeks. Positioned in front of a powerful jet, the bubbles circulated below her, tickling her most intimate areas, creating an even more intense sensation as Asher reentered her.

The floating weightlessness allowed her to tilt her pelvis in various ways and intensified the friction between them. She rested her head back against the edge of the tub. He rocked her hips up and down over him as he continued his own rocking motion in rhythm with hers.

It felt so amazing. The cool breeze on her flushed cheeks, the hot water circling all around them, her nipples rising and falling out of the water, teasing her body with the alternating hot and cold…Asher's full length inside of her…

He paused and she opened her eyes to look at him.

His brow was furrowed and he looked pained.

"You okay?" she asked.

He nodded. "My knee, that's all."

She immediately slid back down toward the seat, allowing him to slide out of her.

"No, don't, its fine," he said, but she shook her head.

"No way. This feels too good for you not to enjoy it, too."

His breathing was as labored as hers as he stood. "Bed?"

She nodded. Taking his hand, she climbed out of the hot tub behind him, and instead of reaching for his robe, he grabbed hers, wrapping her quickly in it before lifting her into his arms.

She stared into his eyes and touched his cheek. "I love you, Ash." At first she wasn't sure if she'd said the words or only thought them, but his grip on her tightened and his gaze was full of so much she couldn't quite understand as he carried her inside and set her down on the bed.

He stared at her a second longer, before his body and his lips made contact with hers and he continued to make love to her.

The intensity of his passion as he brought her immediately to orgasm was almost enough for her to overlook the fact that he hadn't said the words back.

* * *

Exercise used to be his fix for anything. But forty laps in the resort's pool at four a.m. wasn't solving anything.

To say Emma's words had come as a surprise wouldn't be entirely true. Asher had felt it from her the last few weeks especially, and he knew she'd expected more from him than silence to her confession of love. Unfortunately anything he'd tried to say had gotten stuck on his tongue.

He'd been the one to suggest a real date to see if their friendship could be more than just comfortable, dependable, full-of-amazing nights together, and now he was confused and conflicted.

Were these new feelings for her real or simply the fear of losing her?

His mind refused to clear as his arms and legs cut through the cool water. The dark, mysterious mountain sky and the snow falling outside the ceiling to floor glass walls surrounding the pool provided none of the answers he sought. Back and forth, he continued his laps until his knee started to throb slightly and he knew it was time to call it quits. It wasn't helping anyway.

He stopped by the edge of the pool and reached for his towel. What he really wanted was a run, but the swimming was the extent of his doctor-approved exercise, and he sure as hell wasn't dumb enough to jeopardize the progress he'd made with his recovery.

Progress he couldn't have made this quickly without Emma.

Climbing out, he wrapped the towel around his waist and sat on the edge. Reaching for his phone, he saw a missed text message from her.

Feeling lonely in this huge bed.

He sighed, feeling his body spring to life. The effect a simple text from her had on him couldn't be healthy.

And could mean anything.

But until he was sure that his desperation to hold on to her wasn't the reason for these new conflicting emotions, he couldn't pretend to be ready to give her something he wasn't sure he could give. Once he got back on the ice, would he still feel that moving forward with a relationship was the best thing? Or would hockey once again take over, pushing everything else to the sidelines…including the woman he cared about?

The one lying in a bed just a few floors up, missing him.

Grabbing his sandals and robe, he left the pool and hit the button on the elevator.

He may not be ready to give Emma his heart just yet, but he could give her everything else.

CHAPTER 15

～∞～

Text message received at 8:04 a.m.: *Where are you?*

8:32: *Are you okay?*

8:46: *Text me back right away—I'm worried about you. P.S. Sorry I was a bitch.*

Emma wondered if anyone had ever explained the idea behind text messaging or sleeping in on a Saturday to Jess. She didn't think so, otherwise her sister wouldn't assume the worst when Emma didn't respond right away.

Rolling to her side, she sat up and swung her legs over the edge of the bed, glancing at Ash sleeping soundly. He was too gorgeous, sprawled across the sheets, one arm overhead and his sculpted back facing her, and she reached out and touched his shoulder gently before getting up. The night before had been both amazing and terrifying. She'd put everything out there. And now all she could do was wait. Wait for him to feel things as much as she did. And hope that eventually he would.

Grabbing the robe, she slid her feet into a pair of slippers and went out onto the deck. Closing the door as softly as possible, so as not to wake him, she dialed Jess's number.

"Are you okay?" Her sister answered on the first ring.

"Of course I'm okay." She leaned over the deck rail, staring at the snow-covered mountains in the distance. She used to love it there. She'd spent so much of her life there. She'd missed it the last three years, and the dull ache in her chest hadn't disappeared completely. She shivered in the cold mountain morning air and tightened the robe around her.

"So where did he take you?" Jess asked, sounding nervous.

"Breckenridge."

Silence.

Emma waited, feeling her irritation with her sister rise to an unhealthy level with each ticking second of nothing. "Okay, great talk, Jess. I'll text you once we get back."

"Wait!"

She did reluctantly.

"You're not there to compete, are you?"

She felt her chest tighten. She'd never fully understood her sister's problem with her snowboarding days. And sure, she'd suffered a terrible injury, but did that mean she could never snowboard again? While she wasn't certain she would ever be ready to try, Jess's constant criticism and butting her nose in where it didn't belong only made Emma want to.

"No," she said finally. And she hoped they wouldn't be going near the competition slopes. Asher had yet to mention anything about the tour, and while she wasn't fool enough to think he hadn't realized the events started today, so far he'd been smart enough not to broach the subject.

Though they hadn't done much talking about anything.

"Good." Jess sounded relieved. "So…what are you doing there?"

Emma sighed, her exasperation too much. "Crazy passionate sex. Bye, Jess," she said, disconnecting the call at her sister's surprised gasp.

The patio door opened behind her as she slid the phone into the pocket of her robe, hearing the ping of yet another text. No doubt from her sister. One she wouldn't be reading. She was desperate to enjoy the rest of her time there. In a few weeks, Ash would be fully healed and back on the ice…and she needed answers before then.

"Let me guess—Jess?" Asher asked, coming outside and wrapping his arms around her waist. He'd put on pajama pants, slippers, and nothing else, and his bare arms around her were immediately covered in goose bumps, but felt warm to her touch.

She nodded. "She thought you kidnapped me."

"I did," he said, kissing her neck.

His appetite was insatiable, but so was her own. The simplest touch, kiss, feel of his breath on the back of her neck sent her hormones into overdrive and made even more of a mess of her heart.

Staring off toward the mountains, she cleared her throat. She had to know. "So…question."

She felt him tense and her stomach turned. No doubt he thought she was going to pull a girl move and start a conversation about their relationship, demand answers and force him to talk about feelings. She'd let him off the hook on that for now.

"Why are we here?" she asked instead.

He turned her around to face him and his expression was worried. "Not buying the winter getaway angle?"

Her heart fell. "No." Damn, it *was* about the tour. "The Winter Tour?"

"I just thought we'd check out the competitions. There's a lot of great talent here this weekend." He paused. "Maybe even do a little snowboarding…you, not me, obviously," he said with a slightly nervous-sounding laugh.

She looked away.

"It's been a while since you've been on the slopes, and you can't say you don't miss it." He rubbed her arms and crouched to look into her eyes.

She swallowed hard. How often had Ash repeated the same sentiments, trying to encourage her to get back out there? He really wasn't giving up on this. "I'd rather not."

"Oh, come on. Just because you don't compete any-more doesn't mean you can't watch. I still watch every NHL game even though I'm not playing."

She cocked her head to the side. "Hardly the same thing. You know you're going back to it."

He raised one eyebrow.

She shook her head violently. If he suggested she enter the competition, she was packing up her shit and leaving him there on the mountain alone.

"Okay, okay…relax." He paused, looking squirmy as though there was more he wasn't saying.

"What?" She folded her arms across her chest and waited.

"Your old coach is here."

Her eyes widened. "How do you know?" Had he gone so far as to check the listings on the events? She hated that Jess was right. This was his exact reason for bringing her there.

His only reason?

Disappointment crept into her chest. So much for thinking he'd been thinking about the two of them…away together to figure things out. So far, things had only gotten even more complicated.

"I saw his name listed as a judge on the website. He doesn't have any athletes competing in the events."

Her heart fell even more. Her former coach had given up coaching a few months after her accident. The day she'd officially retired, so had he. But he was still an active participant in the snowboarding community. She hadn't seen him since the day she left the hospital, but like her family and Ash, he'd been there every day to visit while she was recovering.

Coach Jarvis had been like family to her. Her coach for more than ten years, he'd helped her rise through the ranks and secure her place on the Olympic team. She knew he partially blamed himself for her accident, but she didn't.

She'd known the weather conditions had been terrible, and she'd taken the chance anyway. Against his warnings. Her accident had been her fault alone.

"What do you say?" Asher asked, looking hopeful.

It would be nice to see Coach Jarvis…Reluctantly, she nodded. "Okay. We can go to today's events and see Coach Jarvis. But I'm not snowboarding, and one word about me competing and I'll kick your ass," she said, only half-joking.

Asher was nodding eagerly. "That's all I ask." He pulled her into him.

She placed her hands on his bare chest and leaned back slightly to look at him. "Just one day, then we forget about the competition and spend more time in the hot tub."

"Deal," he said, kissing her forehead.

And maybe finally do some talking.

An uneasiness filled her, and her stomach was in knots. If Jess had been right about Asher's intentions for the weekend, was it possible her sister was right about more?

* * *

The historic mining town was ready for the holiday season with its streetlights boasting large white and silver snowflakes and the storefront windows competing for the most elaborate Christmas display. Winter wonderland themes, gingerbread themes, and Santa and his elves were everywhere she looked. As a kid, visiting Breckenridge with her family, she'd thought it was the North Pole—certainly the most magical place she'd ever been to during the holidays. At night, the view of the village was truly spectacular, illuminated in white lights, the shadows of the mountains giving the valley a warm, cozy feel. Right now, the sidewalks were bustling with families enjoying the early morning festive events and skiers and snowboarders getting ready for the day's competitions. Shopping bags and snowboards passed on either side of Emma and Asher as they made their way toward the base of the mountain where the tournament was being held.

Of all the places she'd competed, Emma had loved Breckenridge the most. The beautiful village with the variety of challenging slopes made it the perfect combination of adrenaline-seeking fun and relaxation. Tourists and locals blended together in a big, friendly community, where everyone shared a passion for the outdoors and winter sports. And it had been close enough to Glenwood Falls for her family to make the trip to watch her compete, though it was usually only her mother who did.

She took a deep breath, sucking in the cold breeze as she scanned the familiar surroundings through her sunglasses. She knew every inch of the resort by heart. She had practically grown up there, staying in the cheapest lodges, three to a room…no one caring about having to take turns sleeping on the pull-out sofa, as long as they were able to get some sleep before hitting the slopes again the next day.

She'd been lucky to rise above the other competitors in her group. They'd all been talented, daring, amazing snowboarders, but she'd had that little extra spark of drive and determination that had given her the edge.

As much as it pained her to be there, it also felt like home. An odd combination of emotions spiraled through her as they approached the ski school, where the competitors checked in for the events. She expected to see some familiar faces, and she hoped she could handle whatever emotions arose. No one had been able to believe she'd simply walked away four years ago. Most of her friends had tried coaxing her back, but had given up when her fear had started to creep into their own spines, shaking their confidence. Seeing them now might be hard.

No one wanted to be around someone who reminded them of their mortality, their limitations, the possibility that they could fail or worse…

Oblivious to her inner turmoil, Asher squeezed her hand and smiled as they continued along the crisp, snowy path. "See, I knew you'd be okay once you got here."

That's what he thought?

His own excitement was written all over his handsome face. "This is so great."

If he said so.

The happier and more at ease he was, the more edgy and anxious Emma felt. Couldn't he tell this was hard for her? Being around everything she'd walked away from. She fought her annoyance toward him. He was trying to do something nice for her. Something he thought she needed.

She squeezed his hand as they entered the ski school.

Inside, signs directed competitors to the appropriate check-in desks based on their last names, and behind a row of tables, contest administrators confirmed attendance and handed out competitor numbers and tour bags with supplies and swag from sponsors. To their right a large banner announced that the previous year's gold medalist was in attendance as a guest competitor, and her mouth went dry.

Emma had been on that poster once. She'd been that gold medalist, smiling happily, wearing her team colors proudly. She'd once been the source of local pride and the competitor to beat.

Now, she was there, terrified to strap on a snowboard to attempt the bunny slopes.

Pathetic.

Allowing him to drag her here had been a mistake. Walking away, moving on, was easier when she avoided situations like this. Being there now was bringing out an odd sense of longing that she hadn't expected to feel. She didn't like it.

"Come on, let's ask if anyone knows where we can find Coach Jarvis," Asher said, fighting his way through the crowd to the information desk.

Head down, praying no one noticed or recognized her, Emma followed.

No one did.

And *that* was unexpectedly a knife through the heart. Had she been away that long? Had she not left any sort of mark on the snowboarding community? She shook the thoughts away. She wasn't a champion anymore. She didn't deserve any praise or recognition for her previous feats. There were new, stronger, better competitors rising in the sport every day. No one cared about her anymore. Nor should they.

"Hey, we're looking for one of the judges. Frank Jarvis," Asher told the young girl at the desk.

"Sorry. Competitors aren't allowed to…" The pretty blonde's voice trailed as she glanced up and her eyes widened at the sight of Ash.

Right. *He* was recognizable.

"Oh my God. You're Asher Westmore," she said.

He nodded. "Yes I am. I'm not competing…We're not competing," he corrected, moving her forward. "This is Emma Callaway. She was a former competitor and champion and an athlete on Frank's team. We just wanted to see him to say hi."

The girl, wearing a dark blue one-piece ski suit with sponsorship logos on the front, tore her gaze from Ash to nod at her. "Yes. I remember you." Her tone was ice-cold.

Emma searched the girl's face, but she didn't recognize her. Had they competed against one another in the past?

"Of course you remember her," Asher said as the two women just continued to stare at one another. "She was a three-time Breckenridge champion."

Unfortunately the girl was eyeing her with disdain. "She was also the competitor who dropped out of the freestyle at the last minute two years ago, eliminating our division for lack of entrants—meaning *I* wasn't able to compete either that year."

At that moment, Emma would have welcomed real daggers to the chest instead of the ones coming from the young girl's eyes.

Shit.

Asher frowned as he turned to look at her. "You were back here to compete two years ago?"

Shit, shit, shit.

She clenched her jaw. "Let's just go. I'm sure we can find Frank on our own," she said, though she was in no hurry to find her old coach anymore or to run into any more people from her past. She longed for the privacy of the resort. And the hot tub and Champagne…

No doubt if this girl remembered her only for the mess she'd created two years ago by dropping out, for her loss of courage, others would, too.

Asher continued to stare at her, waiting for an answer or an explanation.

He was getting neither. At least not right now, right there in front of this girl. "Can we please just go?" she said.

The girl behind the information desk sighed, ignoring

Emma as she told Ash, "Frank's over at the preliminaries station, helping to check equipment."

"Thank you," Asher said as they walked away.

Emma's legs felt like jelly beneath her, and her mouth was like sandpaper. Her hands shook slightly at her sides and her stomach was in knots. She'd never told anyone about her embarrassment there two years before, and now the man she loved knew what a failure she actually was.

Agreeing to come to the competition grounds had been a mistake.

Outside she headed back toward the rental vehicle, but he stopped her. "Why didn't you tell me?"

"Because I chickened out."

"What happened?"

"I don't know, Ash. I got up there for the trial run and I hadn't slept the night before and the conditions that day were shit…" Excuses. All excuses.

"Well, try now," he said, jumping far too eagerly at the chance to use this new information against her.

"No."

"Come on, Em. If you came back here after the accident, it means you haven't let this go as much as you claim to."

She tried to move around him, as people started to stare, but he blocked her path. She didn't like the twisting in the pit of her stomach suggesting there might be some truth in his words.

"You deserve a shot at this again. You were great once. You could do it again."

"Asher, shut up," she said a little too loudly. Her head hurt and she just wanted to get away.

Surprise made his lips clamp together. But only for

a split second. "What's holding you back? We're here anyway. Competitors drop out at the last minute all the time…"

Like she had.

She shot him a warning look but he pressed on.

"I'm sure Frank could get you appropriate gear quickly. The freestyle is two days from now, if you hit the slopes now and practice…" The excitement rising in his voice made her want to vomit. "Even an old routine would blow this place up…"

"Asher, stop!"

He did and sighed. He studied her for a long moment. "I don't get why you're so afraid."

Really? He couldn't understand her hesitation to try something that had almost killed her? Something she'd been certain she didn't need anymore until she was standing there among the buzz of competition? "Because I could have broken my neck and never walked again. Giving up this ridiculous sport while I could still live an able-bodied life seemed like the best option for me, okay?" she said coldly. Her gaze went past him as several competitors stared a little too long, obviously recognizing them…or maybe just Ash. Either way, having this argument right there on the street only increased her irritation. "Can we go back to the resort now?" At this point, she wasn't sure they could salvage the rest of the weekend but she was willing to try. As long as he stopped this ridiculous conversation.

He didn't. "Just try."

He was seriously obtuse. "I told you, I'm done with snowboarding," she said, her anger rising. Hadn't he promised not to bring up the idea of her competing?

"You're just scared. I get it. But this is your chance, Em…"

"I don't want a chance at this again, Ash." She pulled away from him, an ache in her chest at the look of disappointment on his face. "I left this behind. I'm moving on…" Was he not hearing anything she said? The more she repeated herself, the more conflicted she felt. If he believed so strongly that trying again was the right thing to do, could he be right?

"At the University of Florida?" His tone was cold as he said it. "Busting your butt for a career that won't make you happy?"

He had a lot of nerve to make that assumption. "How do *you* know what will make me happy?"

"Because I know you. You and I are the same. We thrive on the competition, we feel alive when the adrenaline takes over. We work our bodies to breaking points, then push even further." He lifted his sunglasses over his hat to look into her eyes.

She was grateful for her own dark lenses as tears threatened. She shook her head. "That's not me anymore." Damn, she wished she sounded more convincing.

Asher's jaw clenched. He stared at her, his chest rising and falling in a deep sigh. "Where is the girl who won gold at the Olympics? The one who broke speed records three years in a row? The one with the medals and trophies she'd once been proud of? This was your life, and you've been hollow without it."

She was hollow without *him*. Why the hell couldn't he realize what she had—that there was more to life. "I grew up, Ash. This sport was never something that was going to last." Just like hockey for him. "I want a different life." At least she thought she did. Her suddenly conflicted heart betrayed her.

He stared at her as though he didn't know her. As though she were suddenly a disappointment.

Breaking every last piece of her heart.

"Don't you ever want more?" she asked, hating the note of pleading in her voice. If he couldn't figure out that there was a life outside of the arena on his own, what chance did she have? What chance did they have at a future if he continued to put hockey first?

"More than what?"

"Hockey. Life on the road. Putting your body through hell every night. Never settling down…This injury proves you're not the invincible person you think you are. Someday you won't be able to keep up."

He stormed toward her and gripped her shoulders, forcing her to meet his gaze. "Do not put *your* fears and insecurities on me. Just because you're no longer brave enough to go after what you want doesn't mean I'm rolling over and playing dead. This injury is nothing. *Your* injuries were nothing. You recovered, and you could have been great again." He released her and his gaze lowered to their feet. "I guess that's the difference between us."

A lump formed in her throat. What was he saying? That she wasn't the person he'd thought she was? The kick to the gut made her ill.

"You can't allow fear to hold you back from what you want," he said, an obvious attempt to soften the blow he'd just delivered.

Too late.

"You have to go after what you want."

His words resulted in a slightly bitter laugh escaping

her. *Go after what she wanted?* Like when she'd pushed her fears aside and told him she loved him, only to be met with no response? Yeah, 'cause that had worked out so wonderfully for her.

"I think I've taken enough chances that haven't quite panned out the way I was hoping for one weekend."

"Emma…"

Moving around him, she headed down the street. Quickly, through the crowd of blurred faces and away from him.

* * *

Damn. Asher ran a hand over his stubble at his chin as he watched Emma storm away.

"That was smooth."

Turning, he saw Frank Jarvis standing right next him. "Hey, Coach," he said, extending a hand to the man.

He took it with a shake of his head. "Still no luck getting her back on a board, huh?"

Asher's gaze returned to her angry, disappearing figure down the street. "Nope." He didn't get it. She obviously still wanted to compete if she'd come back the year after her accident. And he knew she could be great again if she tried. Allowing fear to hold her back from something she loved, something she was passionate about, was not the Emma he knew.

"Let me buy you a drink," Frank said, nodding toward the Mountainside Ale Brewhouse just as a waitress illuminated the open sign in the window and set out the curbside daily menu.

"It's ten a.m."

"Right. We're getting a late start. Better hurry," the older man said, slapping Asher's shoulder and heading toward the pub.

Asher shrugged and followed the former snowboarding legend. Emma had probably left him stranded miles from the resort by now anyway. At least he hoped that's where she was headed, and not straight back to Glenwood Falls. In all their years as friends and lovers, he couldn't remember an argument with her.

It sucked. He hadn't meant his words to come out as harsh as they had. He just couldn't understand her unwillingness to try. The Emma he knew had never let fear hold her back.

Her words about the chance she'd already taken, telling him she loved him, had made him feel like an asshole. The last thing he'd wanted was to hurt her or upset her by bringing her here this weekend. Yet, he'd done both.

A drink actually didn't sound like a bad idea. He usually avoided alcohol during the season, but well, he wasn't playing. And he probably wouldn't be for a while, seeing as how he'd just pissed off the only woman who cared enough to help him recover quickly.

Inside the dimly lit pub, it took his eyes a second to adjust as he removed his Oakleys and hat from the top of his head. Like everywhere else in Breckenridge, the place was covered in Christmas decorations, reminding him of just how close the holiday was. He'd been hoping to do his shopping in the village and that Emma would help him buy and wrap gifts for his family…

He shook his head. Man, he relied on her for so much.

Sliding into the booth, he reached for a drink menu.

"Don't bother looking. I know exactly what you need," Frank said as the waitress approached.

The woman, who looked about eight months pregnant, was wearing a large black T-shirt with the pub's logo on it over a pair of red-and-green-striped leggings. She grinned upon seeing Frank. "Didn't I just kick you out of here a few hours ago?"

Fantastic. The man had turned to alcohol in his retirement. He wondered if the competition officials knew one of their judges would more than likely be a little tipsy on that day's judging panel. And hadn't Frank been checking equipment that morning? Ash shifted uncomfortably, as Frank laughed. "Can we get two of my usual?" he asked.

The redhead nodded, her Christmas tree–shaped earrings dangling back and forth. She smiled in Asher's direction, but her question was directed at Frank. "You sure your friend can handle your usual? He looks like a lightweight," she said with a wink.

Lightweight? Him? Frank was at least three inches shorter and forty pounds lighter. What the hell kind of drink did the guy order for them?

Frank eyed him, then nodded. "Don't let the baby face fool you. This is one of the NHL's biggest brawlers."

Hardly. Asher shook his head. "You know what, maybe I'll just have a coffee."

"He'll have what I'm having," Frank told the waitress.

She winked at him again as she walked off toward the bar.

"So, tell me what you did to piss off our girl."

Too much. He ran a hand through his hair. "Pushed her too far, I guess."

"Well, you got her to come to Breckenridge…that's a feat in itself. Being back here can't be easy on her."

Asher leaned on his elbows. "I just found out she came this far on her own two years ago." How had he not known that? Why hadn't she told him? He could have tried to be there for her, encourage her, help her get back to what she'd once loved. The fact that she felt she couldn't tell him annoyed him. Like the Florida thing.

Frank nodded. "I saw her name on the competitors list that year…"

"She just needs to try," Asher said.

"Does she?" Frank sat back in the booth and interlaced his fingers on the table in front of him.

"Yeah…I mean, she can't just walk away."

"Why not?"

Was the man playing devil's advocate, or did he truly believe that Emma should give up her passion? The coach may have called it quits and resorted to judging and drinking, so maybe that's where he was coming from, but Emma wasn't a quitter.

"Because she was one of the greatest female competitors in the sport."

Frank leaned forward. "And she retired that way. She didn't keep competing after she knew she only had one way to go. Asher, professional sports have a way of making an athlete feel immortal…but only when they're on top."

He shifted in the booth. He could relate to that feeling, sure. At thirty, his own career was soon going to be on the decline.

"But the inevitable downward spiral can be devastating," Frank continued. "Emma walked away at the right time."

"But…"

Frank held up a hand. "Her injuries had broken not only her body but also her spirit. Without that driving spark that Emma had before her accident, she would never have stood on those podiums again, and that would have crushed her more than the fall."

Asher was silent.

"Right now, she was once the best and she has no reason to feel like that ever had a reason to change…Let her have that," he said as the waitress returned.

The man's words had him conflicted as hell. Was he right? It was a tough concept for Asher to grasp. He planned on playing hockey until they kicked him out and he wore out his last set of blades, whether he was the star or not.

Didn't he?

"Here you are. Two mocha peppermint lattes with a vanilla swirl and double shot of espresso with a candy cane stick on the side," the waitress said, placing two steaming, frothy mugs in front of them.

The scent of coffee, chocolate, peppermint, and a hint of vanilla reached his nose and Asher relaxed a little. "This is your usual?"

Frank raised his mug and grinned over the steam. "It's ten o'clock in the morning, man."

Asher laughed wryly as he picked up his own mug, thinking maybe the coach was right about more than he'd been ready to give him credit for.

He owed his best friend an apology.

Shit, he owed her a hell of a lot more than that.

* * *

"Is there anything I can help you find?"

Emma turned to the salesclerk inside the boutique in the village with a forced smile. "No, thank you. I'm actually just killing time," she said. Two hours since storming away from Asher, she'd yet to clear the argument from her head or rid herself of the uneasiness in her stomach. They never fought. So this odd feeling of not quite knowing what to do next had her wandering aimlessly through the village.

"Well, if you need anything, just let me know."

"Will do. Thanks," she said, browsing the Christmas ornaments on the wall of the shop. Every store she'd wandered into was playing Christmas music, and their displays and décor were warm and inviting, a reminder that the holiday was just a week away. Each store had similar products—Christmas ornaments, scented candles, body lotions in beautiful packaging, cozy knitted scarves…

She was barely seeing any of it, replaying Asher's words.

Can't let fear hold her back.

She could if it meant not getting her heart broken. She'd put her feelings for him out there and had gotten nothing back.

She wouldn't be making that mistake with regard to her former career. She'd thought the risk had been worth it for Asher.

His insistence over her competing again confused her. He'd been there through the days following her accident…he'd been there in the years since. He had to know she'd really moved on. Maybe he just didn't want to accept that. It was as though he couldn't see her for more than just the pro athlete she'd once been.

Her chest ached and the pain deepened as her eye caught an ornament of a cute couple—him carrying skates, her carrying skis—with the caption "Our First Christmas Together."

God…she'd been hoping.

Moving away from the taunting wall, she noticed a selection of snow globes in a glass display case. She wondered if Ash had bought anything for his mother for Christmas yet.

Probably not. Every year they all received New Jersey Devils logo gifts he'd obviously purchased from the arena gift shop…about two weeks *after* Christmas.

The globes were beautiful, and she knew Beverly had a collection of them…

Not her problem.

Asher could do his own damn shopping.

Still, she lingered at the display case. "Excuse me," she asked the clerk. "Can I see this snow globe?" Sigh.

The young woman, wearing a gingerbread-themed smock over a red turtleneck, gingerbread men earrings dangling from her ears, approached with the display case key. "Sure. Which one?"

"Um…the one with the family having a snowball fight." Three little boys and a girl. Just like the Westmores. Beverly would love it for the collection.

"This one just came in, and there was only one. It must be your lucky day."

Hardly. "Yeah, must be."

The salesclerk carefully removed it from the case and handed it to her. "It's so beautiful. It plays three different holiday songs, and the base lights up from the bottom as it rotates," she said.

Emma stared at the children playing inside. It would make the perfect gift for Beverly. Despite her annoyance with Ash, there was no way she could leave the store without it. "I'll take it."

The salesclerk beamed, taking it from her and going to the register. "Are you here on vacation or as part of the tour?" she asked as she wrapped it in paper before sliding it into a box.

Emma swallowed hard. More like an unwelcome trip down memory lane. "Vacation," she mumbled.

"The competitions are great. If you have time, you should definitely check them out," the young woman said, ringing in the sale.

Emma nodded politely as she paid for the snow globe. Could she watch them? Already, just being there was making her doubt her own resolve to having moved on. What would it feel like to watch other competitors, with Asher's words plaguing her? "Thank you," she said, taking the bag.

"Merry Christmas," the clerk said as she exited the store.

She zipped her coat higher as she headed down the sidewalk, back toward the ski hill where she'd ditched Asher. She had to find him. She couldn't make him walk back to the resort on his leg. At least the therapist in her couldn't.

Her cell phone rang in her coat pocket and she stopped on the corner to answer it. "Hello?"

"Hey, Emma?"

The sound of Sean Whitney's voice made her heart race. She'd yet to send him an email regarding her decision to wait until September enrollment. Even in her anger that morning, she still believed waiting was the best thing. "Yes, hi, Sean."

"Am I catching you at a bad time?"

"Um…I've got a second." She lifted her scarf higher around her neck as the shade of the building blocking the midday sun made the temperature drop by several degrees.

"I haven't heard back from you yet, and I don't mean to pressure you, but I'm going to need an answer about the early enrollment," he said, his voice breaking up slightly in the less than ideal reception in the valley.

She sighed. He deserved an answer, and she felt terrible for having put him off this long. "I really appreciate your patience. Unfortunately, I think I'll have to stick to my original timeline of a September start date next year."

He cleared his throat. "Emma, unfortunately, the September acceptance letters went out two weeks ago. The program is full for the fall. I honestly expected you to join us in the new year. That's the spot reserved for you."

Her heart fell. September was full. It was January or nothing.

"Oh…"

"Of course, your name can be added to the course waiting list, but there's no guarantee."

"Not like January."

"Exactly. Sorry, if I'd known sooner…"

"No, please don't apologize. It's my fault for taking so long to decide." She hesitated, biting her lip. Her gaze fell on the mountain, and from the distance she could see the competitors warming up for that day's events. She watched the multicolored figures swishing down the

slopes, the fresh, perfect-condition powder tearing up behind their boards.

"January is fast, I know…but why wait?" Sean continued in her extended silence. "We'd love to have you
here." Anyone could detect the double meaning in his
tone. His obvious interest was one of the things actually
making her choice that much harder.

Why wait? Her gaze was still locked on one of the
reasons—the big, terrifying mountain that despite her
claims to the contrary still had a hold on her.

"Can I think about it? Just for another day or two?" she
asked.

Sean hesitated for a long moment. "Well, okay…but I
need to know by Monday."

Two days away.

"If you don't want the opportunity, we will have to
give it to another candidate," he said.

God, he must think she was so ungrateful for this
chance. She knew other potential candidates would have
jumped at this without hesitation. Especially now that
September wouldn't be an option for her. She'd be looking at postponing her new future career plans by a year or
more. Her hesitation and indecision were crazy. "Thank
you so much, Sean. I really do appreciate this, and I will
give it serious thought and let you know soon. Tomorrow,
not Monday." She couldn't keep him waiting any longer
than that. She couldn't keep herself waiting longer than
that.

"Do that. I'd really enjoy working with you."

Yes, he'd said that already. "Great. Thank you again."
She disconnected the call, then almost immediately hit
Redial on the Florida number. She knew what she wanted

to do. And too much of her decision so far had been based on something—*someone*—she wasn't entirely sure was a safe bet anymore. The last few weeks had been a roller coaster of emotion through this journey with Ash.

She loved him. He was still not ready, or was unwilling, to make the same commitment.

And whether he did eventually or not, she refused to put the rest of her life on hold while she waited.

She was accepting the open spot in January. Decision made, she felt a weight lift from her chest.

Replaced by something else.

As she stared at the slopes, a new sensation filled her—one she couldn't quite define.

She knew one thing. Before she walked away permanently, before she embarked on her new path, she had to conquer her fear of that mountain.

CHAPTER 16

With the main slopes roped off and reserved for competitors, Emma headed to the section of the mountain left open for the recreational skiers.

She couldn't remember the last time she'd had to rent a snowboard and boots, but it didn't matter. Boots on, board in hand, Emma made her way toward the chair lift, through the families and groups of friends enjoying the cloudless day and amazing weather conditions. Holiday music blared from the outdoor speakers, and the smell of hot chocolate and roasted chestnuts from the outdoor café at the base of the mountain made her stomach growl. She hadn't eaten since they'd left the resort that morning, but she couldn't trust her nerves to allow her to keep anything down.

Right after this run, she was heading to the café.

It would be her reward for actually surviving.

At the chair lift, she hung back, allowing several groups and pairs...couples...to get on before her.

"Lone rider?" the attendant asked.

She nodded.

He waved forward another skier and stopped the chair. "You two together," he said.

With one foot strapped into her board, she climbed on first before she could chicken out.

The older man sat next to her and smiled. "I haven't skied in years. Hope I remember how."

"Like riding a bike," she said.

He nodded, turning his attention to the scenery below them and making idle small talk that she was only partially paying attention to as they rose higher to the top of the mountain.

It was a level two slope, a run she could have completed with her eyes closed and hands tied behind her back three years ago. Now, the height and angle of the hill looked slightly paralyzing as she placed her other foot against the back binding and skied off the chair onto the top of the mountain.

"See you at the bottom," the guy yelled, skiing off.

Great.

Arms out straight over the board, she moved slowly away from the chair lift. Choosing a quieter spot at the top, she dragged the toes of her back foot along the snow to stop the board and stood staring at the hill. It was an easy run for her. Or for her former self.

She could do this.

The cold snowy breeze at the higher altitude did nothing to cool her, and her heart pounding in her ears drowned out the festive sounds around her, as she strapped her other foot into the board.

All she had to do was push off, and a simple thirty-second run later, she would be done. She'd have proven to herself what she'd been claiming all along and maybe, going forward, she could snowboard recreationally. She could reclaim her love of the sport without it controlling her, and she could go to Florida with more confidence.

She was suddenly alone at the top, and she forced determination into each breath.

She could do this…She was all alone. No one was watching, expecting anything from her.

All alone…

Except for the familiar-looking ski jacket to her right as Asher climbed off the chair lift and headed toward her.

Damn.

* * *

"Asher? What the hell? Your leg is not healed enough for you to be up here."

"My leg is fine." It was his heart that was a mess. And his mind. "I thought I'd find you here." She hadn't been anywhere else, including the resort. He'd spent hours after leaving Frank searching the village for her. Unsuccessful, he'd walked part of the way back to the resort, hailed a cab the rest of the way, then shuttled it back down to the village when she hadn't been in their room, at the pool, or the resort restaurant. The ski hill was the least of his leg's exercise that day.

"I'm not up here with any plans to compete," she said, apprehension in her voice.

"I don't expect you to," he said. After talking to

Frank, he was finally hearing her. He'd also started to realize that the reason he needed her to hold on to her dream a little longer was so that he wouldn't feel guilty holding on to his. Which was unfair. If she wanted to pursue the doctorate degree, he'd support her one hundred percent.

Emma was smart and determined and driven; she'd be amazing at anything she tried.

"What are you doing up here, Ash?" she asked, brushing her hair away from her face.

God, she was so beautiful, so determined, and so *pissed*. He swallowed hard. "I wanted to tell you I'm sorry. I was wrong. I was wrong to try to tell you what you should want out of life. To make you feel bad about your decision to quit and walk away. You did what you wanted to do…and I should have supported that."

Her expression was unreadable as she stared down the mountain.

"Emma, I said all of that because I'm terrified of what you moving on means for us. No, not for us—for *me*." He paused. "I need you." He hadn't realized how much she filled his life until her absence left him with a big, hollow space that made his chest ache, clouded his mind, and drove him to a dark, lonely place. Which was why he was so damn terrified of her going to Florida. If one afternoon at odds with her had left him feeling this empty, this desperate…How was he supposed to live without her if things changed for her once she started her new life?

Waiting around for a self-centered jock who was focused solely on his career wouldn't be enough for her.

"Which me do you need? The best friend who always

supported you, believed in you…loved you?" she said. "Or the me whose body you could always depend on whenever you passed through town?"

The harshness of the words made his stomach turn. She couldn't honestly believe that he'd only been using her these years…Though what other impression could she take away from his actions? From his unwillingness to commit to the only situation in his life that had ever made sense? From his own harsh words and critical judgment of her and her choices? He moved closer. "All of you. My best friend, my lover…and the woman that I'm falling in love with." He knew it was far more than his own insecurities making him feel this ache for her. He was in love with her. Probably always had been.

She blinked, and he could see tears forming. "Asher, you are scared of losing me, and for the first time you're realizing just how big of a part I am in your life. But that's not love. It's a fear to move on, to find something…someone else…It's an uncertainty you'd rather not face."

She was wrong. How could he make her see that he meant every word? That he loved her. That his life, his career, his dream meant nothing without her to share it all with. "That's not it. I know I messed up. I know I was blind for so long that I might have missed my chance, but Em, I love you." There, he'd said it, and there was no taking it back. He didn't want to take the words back. "I'm not me without you." He reached out for her, but she backed away.

"Asher, I'm not sure I can do this with you. You were right that I was afraid to face my fears, and that's what

I'm trying to do. First with this mountain, then with the PhD program."

With Sean Whitney. But not with him. She was too smart to make that mistake again.

"I'm not ready to be hurt by you," she said softly, her voice barely audible above the breeze.

He gripped his ski poles as he took a step away from her. "Right. Yeah, no, I understand." He did. He was too late. He'd been an idiot, a fool who didn't realize what he had until it was too late. Then he'd hurt her further. She deserved to find happiness with someone who would see the bright light she was from the moment they saw her, touched her, kissed her...

His heart ached to be that guy, but years of not being who she needed stood in the way. "Okay. I'm sorry. I'll go."

"Ash..."

He stopped, a flicker of hope in his heart as he turned to face her.

She looked as tortured as he felt, and he longed to grab her and kiss her and make her believe that she hadn't been wrong to put herself out there for him. That he wanted her fully, completely, and was willing to sacrifice anything to make it happen...but he just stood there waiting. Hoping.

"I really don't think you should be on the slope. This is a level two, and you've never successfully skied it even when you weren't recovering from an injury," she said.

Right. She was concerned about his leg. She really would make a terrific doctor. He didn't doubt that for a second.

"And your big game is in a few weeks," she said, her voice devoid of anything he could grasp onto.

His big game. The one that suddenly no longer seemed to hold as much meaning. "Don't worry. I'll take the trail down," he said, skiing away from her, leaving her alone to take on this challenge she needed to do for herself, deserved to do for herself.

He walked away from her, giving her the space she needed to soar.

CHAPTER 17

*A*fter entering the clinic two days later, Asher hesitated, pretending to read the local community board posted outside the reception office. His gaze flew over the flyers announcing holiday events and local business cards stuck to the bulletin board, but he wasn't taking in any of it. From the corner of his eye, he glanced inside the clinic, but other than several patients waiting in the reception area, he didn't see anyone else inside.

His mouth was dry as he checked his watch. His session was scheduled to start in five minutes.

His leg was feeling much better though, and he could do the exercises just as well at home...

"Going in?" Jane's voice behind him made him jump. She laughed. "Sorry. I'm pretty good at sneaking up on people," she said, as she struggled to open the office door, balancing a tray of coffees.

"Let me," Asher said, holding the door while she entered. Then, releasing a deep breath, he followed behind.

Jane set the coffees down on her desk and removed her dark green winter coat, hanging it on the hook behind the desk chair. "I didn't know you were still in town."

He nodded. It was just a week before Christmas, and he'd never hear the end of it if he left now. But man, was it tempting. He hadn't heard from Emma since she'd taken the Greyhound bus back to Glenwood Falls instead of driving back with him.

He'd been on his way back to the room with a well-rehearsed better apology, when the resort's front desk attendant had handed him the note she'd left.

Need some time and space. We'll talk soon.

That was it.

And in the last two days he'd been progressively in a worse mood the longer the time and space continued. He'd texted to make sure she'd gotten home and received a one word reply: *yes*. And he'd texted to say he was sorry. To which he'd gotten silence.

That morning, he'd struggled with the urge to cancel his appointment. He didn't want to see her for the first time after their disastrous weekend like this…but this may be the only way he would.

"I'll be sticking around until after Christmas." He had four more therapy sessions before they'd think about letting him back on the ice, but he'd go crazy in Glenwood Falls if Emma continued to ignore him.

"That's nice. I'm sure your family will be happy to have you here this year."

He nodded distractedly as he heard one of the therapy doors opening. He turned slightly. Not Emma, but the older male therapist that worked there. He nodded in greeting, then turned back to Jane. "Can you let Emma know I'm here?"

She nodded, then frowned, looking at her open schedule on her computer. "Actually, your appointment this morning is with Dr. Masey."

His mouth was like chalk. "Nope. Emma's my therapist." His only therapist. Also the woman he was going crazy without, one he was certain he was in love with and one whose silence was torture.

Jane frowned as she looked at the computer. "Not today. This is weird. A lot of Emma's patients have been reassigned to Dr. Masey."

The doctor nodded as he approached. "That's right. There isn't a mistake on the schedule. Unfortunately, Emma's leaving us to pursue her doctorate at the University of Florida," he told Jane. "So she's reducing her hours and transitioning patients to me in the next two weeks."

Asher's mouth gaped. She'd handed him off? And she was going to Florida for the January semester?

Damn. He hadn't thought his disappointment and regret over their argument could get any deeper. He was wrong.

"Are you ready to go in?" Dr. Masey asked.

No. Unfortunately, he knew he wouldn't get clearance to get back on the ice unless he successfully completed his therapy sessions and they sent a letter to the team's doctor and his coach. He swallowed hard, fighting to conceal his feelings as he nodded. "Yes, yeah…Thanks, Jane."

She shot him a sympathetic look, obviously able to

read the situation. No doubt his turmoil was written all over his face. "No problem, Asher. Good luck," she said.

Following the doctor into the therapy room, he glanced toward Emma's office. She was leaving Glenwood Falls for Florida. Leaving her past behind...

Damn, but he refused to let that include him.

* * *

"You're not going to need all of these sweaters in Florida," Jess said, watching Emma box up her clothing two days later.

Emma stared at the stack of heavy sweaters, leggings, and jeans she'd just packed into the oversized box and sighed. "You're right...Can I store this stuff at your place while I'm away?" Thankfully, she'd been going month to month on her apartment, so she'd only had to pay one month's rent to get out of her lease. Her landlord had said it wouldn't be any trouble renting out the space after Christmas, and it had eased Emma's guilt over the lack of notice.

Dr. Masey, too, had been willing to accept two weeks as her notice, and he was happy to help her to transition her patients while she was still technically there. He was hoping she'd return to work at the clinic once she graduated, but at that moment, she had no plans beyond the immediate future.

So why she had this sense of dread weighing heavy on her chest, she didn't know.

Actually she knew exactly why her excitement over the opportunity was slow in coming. She didn't have Asher's support in it.

In fact, she wasn't sure she had Asher at all.

He'd texted twice since she'd left him on the mountains, but she wasn't ready to talk to him yet. If there was a chance he could mess with her mind about her decision or make her doubt her choice, she didn't want to talk to him at all.

She felt guilty for not telling him that she'd rescheduled the rest of his appointments with Dr. Masey, but he was almost fully recovered. He had only a few more sessions, then he'd be back in New Jersey and back on the ice. His mind would once again be on his milestone game and his future in hockey.

"Emma—are you hearing anything I'm saying?" Jess asked, taping up the box and writing WINTER CLOTHES on it.

Emma blinked. "No. Sorry. Just trying to figure out what the hell to pack." Her summer shorts and tank tops? Her flip-flops? Her bikinis? For most people, the idea of moving away from the cold winter months in Glenwood Falls would be a dream come true, but she loved her winters…and now that she'd braved several hours on the slopes, the snowboard in the corner of her closet was beckoning once again. She'd miss Colorado.

But she didn't have to stay in Florida forever.

Jess stood and opened the closet, taking out several skirts and casual dresses. "These would work…"

Emma raised an eyebrow. "I'm going out there for school, not to date."

Jess ignored her, placing the items into the suitcase she was packing for the plane. Her flight left January 2. Less than two weeks from now. "You can still look nice."

For Sean? She didn't ask for fear of starting another

argument with Jess. They'd just gotten over the last one.

But in truth, the head of the department was the only part of the program she was wary of. Her heart was a mess, and she didn't need Sean complicating her life any more. As soon as she met with him again face-to-face, she planned to make it very clear that she was there for the education only.

Reaching into her drawer for some T-shirts, her hand touched the silky fabric of her New Jersey Devils jersey. A lump immediately rose in her throat as she took it out of the drawer.

Ash had given her the jersey with his name and number on the back. Leaving home without it wouldn't feel right.

Nothing the last few days had felt anything close to right.

Jess's perceptive gaze didn't help as she tucked the jersey into the suitcase.

"Have you talked to him?" she asked.

Emma shook her head. The last person she wanted to talk to about Ash was her sister. The "I told you so" conversation would destroy her. She just wanted to get through the holidays with her family, then get on a plane and hope that her study schedule would fill her days and thoughts, drowning out the dull ache in her chest that she was currently suffering.

Approaching, Jess took her hands, forcing her to sit on the bed. "You're doing the right thing," she said.

Emma nodded. She knew she was. Being on the slopes had helped her overcome her fear, but it had also helped her say goodbye to her professional snowboarding past.

She loved being on the mountains, and they would always be a part of her—a part she was proud of—but she was ready for her new future.

"I'm sorry I was so pushy in this…" Jess started.

But Emma stopped her. "You were right, Jess." She paused. "About everything." She hadn't gone into detail about her argument with Ash, but her early return from the mountains and the fact that she'd had to call Jess to pick her up from the bus station had said enough. Tears burned the back of her eyes, and Jess moved closer to hug her tight. "Asher is something else I have to let go of."

CHAPTER 18

❦

The Avalanche were unstoppable. As much as Asher hated to admit it, they might just be the Devils' biggest competition for the cup again that season. Going head to head against his brother in the playoffs would be déjà vu, and he hoped for a different outcome this time.

He was itching to get back on the ice, and his mood was worsening with each passing day as Christmas drew closer. The sight of Christmas lights and decorations, the sound of the familiar carols, and the deliciously tempting aromas of the season were doing nothing to make him feel better. If it weren't for his last therapy session with Dr. Masey, he would have been tempted to go back to New Jersey.

Abandoning his family a few days before Christmas would be an asshole move though, so he continued to suck it up when they insisted on decorating the family tree together and forced him to attend the children's Christmas concert at school. He'd sat in the crowded gymnasium, knowing Emma was there somewhere with her family watching her nephews, and unable to think about anything else.

He couldn't believe she still refused to talk to him six days later, but three unanswered text messages were ringing loud and clear.

He watched the final seconds of the third period count down as he stretched his leg. Between his sessions with Dr. Masey, he was working the leg like crazy. Walking into the clinic knowing that Emma didn't want to continue his rehabilitation and had purposely arranged her schedule so she wouldn't be there when he was there depressed him further, but he had to see this through.

He tried to focus on the game, but his gaze constantly shifted to his unringing cell phone.

Come on, Emma!

She couldn't really be done with him. Could she?

The thought made his stomach turn. They'd never gone this long without talking. He missed her, but he didn't even know where to start to get them back to where they'd been before the trip. Her words had struck a chord with him—one he didn't need struck. The injury had already reminded him that he couldn't continue this dream forever, and he hadn't needed to hear it from her.

But his words to her had been unfair. She'd had a fantastic career, and she was smart enough to know that snowboarding wouldn't be there forever and find a new path for her future. A great path. She was going to be a doctor—wow! Any patient would be lucky to have her. He wished he still had her—in all capacities.

Onscreen, the third period had ended and Ben approached an ESPN reporter for the after-game interview. Awarded a star that evening, his brother was first up to the hot seat.

"Great game tonight. The team looks like it's headed right back to the playoffs this year, with fourteen straight wins," the reporter said.

Ben nodded. "We're playing well. Everyone feels good. We haven't had any injuries this season so far…It's looking good." He ran a hand through his sweaty hair and looked more tired than usual after a game. Asher leaned closer to study his brother. His normal post-game high seemed to be missing.

"You're leading in points again this season," the reporter said. "With all the new, younger players on the team, that must be a great feeling."

Ben smiled as he shook his head. "Not as great as finding out my fiancée is expecting our first baby," he said.

Asher's mouth dropped. Had Ben just said that on national television? Readily given the tabloids shit to go nuts over? After his brother's previous year in hot water, Asher had expected him to keep his personal life a little more low-key these days. Apparently not. His brother loved the spotlight.

He glanced at his mother, who'd just entered the living room, her pleased-as-shit grin matching Ben's. "You knew?"

She nodded. "Olivia called me just after she told Ben before the game tonight."

Wow. This was great news…but he couldn't help but wonder how a pregnant fiancée might interfere with his brother's focus for the rest of the season.

Ben's voice drew his attention back to the TV. "And I also have another announcement to make. I was going to wait until the end of the season…In truth, I hadn't felt confident enough in the decision until earlier today…"

What the fuck? Asher leaned closer to the screen and shot a look at his mother, but her expression looked just as surprised, though not as concerned as his.

"I'm retiring at the end of the season when my contract with the Avalanche is up," Ben said.

"Shit."

"Retiring?" Even the reporter looked surprised— surprised and thrilled that she was getting the first official announcement.

Other mics appeared on screen, shoved in Ben's face, as every reporter in the stadium tried to get the story.

"But you're only thirty-four. You still could play for years…"

Ben nodded. "I could. And I feel great. But I've got a Stanley Cup win, I've hit every professional goal I've set for myself…I've done what I wanted to do, and now there's another life, another set of goals I'm looking forward to achieving."

"Wow. Well, you'll certainly be missed."

"Good," Ben said in true Ben fashion. "I'd hate to go out on bottom and be forgotten about." He winked, and as usual the reporter swooned.

Go out on bottom and be forgotten about.

"Thanks for the exclusive, Ben. Good luck with the rest of your season. Your *final* season," the reporter said, turning back to her cameraman.

As Ben disappeared through the sea of reporters, Ash

turned off the television. Final season. His brother was hanging up the jersey…for a new life.

That there was more to life than hockey had never sounded so true as it did when the one person he'd foolishly thought would wear skates until they pried them off his cold, dead feet was hanging them up early.

Asher sighed, resting his head back against the couch cushions. Ben and Emma might be right to be moving toward other goals, but he still had milestones he wanted to achieve for himself in the sport.

He couldn't give everything up or walk away just yet.

But damn, if he didn't hate that—unlike his brother—he hadn't discovered a way to have it all.

* * *

Decorating an artificial pink tree alone was depressing as hell.

Emma draped strands of tinsel over the edges of the branches on the barely four-foot-tall rotating musical eyesore that she'd bought mainly to piss off her ever-traditional sister. She was only decorating it because her nephews were coming over the next day. Now that they were out of school for the holidays, she was watching them while Jess and Trey were at work, and she'd promised them that they could pop popcorn and string it for her tree. In the background, *It's a Wonderful Life* was on the television, and she raised an eyebrow as she watched George Bailey hugging his family after the angel had shown him all the wonderful things he had in his life.

The guy couldn't just figure it out on his own and save his family a ton of heartache? Picking up the remote, she switched the station. *Miracle on 34th Street.* Nope. *White Christmas.* Nope. Ah, *Die Hard.* Perfect. The only holiday movie that wouldn't destroy her completely.

Looking at the tree and the remaining tinsel in her hand, she flung it in the air over the branches. It fell, clinging where it would.

There. Done.

Now, no one could say she wasn't festive.

She glanced around her living room, where half-packed boxes were stacked. She'd been renting her apartment furnished—never fully ready to commit to small-town life—so she only had her personal items to pack and store at Jess's while she was away. She'd rent another furnished apartment in Florida.

Sitting on her couch, she reached for her laptop and saw a notification flashing in the corner.

A new IM message from Sean.

She sighed. Since she accepted the January enrollment spot, he'd emailed her six times with course information, a book list, apartment listings near the campus…

She appreciated his help, but it was all a little too much. She really hoped he wasn't expecting anything more than just faculty friendship once she arrived in Florida. Ignoring the blinking message, she closed the laptop and tucked her leg beneath her on the couch, her thoughts wandering, settling on nothing concrete. Just a slightly overwhelming feeling of uncertainty enveloping her as she scanned her apartment. In two weeks she'd be living almost two thousand miles away…

Her gaze landed on the nutcracker centerpiece from the fashion show, standing near her electric fireplace in the corner. Tears burned the back of her eyes as the tender expression of love carved in the wooden figurines reminded her of everything she wanted that was just out of reach.

Picking up her cell, she stared at the picture of her and Ash taken at the NHL award ceremony. It was one of the best nights of her life. Everything in the world had felt right that evening.

Would it ever feel that way again?

* * *

"Congratulations," Asher said, sliding onto a stool at the Grumpy Stump next to his brother the following evening.

"On both—the retirement and the baby—or just the baby?" Ben asked, handing him a shot from those lined up on the bar, as the hometown crowd celebrated the good and unexpected news.

"Both in time…the baby for now," Asher said, raising the shot.

Ben held his up. "Look at it this way, with me out next season, you may have a shot at the Stanley Cup."

Asher laughed. "Fine. I'll think about letting you have it again this year."

"I'd appreciate that," Ben said, and the two tipped back their drinks.

Setting the shot glass down on the bar, Asher ordered a round of drinks and tossed several bills down.

Ben looked around the full room. "Flying solo? Where's Emma?"

Asher reached for his beer and chugged it back. He knew his family would notice that he was alone tonight. "I blew that."

"Naturally." Ben nodded. "But fix it."

Ben knew all about fixing things, but Asher wasn't sure he could change things between him and Emma even if he did have his brother's *GQ* model smile and charm. He shook his head. "It's too late. Besides, I gotta get back to New Jersey. Start training again." And she had a new future to start. One that didn't involve sitting around waiting for him.

"Do you love her?"

"Wow. Who are you, man?" Love? A year ago, his brother would have choked on the word. Olivia coming into Ben's life had transformed his playboy brother. He barely recognized him anymore…in a good way. Until he started talking about feelings—that shit was just weird.

"Come on. Answer the question." Ben elbowed him.

He knew the answer, but having this discussion with Ben seemed pointless. In a town as small as Glenwood Falls, he'd been expecting to see her around more, but there had been no sight of her…even coming or going from her father's house. She was clearly going to all lengths possible to avoid seeing him. So, what did it matter that for the first time in his life, he was experiencing the soul-crushing defeat of love? Admitting it would only hurt more.

"Asher, it's not a trick question, man."

He chugged another mouthful of beer. "Yeah, maybe… I don't know," he lied.

Ben shook his head. "You're right. It's too late, and she deserves better."

Asher shot his brother a look. "All right, yes. I love her. I can't stomach the idea of another day without her. But she's avoiding me, and she'll be leaving for Florida soon." He shrugged. "I can't keep getting in the way of what she wants."

Ben tapped his shoulder as he stood. "She wanted you, man. But if you're not ready to commit, then you're doing the right thing by letting her go."

His brother headed toward his fiancée in the corner booth where their family was gathered. Ash had never felt so alone as he weighed his brother's words.

He knew Ben was right. But could he let Emma go?

The decision didn't seem his to make anymore.

CHAPTER 19

◦⤳✿⤶◦

S o, it looks like your determination has paid off.
You're clear to start playing again. But ease into it,"
Dr. Masey said the next day.

His final session had gone well. He had no more pain
and had regained full movement in the knee joint. He
knew his determination had definitely played a role in
his quick recovery, but most of the credit went to Emma.
She'd known how hard and fast she could push him.

She knew him.

Asher pushed the thought away as he sat up on the
therapy bed.

Five weeks. Not the two to three he'd boasted, but at
least not the six to ten they'd recommended. He'd be back
on the ice by New Year's Eve. "Thanks, doc," he said,
taking the clearance letter Dr. Masey had prepared for
him and climbing down from the table.

"Will your milestone game be here in Denver?" he asked as Asher put on his coat.

"Yeah. On New Year's Eve." It would be the last game he'd play in Denver that season unless the two teams made the playoffs. And oddly enough, his injury had made reaching his milestone on "home" ice possible… which he was reluctantly grateful for. "I'll try not to beat the Avalanche too badly," he said as he opened the therapy room door.

"Merry Christmas, Asher." The doctor shook his hand. "Good luck with the rest of your season."

"Merry Christmas," he said, leaving the office and entering the empty reception area. He was the last patient of the day…for the year actually, as the office was now closed until after the holidays.

Emma's door was open, but the lights were off and she wasn't there. He didn't know when she planned to leave for Florida, but he suspected it would be right after the holidays.

How was he going to spend the first Christmas in years in his hometown so close to her but not spend it with her?

Man, he'd messed up. If he could go back and change things, he would.

Pushing through the door, he pulled the zipper of his jacket higher as he walked home. The snow was falling in large, fluffy flakes, collecting on his jacket, his boots, and the crunchy ground beneath his feet. This part of town in the late afternoon was quiet as offices had closed already for the Christmas break and only a car or two passed as he walked, head down against the blowing snow.

Arriving home, he shook his head, seeing Mr. Callaway stapling another row of multicolored lights to his doorframe. He must have noticed Beverly's latest addition: an inflatable Santa Snoopy on the front lawn.

It was the day before Christmas Eve, and their feud was still going strong.

At least their parents were only fighting over holiday lights…

Opening the front door, he stomped his boots on the outdoor mat before entering.

"How did it go?" his mother asked, coming out of the kitchen.

"Great," he said. He removed his coat and hung it on the hook near the door. "Got my clearance." He took off his boots and set them on the drying rack. "I'll be back in Jersey and on the ice after Christmas. Coach agreed to let me play here against the Avalanche on New Year's Eve for the milestone game."

She wiped her hands on a Christmas apron that was covered in flour and gave him a quick hug. "I'm glad we will all get to be there," she said.

Would they *all* be there?

As if reading his thoughts, she said, "Emma stopped by."

His mouth went dry. "When?"

"About an hour ago."

When she knew he wouldn't be there.

"She brought over some things, left them in your room. Are you two okay?" Her perceptive gaze studied him. He suspected she already knew the answer. He and Emma had never gone this long without seeing one another, without talking…and his mother had noticed his depressed mood since he returned from Breckenridge.

He shrugged. "Yeah, fine…"

"She wasn't going to wait for you forever, you know," his mother said gently, touching his arm.

He did now. "I just wished I'd known time had run out," he said with a sigh and headed upstairs.

On his bed was a bag from Trinkets & Such—a shop in Breckenridge. Opening the box inside, he found a snow globe with a winter scene that could have been captured in his own front yard years before. Reaching into the bag, he read the note.

For your mom…

He sat on the bed with the snow globe as his mother appeared in the doorway.

"Is that for me?" she said, leaning against the doorframe.

Of course she'd already checked out what was in the bag.

"Yes." He stood and handed it to her. "Merry Christmas. I have fantastic taste," he said, desperate to ease the mood in the room and the ache in his chest.

His mother took the globe and hugged it to her chest. "She's a wonderful girl, Ash."

He nodded. He knew that. "The best."

"So, what are you going to do?"

"Play hockey." The only thing he could do.

* * *

So, she'd chickened out. Dropping off the snow globe for Beverly when she knew Asher wouldn't be there had been a gutless move, but she couldn't face him. Not a day be-fore Christmas Eve, when her heart was still in a mess.

She couldn't trust herself not to fall right back into his arms.

At the clinic, she packed her belongings and looked around the quiet, empty space. She hoped to be back working there once she finished her program, but in re-ality, with a specialization in sports therapy, she'd have little chance to use her skills in the small town.

It was more likely that she'd find new work in Denver…or maybe Florida, or wherever else the wind might take her.

For the first time in her life, the uncertainty of what came next made her nervous. She used to love to travel and explore different parts of the country and other coun-tries. Her snowboarding days had been all about adven-ture and unpredictability…but now she craved the safety and security of a stable, solid future.

She picked up a frame from her desk, a picture of Ash and her taken the year they'd met. They'd been hiking on Pikes Peak and had stopped to snap a selfie before self-ies were cool. No one else had been around that day on the mountain, and it was probably the first time in her life she'd truly felt connected to someone. She sighed, setting it carefully in the box. Then, putting in a few other items, she closed it, noticing an envelope with her name on it on her desk.

Opening it, she saw a party invite from Jane, addressed to her and Asher for New Year's Eve.

She tucked it into the box, knowing Asher would most likely be playing his one-thousandth game, and the chances of her attending alone were slim to none.

What she would be doing on New Year's Eve wasn't something she wanted to think about. All she knew was that it would be the first New Year's Eve she'd spent in ten years without blowing Asher a kiss through a Skype connection.

CHAPTER 20

◦◦◦

The smell of smoke woke him, and before his eyes could adjust to the darkness, Asher shot out of bed. Opening the bedroom door, he peered into the hall. The hallway smoke detector wasn't going off, and it was eerily quiet for just after midnight. He walked down the hall toward his mother's room, checking the other bedrooms as he went. No sign of fire…No smoke…In fact, the farther he moved from his own room, the less the heavy, putrid smell reached him.

He stopped at the top of the stairs and scanned the area below. The Christmas tree lights, which his mother insisted on leaving on, cast a glow over the room and entranceway, illuminating his view of the space as he went downstairs. He checked the kitchen first, then the living room and bathroom…Nothing.

And the smell of smoke was gone.

Was he having a stroke or imagining things? The smell upstairs in his room had been undeniable.

Outside, maybe?

He flicked on the outside light above the door and opened it. A flash of orange to his left caught his eye, and he rushed outside.

Mr. Callaway's porch was engulfed in flames.

The obvious source of the fire, the tiny evergreen tree he'd decorated with old fifties-style bulbs, blazed close to the house.

Shit.

Running back inside, he grabbed his boots and shoved them on his feet, then ran toward the neighbor's house. The fire had already covered one side of the porch, and the flames were spreading to the siding. The path to the front door was blocked.

How was he supposed to get inside? And why in the hell hadn't a smoke detector gone off yet? Immediately regretting not taking his cell phone as he'd rushed out in his boxer briefs, he contemplated going back inside to call 911, but what if the rest of the house caught quickly from all of these wires and electrical cords draped everywhere?

Fuck these stupid holiday lights.

Oblivious to the cold, he headed to the side of the house, looking for a back door. The last time he'd been inside the house was years ago, before Emma's father had bought it…he hoped the layout was similar to his mother's interior. Seeing the screen door over the fence through the yard, he tugged on the gate, but it didn't move. Reaching over it, he found a padlock on the inside.

Damn!

Moving away, he took several steps backward and then ran toward it, hiking himself up and over. Then, running up the back steps of the deck, he tried the handle.

Locked.

Seriously? Mr. Callaway had to be the only person in Glenwood Falls worried enough about security to lock their back door *and* fence. He banged on the glass with his hand, and immediately Terror came running.

"Good. Bark, little guy…wake up Delaney." He nodded encouragingly at the dog as he tried to see into the house. The kitchen was fire- and smoke-free, but this was the back of the house. By now, the living room could be up in flames. Sweat gathered on his forehead, despite the chilling air, as adrenaline made his heart race.

He continued to hammer on the door and the dog continued to bark, but Delaney didn't appear.

He had to go in. Depending on where the old man's bedroom was, he could already be passed out from smoke inhalation.

Using his elbow, Asher smashed the window, wincing as a shard of glass tore into his flesh. Ignoring the pain and the blood dripping onto the snow at his feet, he reached inside for the handle, unlocking and opening the door. He scooped Terror into his arms and headed toward the hallway, checking the way before moving on. A set of stairs leading to the second floor was on his right, so he took them two at a time, calling out as he went. "Delaney! Mr. Callaway!"

No response.

Glancing toward the ceiling, he saw the reason for the silence. The smoke detector hung open, no batteries inside.

His jaw clenched. Emma's father shouldn't be living alone. Unlike Asher's mother, the man had never fully learned to take care of things, depending on Emma and Jess far too much since their mother died.

With Emma gone, Jess would be completely responsible for the man. A rare sense of sympathy for Emma's sister filled him. He continued to call out as he checked the three bedrooms and the bathroom at the end of the hall. In his arms, Terror barked loud enough to wake the dead, but still no response.

And no Delaney. Where the hell was he? Was the man not even home?

As Asher ran back downstairs, he could see the flames had worked their way into the entryway. Heavy, thick, dark smoke filled the air and he bent low as he moved through it.

Crouching made his knee throb slightly. Maybe he wasn't as fully recovered as he'd thought. He hurried past the hall bathroom, checking it quickly, then continued on toward the living room at the front of the house.

Finally, he saw the older man, asleep in an old rocking chair near a burnt-out fireplace. He sat under a quilt, his head tilted to the side. His right hand hung limp over the arm of the chair, and a picture of his wife, Clare, had fallen to the hardwood floor.

Flames were working their way into the room through the front wall and had already shattered the glass window. The smoke was bitter to his nostrils, and Asher held his breath against the pungent air.

"Delaney," Asher said through his hand as he stooped next to him. "Hey, wake up. I need to get you out of the house." Please, God, do not let him be passed out.

Emma's father was not a small man, and unconscious he would be difficult to move, especially with Terror in his arms as well.

The old man's eyes opened slowly and he blinked and coughed. Dazed, confused…he stared at Asher as though he didn't recognize him before his eyes closed again.

"Mr. Callaway, wake up!" He shook him hard, but the man's head just fell forward.

Shit. How long had the smoke been filling up the house? He had to get him out into fresh air.

Coughing, he blinked through the smoke burning his own eyes as he lifted the blanket back, picked up the photo, and hesitated momentarily before tucking it awkwardly under his arm. He set the dog onto the floor. "Go outside," he told him.

The dog stayed by his side and yipped.

Loyal, if not smart.

Placing one arm under Delaney's legs and the other at his back, he lifted him as best as he could and scanned the area for a clear, safe path outside. The thick smoke made it hard to determine whether the back door was still an unhindered path, but the front door certainly wasn't an option, so he headed toward the back of the house. Coughing and struggling to breathe, the lack of oxygen tiring his muscles faster, he made his way through the smoke, struggling under the man's dead weight, checking to make sure the dog was following.

A glance toward the front of the house revealed that the porch was now completely engulfed in flames, so he went back through the kitchen, breathing in the thick, poisoning air slowly, as his own consciousness started to struggle. He had to make it outside. If he passed out, they were both screwed.

Picking up the pace, he went into the kitchen, and in the limited visibility, he tripped over a chair.

Pain seared through his newly recovered knee and he blinked through the haze. The weight of the man made his forearms burn, and the thick clouds spiraling around him threw off his sense of direction.

He could barely make out the open door.

Almost there.

A few more feet and they were both outside.

Terror ran out behind them, and Asher inhaled a large gulp of air as he looked around for a place to set Delaney a safe distance away from the house. There was no way he could climb over the fence carrying the man, and he couldn't risk injuring him by throwing him over unconscious.

He set him near the back fence and removed his winter boots, putting them quickly on the man's bare feet.

Running back toward the fence, he could hear yelling near the street. Peering through the planks of wood he could see a crowd gathered there, and hearing a fire truck siren wailing in the distance, his shoulders relaxed.

They were outside. Delaney was okay. Terror was dancing around his feet, yapping incessantly…

"Asher!" he heard his mother call out from the back deck of her house next door.

Turning, he saw her and relief flowed through him, despite the panicked expression on her face.

"We're okay. Send the firemen back here. Delaney's unconscious." He struggled to yell, as his chest felt like it was full of thick smoke. Breathing was still difficult, and his sight was slightly blurry.

Picking up Terror, he carried him, oblivious to the numbing cold of the icy snow crunching beneath his bare feet, back to where Delaney lay slumped, still unconscious near the fence.

Then, exhausted, his knee aching, his feet numb, and his lungs torturously struggling to breathe, Asher set the dog down next to his owner and collapsed beside them both as he heard the fireman cutting through the padlock on the gate.

Those stupid Christmas lights.

* * *

Emma rushed through the hospital doors in Denver two minutes after three a.m. In her pajamas and winter coat, mismatched running shoes on her feet, her heart was in her throat. Exhausted from reading the course prep material, she'd basically passed out around midnight and hadn't heard her cell phone ringing the first two times Jess had called. Thank God, her sister had kept trying. Running up to the information desk, she gave the nurse her father's name.

The older woman checked several files on her desk then pointed to the elevators down the hall. "He's being treated on the third floor in the burn unit…"

Burn unit. Emma didn't hear anything else as she sprinted toward the elevators, not feeling her legs beneath her. As she rode the elevator, she swallowed back tears. Those damn Christmas lights. She'd said they were a bad idea. Her father living alone was a bad idea. She hoped her sister realized that now.

The fire may have been an accident, but she couldn't help but have a feeling in her gut that accidents like this would happen often. Her father was more than just a little lost without their mother. And being in Florida, where she couldn't help Jess take care of him, would be torture.

She bit her lip as the slowest-moving elevator in history finally stopped on the third floor. Following the signs to the burn unit, she hurried there.

She saw Jess and Trey in a waiting area. "Where is he?"

"He's okay," Jess reassured her, hugging her, though the mascara stain tracks on her sister's cheeks revealed she'd been just as concerned. She couldn't remember ever seeing Jess disheveled or not put together, but this evening, her sister's blond hair was tangled and she wore her husband's winter coat.

"The doctor has him hooked up to oxygen," Trey told her, handing her a steaming cup of black coffee, like the one Jess clung to.

She took it with a shaky hand even though she knew she wouldn't be able to get the liquid past the lump in her throat. "Oxygen?"

"He'd inhaled a lot of smoke before Asher found him and got him out of the house safely."

She blinked. Ash had found her dad? Had *saved* her dad? Jess hadn't mentioned that little detail on the phone. "Can I see him?" she choked out.

"In a few minutes. The doctor just wants to check him out a little bit more first," Jess said. "But he really is okay. They both are. No burns...just smoke."

Emma collapsed in a seat. Asher had saved her father's life. They were both okay. The emotions welling up in her chest nearly strangled her. "The house?" She'd been in too much of a hurry and terrified to drive past it on her way.

"Not as lucky," Trey said. "Fire damage to the left side, mainly the porch and front living room."

Damn. "That sounds like a lot."

Trey nodded, wrapping an arm around Jess. "But honestly, your dad and Terror were lucky to get out. He was asleep in the living room."

Her heart fell. Not exactly the way any of them had expected to be starting Christmas Eve. A Christmas Eve she already had been dreading. She'd never thought it could go from depressing to absolutely devastating.

Thank God everyone was going to be okay. She swallowed the lump of fear that had taken up residence in her throat since the moment she'd answered the call from Jess.

"How's Asher?" she croaked. He'd saved her dad's life. She still couldn't wrap her mind around it. Jess had said on the phone that the smoke detector had been disabled. That didn't surprise her, but it definitely angered her. Her father was always complaining about it going off when he tried to cook. The fact that he'd disabled it was just another reason Jess could no longer argue against him moving into a retirement community.

She was confused about how Asher could have known about the fire in time without the silence-piercing noise going off next door.

What if he hadn't discovered it? The thought made her blood run cold, and she shivered.

No, she wouldn't go there.

"He's being treated for smoke inhalation as well," Trey

answered. "Although I think Asher's more concerned about his knee."

Emma frowned. "What happened to his knee?"

"Tripped over a chair carrying Dad out of the house," Jess said quietly.

"He carried Dad out?" Her mouth gaped. Her father was over two hundred pounds.

Trey nodded. "In his boxer briefs…And he also gave Delaney his boots, and the two of them sat in the snow near the house for a little while until firemen could get them, so the doctors are treating Asher for hypothermia."

Emma blinked. Sounded like Asher had gotten the worst of things.

"Where's Beverly?" Emma asked.

"She rode in the ambulance with Asher and Dad," Jess said.

The elevator doors opened and Jackson and Abigail stepped out. They rushed toward them, looking as terrified as she'd felt moments before.

"Everyone okay?" Jackson asked.

She nodded.

Trey spoke, filling them in.

Jackson sat next to her. "Shit," he muttered, echoing everyone's thoughts.

Sitting in silence for what seemed an eternity, each of them no doubt going over the inevitable what-ifs that could have made this Christmas a hell of a lot worse, they all stood immediately as Beverly came out of a room and walked toward them.

She raised a hand as a million questions flew her way. "Asher's good. They both are."

They were both okay. She sank back onto the chair, not trusting her legs.

Beverly continued. "Jackson, did you bring a change of clothes?"

He nodded. "In the car. I wasn't sure if they were letting him go home tonight."

Beverly nodded. "Yes, in a few hours…" Then turning to Emma and Jess, she said, "Unfortunately, they will be keeping your dad overnight, since he did get the worst of the inhalation."

Emma nodded.

"We're not going anywhere," Jess said.

"And don't worry about the house…I know a contractor who can help your dad rebuild quickly," Beverly said, winking at Jackson.

He smiled and nodded in agreement, wrapping one arm around Abby and one around his mom.

Emma gulped. The Westmores were so close. And their kindness extending to her family had more tears threatening to fall.

She glanced at her sister and Trey, and her stomach twisted.

So much of her time as an athlete had been spent on the road, traveling, training…she'd never developed a strong bond with her family. She never felt the void as much as she had the last few days, especially tonight. In this emergency setting, she felt slightly like an outsider among people she'd known her entire life. People she loved and cared about. She'd spent years away, being too busy for what mattered, and now another dream was taking her away from them as well.

"Can I see Asher?" she croaked, needing to at least be

in the same room with the one person who'd always made things okay.

Beverly glanced at her and nodded. "I'm sure he'd like that." Her expression was soft, kind, as though she knew the pain Emma was going through. It made her chest tighten even more.

Turning to her sister, she laid her coat on the seat. "I'll be back. Come get me if they say we can see Dad," she said, before disappearing down the hall.

At Asher's door, she lingered in the hallway.

Start with a thank-you for risking his life to save Dad.

With a deep breath, she went inside and relief mixed with disappointment to see that he was sleeping. Lying on the bed wearing an oxygen mask, his leg elevated with the knee wrapped, the rest of his body wrapped tightly in a heated blanket, he looked even worse than he had the night of his own injury, and she swallowed hard.

He's fine. They are both fine. Deep breath.

Those stupid Christmas lights, she thought again as she sat next to him and tears gathered in her eyes. If nothing else, she hoped their parents would finally put their silly arguing and competing behind them. Though it wouldn't matter. With or without Jess's support, Emma needed to talk to her father about a retirement home.

Asher's face looked peaceful, and she released a deep breath as she touched the blanket, so grateful that he'd been there…so grateful that he and her father were okay. She'd missed him so much in the last week, and as each day had passed, reaching out to him and making things right between them again had seemed less and less possible.

His eyes opened, and a small smile appeared on his lips beneath the mask.

"Hi," she said, not trusting her voice to say more.

He reached up to remove the oxygen, but she stopped him. "Don't. You need that. I just wanted to see you…To say thank you." Her voice broke and he covered her hand with his own, squeezing hard.

His gaze locked with hers, and the sight of his own tears glistening in his icy blue eyes was too much. There were too many questions, too many emotions to decipher, and she was too mentally and emotionally drained to try to start figuring them out.

Their friendship had always been easy, and their physical connection had never left her any doubt of their chemistry…but love was the hard part, the mystery she'd yet to solve.

She squeezed his hand and leaned forward to kiss his forehead, as tears fell down her cheeks. "Thank you again," she whispered, letting her lips linger against his warm skin just a fraction of a second longer. "Merry Christmas, Ash," she said, turning to leave.

Walking away from the man she loved, she wished for a metaphorical fire of their own.

CHAPTER 21

⁓∾

"Have you read this?" Beverly held out a copy of that day's *Glenwood Times* as Asher entered the house.

He didn't need to. Everywhere he went, he'd been showered with praise and admiration. How Jess had gotten a write-up done and submitted in time for that day's paper was a mystery, but she'd obviously painted him as a hero. "I was lucky to get any shopping done with people coming up to me…" He hesitated before taking the paper from his mom.

LOCAL HERO TURNED ACTUAL HERO.

Sigh.

He handed it back. He couldn't believe it had been only eighteen hours since he'd rescued Delaney. It felt like three days. After being released at five a.m., he'd slept the morning away before heading out to do his last-minute Christmas shopping.

He'd avoided walking past the house next door. It was too soon to see the aftermath of what could have been a more tragic night.

"It's a great pic of you this time, at least," his mom said, placing the paper in front of him once more. "Unlike the last one Jess printed."

He glanced at the pic of him that he knew had been taken the summer before at a barbeque he'd attended at Jess's house with Emma. Emma had been in the original picture, too…wearing a strapless yellow sundress that had showed off her tan to perfection. He'd teased her about her manicured, pretty pink toes in her open-toed sandals all evening…

Damn. He'd missed so much that was right in front of him all this time.

Seeing her in the hospital that morning as he'd left with his mother without talking to her had been tough, but she'd been in with her father and Jess and Trey, and he hadn't wanted to interrupt the family's time together. But he had called the hospital that afternoon and been relieved to hear that Delaney had been discharged just hours after him.

The man would be home for Christmas with his daughters.

"Where can I wrap this stuff?" he asked, holding the bags from Rolling's Sports and Bath & Body Works.

Shopping for his family had been surprisingly easy. Hockey gear for the guys and his nieces, and some fruity-scented body shit for his sister and soon to be sisters-in-law. Done.

At least it wasn't New Jersey Devils sweatshirts again this year.

"There's wrapping paper and everything you need in my bedroom closet," his mother said, tearing out the article from the newspaper.

"And I can't convince you to wrap these for me?"

Her laugh was his answer as she walked away toward the kitchen.

"I'm a hero, you know!" he called after her, knowing it made little difference to his mom.

*   *   *

Spending Christmas Eve telling their father that they thought he should move into a retirement community would have made for an even crappier holiday, so Emma and Jess decided to wait until after Christmas to break the news.

Their father would be staying with Jess until the house was fixed anyway…and at least her sister was finally on board with the decision.

"Sorry about your gifts, girls," their father said, the raspiness from the smoke inhalation making it difficult to understand him.

"Dad! Don't even give it another thought," Jess said, taking a blanket from the couch and placing it over him in the chair next to the fireplace.

"Yeah, how many pairs of socks does a girl need anyway?" Emma teased, the permanent lump in her throat never backing off. Looking at him, all she could think was that he was lucky to be alive. Because of Ash.

He wagged a finger at her, but a bout of coughing prevented him from replying.

Emma frowned and Jess handed him a cup of hot

water, as the nurses had suggested, to help with the congestion he was suffering.

Terror sat up at the sound and immediately jumped into the man's lap.

Emma felt another tug of guilt as she watched her dad affectionately pet the puppy. Finding a retirement home that would also accept Terror would be a challenge.

"It's your turn, Aunt Emma," Brayden said, touching her arm.

Sitting on the floor around the coffee table, she was playing Life with the boys.

"Oh, right..." She scanned her game pieces. So far she was the lone occupant in the pink minivan game piece, and she was en route to a college education, taking the much longer path to the finish line at the end of the game board.

So much like real life it was terrifying.

She rolled the dice again as the doorbell rang. Standing, she moved the piece three spaces and collected her measly coffee shop pay of fifty bucks before heading to the front door.

She opened it and shivered as a gust of wind blew her hair into her face. Tucking it behind her ear, she stepped outside. There was no one out there.

Looking down, she saw a small box.

She picked it up and carried it inside.

"Who was it?" Jess asked, meeting her in the hallway.

She shrugged. "No one there, just this."

"Open it."

She did, reaching through red tissue paper to take out an old photo frame she'd have recognized anywhere. Her heart raced as she took out the photo of her mother that had sat on her father's mantel for years. "It's Mom," she said, handing the photo to Jess.

Tears gathered in her sister's eyes as she took the frame and hugged it to her chest.

Inside the box was also a note.

Merry Christmas, Love Asher.

Emma swallowed hard as her sister's gaze fell on her. "You sure things are really over between you two?" Jess asked.

"You don't even like him, remember?" Now was not the time for her sister to get soft.

Jess sucked in her bottom lip and nodded, then carried the photo into the living room and handed it to their father.

Tears reflected in his eyes as he smiled, touching their mother's face in the frame.

In the living room doorway, Emma struggled with the need for a bathroom break to escape the emotions strangling her, or at least set them free, but her feet refused to move.

"He's a good man." Her father's words broke her completely.

Asher was a good man. The only one she wanted.

But until she was sure what he felt for her was real, until *he* was sure…she refused to wait in vain for the love they both deserved.

* * *

Asher had just returned from delivering the photo to Mr. Callaway and barely placed the last gift under the tree when the front door opened. The family was exchanging gifts that evening because Ben was in town and Jackson was spending Christmas Day with Abby's parents.

He hoped the large crowd and the spiked eggnog would help numb the dull ache in his chest at not being with Emma.

"Hey, Uncle Ash!" Taylor said, hurrying into the living room. She laughed when she saw the mess of wrapping paper duct taped around the new hockey pads with her name on it. "Oh my God—you're worse at wrapping than Neil," she said.

"Hey! I offered to pay you to do it, but you and your mom insisted that it's the effort that counts," his brother-in-law said, extending a hand to him. "Hey, how's the knee?"

Asher accepted the handshake. "Good to have you back, man." He knew Becky and Taylor were relieved that Neil had just completed his final active tour overseas. They all were. "The knee is good," he said. Thankfully the pain from the night before had subsided rather quickly, and other than a persistent cough that the doctor said was normal after smoke inhalation, Asher felt fine.

Oh, and other than the fact that his heart was aching for the woman he loved.

And it was quickly apparent that being around his siblings and their significant others wouldn't help.

Asher tried to ignore them paired up and cuddling on the sofas as he sat on the floor an hour later to hand out the gifts, fighting the tug of disappointment in his chest that he hadn't heard from Emma. A mixture of fear and dumb stubbornness was preventing him from reaching out. He'd saved her dad's life...and then returned the photo of their mother that the firemen had recovered from the backyard. The least she could do was a thank-you text…Even Jess had reached out on behalf of the family.

He shook it off, reaching for his poorly wrapped packages and handing them around.

Abby took hers with a grin. "It's heavy this year… What? No New Jersey Devils dish towel?" she teased.

He took the box back. "It's not too late."

"No! I'm sorry. I want my gift," she said with a laugh.

He handed it back, then handed similar ones to Becky and Olivia. "You should all open at the same time," he said.

They tore into the packaging and removed the various lotions and scented candles in the gift boxes that the store clerk had insisted he needed for presentation value, then had charged him almost double for…

Then a gift exchange between the three women quickly followed.

He frowned as his brothers laughed. "What are you doing?"

"Switching scents. Vanilla makes Becky gag, and Olivia already had the jasmine one," Abby explained.

As if there was even the slightest chance that he could have known either of those things. He faked a look of hurt. "I put a lot of thought into picking those out for each of you."

Ben and Jackson snickered.

"Right," Jackson said, picking up one of the lotion bottles. Hiding the label, he said, "Can you even guess what scent this is?"

Point taken. "Moving on…" He selected the gifts for

his nieces next, and their squeals of delight at the expensive new hockey gear made up for their mothers' rudeness.

Then reaching under the tree, he found the one with his mother's name on it. He swallowed hard as he handed it to her. Emma had really knocked it out of the park for him with this one.

His mother opened the box and removed the tissue inside, pretending not to know what was inside already. Then taking the snow globe out, she smiled and winked at him. "Someone knows his mother well."

Abby, Becky, and Olivia rushed closer to have a look. The *ohhh*s and *ahhh*s that followed made him grin at his brothers. "Guess who just leaped to the front of the pack as favorite son?"

Ben shrugged. "That's not fair. Emma must have helped."

The sound of her name was a kick to the gut, evaporating the momentary joy he felt. He nodded, admitting defeat and busying himself collecting the discarded wrapping paper from the floor. Carrying it to the kitchen, he stashed it in the trash can near the door and stared out the window as the snow continued to fall outside.

His milestone game was a week away, as the year came to an end. How was he supposed to start a new one without Emma, without his best friend and the only woman he'd ever loved? Without the only woman he would ever love?

Too soon, he'd find out.

* * *

Opening her apartment door after midnight Christmas morning, Emma felt the weight of loneliness like never before. In the corner of her living room, her artificial pink tree gave a warm, welcoming glow in the otherwise cool space. Maybe she should have accepted her sister's offer to stay the night, but being there with the family had just reminded her of everything she'd never thought she'd wanted until recently.

Seeing her sister and Trey together—so in love, so happy with the life they'd built—filled her with a sense of longing…

She'd never experienced a maternal ache for kids, but lately, as the possibility of having a family got slimmer with each passing year, a mild panicky feeling was starting to set in. She'd once known where her life was headed, the path she'd been on had been clear, and she'd been happy with it. Now, things were different. She had a new plan…but one that didn't bring her any closer to a family…to the other things in life she wanted.

Going into the living room, she tossed her purse onto the floor next to the couch. Then she grabbed a blanket, curled up on the sofa, and reached for the remote. She flipped the stations until she found an old black-and-white holiday movie and settled in for another Christmas alone.

CHAPTER 22

⟿∽

*H*is apartment had never seemed so quiet or empty. After tossing his bag onto the floor and his keys onto the hall table, Asher flicked on the light, illuminating the open-concept bachelor pad, and shivered in the cool air. It hadn't felt as cold in Jersey in November, but now the frigid, damp, late-December air penetrated the walls of his home, further depressing him.

The only sound was a distant dripping of a faucet in the kitchen that he'd planned on fixing...before his life had gotten rocked with the hit on the ice. No holiday music to drive him insane. No sound of his mother and Mr. Callaway fighting to distract him from his own problems. And no festive decorations or holiday lights to remind him of the season.

He'd thought he couldn't feel any worse than when he'd been surrounded by love and holiday cheer with his family in Glenwood Falls, while he was missing Emma.

He'd been wrong.

Squaring his shoulders, he grabbed his bag and shook off the feeling of loneliness.

He was back. He needed to get his head on straight and start focusing. He was fortunate that the reinjured knee seemed to be healing just fine, and in a few nights, he would play his one thousandth game.

Back in Denver.

His family hadn't understood why he insisted on flying all the way back to New Jersey for just a few days when he was scheduled to play his next game against Colorado anyway, but he couldn't stay.

He'd felt claustrophobic and on edge in the small town…so close to Emma, longing to go see her, and not having the courage to.

Mentally and emotionally drained, he undressed and slid beneath the cool, unwelcoming sheets on his bed. He was exhausted, but he lay awake for hours, unable to sleep. The sound of his alarm couldn't come fast enough.

It felt like he'd finally just closed his eyes when the buzzing sound filled his room. Reaching across, he slammed it silent and tossed the sheets aside, then prepared for his first practice in six long weeks.

His muscles ached to be put to use. Arriving at the arena just after seven a.m., the familiar routine eased the tension from his body.

His team was happy to have him back, and a round of applause filled the locker room as he entered.

It was good to be back, surrounded by the only thing in his life that had ever made sense, the only thing he was good at, the thing that he could depend on. For now.

His coach was still dodging him on the issue of his contract renewal.

"Look, why don't we sit down in the new year—you, me, and your agent…and figure out what's next for you," Coach Hamilton said, his gaze drifting past him to the players practicing on the ice.

Not the most encouraging answer.

When his coach wanted to re-sign a player, he acted as though the contract wasn't running out. An assumption that the player would continue on the team was the normal protocol. Obviously not in Asher's case.

Asher nodded. "Okay."

"Don't worry about it for now, okay?" his coach said, tapping him on the shoulder. "Get out there. Go warm up those skills. Fans want to see that you're back and better than ever."

The message rang loud and clear. It wasn't just the fans needing to see if he still had it.

Skating out onto the ice, he moved a little slower at first, his confidence just a little off. Part of him wanted to play it safe at practice, make sure his leg held out for the game against Colorado…his thousandth game, finally. But a bigger drive, a different need was a source of fuel for him now. While the milestone game mattered, so did game 1,001, 1,002…and every other game he could squeeze into his lifetime.

He needed to prove that he still had what it took to be one of the greats…like his brother. But not to beat his brother or to compete with him, but because he knew he was that athlete. No one else on the ice that morning had the same devotion and dedication to the sport as he did…no one else needed the sport as much as he did.

Right now, it was all he had.

So, he left it all out on the ice.

He'd messed up his shot with Emma. He refused to let something else he was passionate about slip away.

He skated hard and fast, body-checking players and taking hits from all sides. He stole the puck and took every shot given to him. He played like the hungry kid he used to be.

And three hours later, exhausted and dripping with sweat, he was the last one to leave the ice.

"Westmore," his coach said as he headed toward the showers.

He turned. "Yes, coach?"

"Next week after the game—you, me, and your agent." The man's attention was definitely focused on him now.

Relief flowed through him and he felt the tension of the last few weeks start to melt away. "Yes, sir."

"Good to have you back."

"Yes, sir."

* * *

Emma slowed her vehicle as she passed the Westmore house, knowing it was stupid. Asher had left already. She'd run into Beverly at the grocery store the day before and the woman had seemed as disappointed as Emma was.

He'd left without saying goodbye.

She stopped the car a block away and climbed out into the freezing air. The bright sun reflecting off the frost covering the ground did nothing to warm her and she put on her gloves before opening her father's mailbox.

Possibly for the last time.

The day after Christmas they'd driven to Willow Springs, the retirement community just outside Glenwood Falls, and her father had agreed it was for the best. Jess would look after the sale of the house in the spring once the repairs were finished.

Taking the stack of late Christmas cards and several flyers out of the mailbox, she flipped through for any bills or anything urgent.

Her heart stopped seeing an envelope with the New Jersey Devils logo in the corner.

Addressed to Jess?

She tapped the envelope against her gloved palm. Her sister wouldn't care if she opened it, would she?

Damn.

Locking the mailbox, she hurried back to the car and drove straight to her sister's house.

The smell of chocolate and cinnamon wafted out to greet her as she entered through the front door. How her sister and family didn't collectively weigh a thousand pounds from all of Trey's delicious baking, she'd never know. Emma had certainly indulged that past week and was feeling the tightness in her clothes.

"Jess!" she called, leaving her coat and boots on as she rushed through the house. Stopping in the living room, she checked to see if her father was awake in the chair in front of the football game before asking, "Dad, do you know where Jess is?"

He ignored the question, instead pointing toward the television. "They better have ESPN at Windy Old Geezer Springs."

Emma rolled her eyes. "Dad, where's Jess?"

"Is that my mail?" he asked, nodding at the pile in her hand.

"Oh, yes, here. Looks like Christmas cards and junk mail," she said, handing him everything but the letter for Jess.

Braxton entered the living room with a plate of cookies and glass of milk. "Here you go, Grandpa," he said.

"Braxton, where's your mom?"

"Downstairs in our playroom trying to convince Brayden to throw away a bunch of old stuffies…"

She didn't wait to hear the rest as she hurried down the stairs to the boys' playroom.

Braxton followed.

"Jess, this came for you," she said, extending the envelope toward her sister.

Jess held two stuffed toys—a giant elephant in one hand and a long green snake in the other. "Pick one, Brayden," she said, her patience with the after-Christmas playroom organization waning thin.

"I like both."

"Brayden!"

"Jess!" Emma said, taking both toys and handing them to her nephew. "Open this," she told her, handing her the envelope.

Jess shot her an annoyed look, but then her eyes widened as she saw the logo. "What is it?"

"Open. It." The words were said through clenched teeth.

Jess ripped the corner off and pulled out a stack of hockey tickets. She read the sticky note attached. "As promised, tickets for the New Year's Eve game in Denver. Hope you all can make it." She flicked through. "There're seven."

Enough for her sister's family, her father, and her.

Emma swallowed hard.

"Are you going to go?" Jess asked the question she'd just been asking herself.

One she didn't know the answer to.

CHAPTER 23

❦

$\mathcal{N}$ew Year's Eve and back in Denver.

Sitting on the bench in the locker room, Asher stared at his phone. Other than her brief visit to the hospital, no contact from Emma in almost two weeks. Only two weeks, but it felt like a lifetime. He couldn't remember a time when they'd gone this long without talking. She'd always been the one constant in his fast-moving world, the one thing he could grab hold of when the stress of the whirlwind pace got too much. She'd been his best friend. His only real friend. The person he depended on and trusted even more than his family…yet she'd been so much more than that. And he'd been completely blind to it.

He'd thought getting back to his rigorous training schedule and the anticipation of the thousandth game would have helped to take his mind off of her, but countless hours on the ice, pushing himself to his limits, hadn't erased images of her scrolling through his mind. No amount of game strategy talk or hints about a big contract renewal had helped put things back into perspective.

The problem was, he knew what mattered most now.

And it didn't come with a big payday, fan adoration, or hitting every professional goal he set for himself.

"You nervous?" Anderson, a young rookie forward, asked, pulling his own jersey over his head.

"Nah." He knew his teammate meant about the thousandth game and once again facing off against his brother on ice that was more home than away for him.

But it was true. None of that bothered his nerves. What did was whether or not Emma would be there. He'd received a thank-you text from Jess, saying that they would be there tonight…but he hadn't had the balls to ask if *they* included Emma.

He needed her there.

"Well, suit up, man, and try to steer clear of your brother," his teammate said with a grin.

"Yeah," Asher said, reaching for his skates. "I'll certainly try."

*   *   *

Holding a bottle of Champagne, which she had no intentions of sharing, Emma knocked on Jane's front door. The lights were dimmed and she could hear holiday music coming from inside, mixed with the sounds of chatting and laughter.

Why was she here?

She certainly wasn't in any mood for a party. The idea

of ringing in the New Year among co-workers and people she barely knew was slightly depressing.

She was there because she was desperately trying to avoid being somewhere else.

All day she'd gone back and forth on whether to go to the game with her family, to be there for Ash, but she'd successfully convinced herself that going wasn't the right thing to do.

Meaning, she was full of shit and capable of lying even to herself.

Ten years of friendship…years of love should have been enough to patch the hole in her heart long enough to make it to his big game, but the pain was still just a little too much.

She wasn't interested in getting hurt anymore. Despite his claim to be in love with her, she knew the truth: he was terrified of losing her. That wasn't real love. And she needed to remain true to herself and move on…and away from the hold he'd always had on her.

Going to the game would have been a mistake.

She knocked again, and Jane answered with a welcoming smile. "Hi! So glad you were able to make it. Come in," she said, moving back to allow Emma to enter.

"Thanks again for inviting me." Otherwise, she'd probably be sitting in the Denver arena parking lot right now, continuing to do battle with herself.

"Make yourself comfortable…there are people mingling everywhere," she said, reaching for Emma's coat.

Emma unzipped it, then shook her head. "You know, I'm a little chilled. I'll leave it on for now." Easier to make a quiet exit later if necessary.

The smell of baked goods coming from the kitchen

made her stomach growl. She knew she wouldn't be able to eat a bite, but the laughing, jovial crowd in the living room looked like more than she could handle tonight, so she headed straight for the kitchen. If she didn't get this liquid into a wine glass soon, she was popping the cork and drinking straight from the bottle.

She knew one thing, she'd never make it to the count of midnight sober. Not when she'd be missing her usual New Year's Eve Skype "kiss" with Ash.

"Hey, Dr. Masey," she said with as much enthusiasm she could muster as she entered the small kitchen. He was leaning against the island chatting to several doctors from the medical clinic. "Happy New..."

"What are you doing here?" he interrupted, turning from his conversation.

"I was invited." She reached for a glass and set it on the counter.

"But Asher's game is tonight."

She sighed. *She knew that!* All day she'd unsuccessfully tried to forget. Her nephews had been practically bouncing off the walls at the idea of going to a game, and even Jess had tried to talk her into going.

"Put everything aside for one night. For him," she'd said.

Who knew she'd be wishing for her anti-Asher sister to come back? Since the fire, her sister was pro-Asher, and it was coming a little too late.

"I'm sure he'll do great," she mumbled, peeling the foil from the rim of the bottle and tossing it into the trash.

She unscrewed the metal cage and gripped the cork tight as she yanked.

It didn't budge.

She pulled harder, wincing as she expected the cork to come flying out, shooting Champagne everywhere.

It still refused to move.

Oh come on! She handed the bottle to Dr. Masey. "Can you open this? Quickly."

"I'm not opening this," he said. "You can't be serious, Em. You're going to miss this important event in his—"

She held up a hand. "Stop." She didn't need anyone else telling her that she was wrong not to go. Besides, the game started in ten minutes. It was too late anyway. "Please just open my Champagne so I can get sloppily drunk and kiss some random stranger at midnight."

One of the other doctors winked at her, and she immediately regretted saying the words out loud. She certainly didn't mean them. At least not the kissing a stranger part.

Dr. Masey reluctantly popped the cork and poured half a glass. But he held it back out of reach when she reached for it. "You should be there for him tonight. This is a big deal," he said.

Emma stared at the glass of Champagne that was supposed to be her savior that evening, and doubt over her decision returned. Even if they'd been fighting, Asher would never have missed a big moment in her career…in her life. They'd been best friends for so long.

Did it matter that seeing him would break her heart even more?

Could her heart possibly break any more?

Damn! She glanced at the clock on Jane's kitchen wall. "The game starts in six minutes. I'll never make it to Denver in time anyway." What was she saying? What happened to her resolve? "And I don't even have a ticket."

She'd refused to take one from Jess in case she changed her mind.

Think about the fact that he hurt you. Think about the fact that he could hurt you again…

"You have to at least show up," Dr. Masey said.

Emma bit her lip. "And what? Just wait outside the players' gate at the arena until he appears and yell at him to get his attention like the other puck bunnies?" Her mouth went dry. She wouldn't have to. She knew he always booked the same suite in the Fairmont Plaza hotel, and he always left a room key at the front desk for her, since she'd always beaten him back to the hotel, as he'd needed to shower and change and often had post-game interviews.

Would he leave a key this time? If he did it would mean he still had hope for them.

Suddenly *her* faint spark of lingering hope needed to find out. "Okay. I'm going to Denver," she said, feeling her stomach flutter. She thought she might actually throw up. Grabbing the Champagne bottle, she struggled to stick the cork back in, then stole one from the top of a wine bottle and jammed it in.

Suddenly she did feel like sharing. With the man she was in love with.

Dr. Masey smiled as she exited the kitchen. "Have a happy New Year, Emma," he called after her.

With any luck…

CHAPTER 24

❧

*R*eleasing a nerve-filled breath, Asher left the locker room.

This was it. The moment he'd busted his ass for since he was four years old. And it was happening in the one stadium that had always felt like home. At the covered entryway to the ice, he held back, allowing each of his teammates to go first. Each player shook his hand as they passed. Asher's heart raced and blood pumped throughout his body on an adrenaline rush.

His coach was the last one to pass him, and the silent nod of respect had Asher itching to get out there. For sixty minutes of play time, everything would make sense.

He headed toward the arena door, and the moment his blades touched the ice, the stadium erupted in a standing ovation. The sea of New Jersey Devils colors in the stands boasting his name and number made it hard to believe he was on Colorado ice.

He stopped to wave to the crowd of supporters, but unfortunately, the spotlights dancing across the ice in the otherwise dark stadium made it impossible to see if the one person he longed to see was there.

He gave another quick wave to the crowd as he skated his first lap around for his warm-up with his teammates.

A moment later, the music changed to the Colorado theme song, the lights changed from red and black to burgundy and blue, and the Avalanche players skated out.

As his brother skated past, he held out a fist and smiled as their knuckles bumped. "Proud of you, bro," Ben said before skating off to join his own team.

The words were almost enough to ease the ache of disappointment in Asher's chest as the lights came on, the anthem was sung, and he didn't see Emma sitting with her family in the stands.

She wasn't there. She hadn't shown up.

He knew why. She loved him. A friend could move past their argument, but what they had went far beyond friendship. For both of them. He was done putting his feelings on ice, compartmentalizing his life. He wanted his hockey career and he wanted Emma—simultaneously. It might be complicated. It might mean sacrifices, but he didn't care.

His heart raced, and he couldn't get this game started quickly enough. The faster it started, the faster it could be over and he could get his shit from the hotel and be on his way to the woman he loved before the stroke of midnight.

This was one New Year's Eve he would be kissing

his best friend for real, whether she was still angry at him or not.

* * *

The game would be over in twenty minutes.

Emma had listened to it in her car all the way from Glenwood Falls and knew the Devils were leading 4–2 going into the last period.

She'd been white-knuckling it the whole way as unexpected snow had started the moment she'd taken the exit for the highway, but nothing—not even an abominable snowman appearing on the road—could have stopped her from getting there.

She missed Ash. She loved him. She wanted to be there for him, even if she wasn't sitting in the stands. She hoped what she had planned would be better, anyway.

God, she hoped.

Dragging her small suitcase and slightly out of breath, Emma rushed toward the front desk of the Fairmont Plaza hotel.

She wasn't sure if she should be relieved to see the familiar desk clerk smiling back at her as she approached.

Guess it depended on whether or not Ash had left a key for her.

Maybe she should just check into her own room and text him to come to her…to save herself from the embarrassment if he hadn't.

"Hi, Evan…" she started nervously. Maybe this wasn't a good idea. He would probably go out with the team to celebrate after the game…or his family. It *was* New Year's Eve. And this was a huge night for him.

Guilt for not being there washed over her. She'd make it up to him.

"Miss Emma! So great to see you," Evan said with a happy smile. "He didn't think you were coming." He nodded behind her toward the lobby television that was playing the final period of the game.

Her heart echoed in her ears. "What?"

"Mr. Westmore," he whispered, leaning forward, shooting her a conspirator's wink. "He looked so torn when I asked him if he needed a key left here for you this time."

Emma swallowed hard. What had Asher decided? "Did he?" she asked, almost hating that the desk clerk had essentially been privy to their secret affair for years…yet kinda grateful to have an ally in this moment of stress.

Maybe he'd have a drink in the lounge with her to ring in the most depressing, stressful New Year's ever if the answer was no.

But instead he reached into a folder on his desk and produced the swipe card key.

Happiness and relief filled her chest and tears stung the back of her eyes as she accepted it. "Oh, thank God," she said.

Evan laughed. "Can I send up some Champagne and chocolate-covered strawberries?" he asked.

She nodded, then shook her head. "I have my own Champagne, but chocolate-covered strawberries, yes."

"No problem, Miss Emma."

In the room five minutes later, Emma unpacked her small overnight suitcase and flicked on the television, tuning to the last five minutes of the third period. The Devils were still winning by one point, and Ash was on the ice. It was the first time the home crowd wasn't upset by what was sure to be a loss for the Avalanche.

She held her breath as she watched the man she loved finish off the one-thousandth game in his impressive career. Tears sprang to her eyes as the game ended moments later and the fans erupted.

The camera zoomed in on Asher's expression as he waved to the crowd with one final lap around the ice. No one else would detect the glimmer of disappointment in his eyes as he searched the stadium…for her? But she saw it and it broke her heart a little more.

She should have been there for him.

Well, she was right here waiting now.

She continued to watch as the team officials and an ESPN reporter carefully made their way out onto the ice, her impatience growing as they droned on about the significance of the milestone game.

Coach Hamilton presented Asher with the award he hadn't received at the annual year-end event, and he gratefully accepted it, taking the mic from the man.

Emma sat on the edge of the bed, holding her breath as the stadium quieted and he spoke. "I can't tell you how happy I am to receive this honor tonight. Thank you, Coach Hamilton, for not making me wait another whole year to get my hands on this," he said, raising the award a little higher.

Emma smiled as she watched the man she loved on screen thanking his family for their support and encouragement. He looked so impossibly irresistible, and she wished she could reach through the screen to touch him. She couldn't wait any longer to be near him, to kiss him, to tell him she loved him and that that would never change. She could wait until he was ready. She had no other choice, really. There was no one else she wanted.

"I learned a lot these last few weeks," Asher continued. "Being injured and not having every waking moment dedicated to this sport, I realized how important other things in my life truly are. I've overlooked a lot and I've taken a lot for granted," he said, staring into the screen. "One person in particular."

A lump rose in her throat and her hands clenched together on her lap. "Emma, this…" He held the award toward the camera. "None of this means anything without you here to share it with," he said.

A murmur went through the stadium and Emma's mouth dropped. Had her media-phobic, private best friend—love of her life—just said that on national television? In the middle of the biggest speech of his career to date?

"I know you're watching, Em," he said. "And in case you didn't already know, in case you still have any doubt…I love you."

The stadium erupted in applause and cheers once more.

He loved her. Tears of happiness slid down her cheeks as she watched him take a deep breath and raise the award to the crowd. He handed the microphone back to the reporter before doing one final lap around the arena and skating off.

Sitting back on the bed, Emma's heart felt like it was about to explode.

Every second from now until he walked through the hotel room door would be an eternity too long.

* * *

Sliding the room key into the lock and opening the hotel room door an hour later, Asher blinked.

Shit, did he have the wrong room?

Sticking his head outside, he checked the number. No, this was his room and his key worked.

But it certainly didn't look like the room he'd left earlier that evening.

The lights were off but the room was illuminated by a delicate glow of candles burning on the desk and bedside tables. The flickering reflected against the window overlooking the snow falling softly on the quiet city of Denver, awaiting the stroke of midnight. A bottle of Champagne sat chilling in an ice bucket next to the hot tub already overflowing with bubbles, and Champagne flutes were filled on either side of a plate of chocolate-covered strawberries.

Anticipation made his mouth go dry and his palms sweat as Asher dropped his hockey gear and locked the hotel room door. It looked like he wouldn't need to grab his things and drive like crazy to get to Emma before midnight. She'd come to him. Kicking off his shoes, he smiled as he crossed the room to the partly open door to the bedroom in the suite.

He paused for breath, knowing that in a second the sight of the woman he loved might steal his ability to breathe completely.

Pushing open the door, he felt the tension of the last several weeks lift from his shoulders, as he leaned against the doorframe and took her in.

"You left a key," Emma said from where she lay on the

bed with her back against the oversized pillows, wearing the sexiest short red silky nightgown he'd ever seen on her perfect body.

His mouth was dry, but his pulse raced. "You used it," he said, enjoying the moment he'd been hoping for but hadn't the confidence to expect.

"Get over here." She crooked a finger at him.

He strode across the room, tossing his coat aside as he went. Reaching for her, he lifted her from the bed, and her legs went immediately around his waist as he held her in his arms. "I didn't think you'd come," he said gruffly against her lips. His body craved her, but his heart was doing the driving at the moment. And it terrified him. But not nearly as much as the idea of never having this chance with her.

He'd meant what he'd said on the ice in front of his family, his team, his fans…and millions of strangers watching at home—he loved her. "You were watching the game tonight, right?"

She kissed his lips gently, cupping his face between her hands as she nodded. "I'm sorry I wasn't there," she said.

"This was a much better surprise."

"You hate surprises," she said, kissing him again, wrapping her arms around his neck.

"Surprises that involve you looking so amazingly beautiful in my arms, I can learn to love. In fact, I can't imagine anything better."

She pressed toward him, but he held back before her lips met his again. "I love you, Emma. I'm so in love with you that nothing else matters when you're not a part of my life," he said, swallowing the emotions threatening to strangle him.

"I know," she said with a smile. "And now so does the rest of America."

He didn't care. It had taken almost losing her for him to realize how much he loved her, and he'd shout it from the hotel rooftop if she needed him to.

"I love you, too," she whispered.

He shook his head. "No. Not like this," he said, laying her back gently on the bed and lying next to her. "You can't possibly be feeling as strongly as I am." He hadn't known it was possible to feel this much, this deep. "The thought that I'd never get the chance to touch you…" He trailed his fingers along her soft bare skin. "Kiss you…or be near you again practically killed me…and this overwhelming sensation of knowing that the one thing I can't live without is right here next to me…"

"Feels wonderful, doesn't it?" she asked, rolling him onto his back and straddling him.

"So we're on the same page?"

"I think we always were," she said against his lips as she leaned forward to kiss him.

He quickly flipped them so he was on top as he reached for his shirt to pull it off over his head.

"You know what the good news is about fighting with you?" she asked, trailing her fingers along his abs. His body sprang to life, and as usual the overwhelming desire to make love to her took over.

"What's that?" he asked, sliding the straps of her negligee down over her shoulders to expose her beautiful breasts.

"We get to have make-up sex. We haven't tried that before," she said, an innocent expression on her pretty face, as she unbuttoned his jeans.

He laughed as he kissed his best friend, the sound of the New Year's Eve countdown echoing somewhere in the night.

Nope. Innocent was definitely not a look Emma Callaway could successfully pull off.

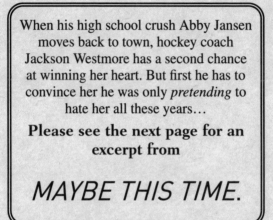

When his high school crush Abby Jansen moves back to town, hockey coach Jackson Westmore has a second chance at winning her heart. But first he has to convince her he was only *pretending* to hate her all these years…

Please see the next page for an excerpt from

MAYBE THIS TIME.

CHAPTER 1

*O*f all the mistakes she'd made in her twenty-nine years, Abigail hoped her decision to move back to Glenwood Falls wouldn't be the biggest one.

The silent treatment she'd received from her daughter on the exhausting fifteen-hour drive from California to Colorado made her think that maybe it was.

She waved to Dani from the sidewalk as the school bus pulled away from the curb, but her nine-year-old ignored her.

Great.

As the bus rounded the corner, Abigail pulled her cardigan tighter around her and turned to walk back toward her family home. The mid-September mountain breeze felt even cooler to her, having spent so many fall seasons living in sunny Los Angeles, where the palm trees and green grass never gave way to the gold and red leaves crunching beneath her feet as she walked.

The wind blew her long blond hair across her eyes, and she tucked it behind her ears. The sunshine reflected off of her solitaire diamond ring, nestled safely next to the platinum wedding band that used to hold a promise of forever.

She'd have to take them off soon. She probably should have already.

Dean's wedding band had been sitting on the night-stand on his side of the bed for almost ten months.

Some people had an easier time letting go and moving on.

She took a deep breath as she opened the front door. The smell of coffee and blueberry pancakes greeted her, and she forced a smile, hoping it would dull the constant aching in her chest.

Time to face another day.

Another day in Glenwood Falls—her former home-town. Another day with her parents trying to make her feel better about her divorce. And another day she had to get through with a heaviness weighing on her whenever she thought about her future.

Hers and Dani's.

Following the smell of coffee, she went straight to the kitchen.

"Good morning," her father said, pouring her a cup.

"Hi, Dad," she said, glancing around the kitchen that hadn't changed in years. The same harvest gold fridge and stove that had been popular in the seventies and that her father miraculously managed to keep running, the round glass-topped table near the window that seated four, and the same butterfly-patterned curtains she'd sewn one year in home economics class—the only thing she'd ever successfully made. In ten years, nothing had changed, and she'd expected that sense of familiarity to make her feel better.

Instead it made her feel as though her attempt to move on with her life had taken her two steps backward.

"Dani got off to school okay?"

"Yes, although she still refuses to speak to me," she said, sitting in her old familiar place at the table. She took a sip of the tar-like coffee and winced, but immediately took another one. She used to hate how strong her father made it, but the last three mornings, she'd needed the strength it provided to deal with Dani's anger at her for moving them away from her father in L.A.

"She'll come around," he said.

Abigail knew it was true. She just hoped it was before her little girl started college.

On the table was that day's *Glenwood Times*—the local newspaper. Picking it up, she opened it to the classified section as she had the day before.

Nothing new added. Still just three open positions in the town of five thousand residents—the deli counter at the supermarket, early morning flower delivery, and sawmill operator.

"Dad, how hard is it to operate a saw?" she asked with a sigh.

He chuckled. "Just the fact that you need to ask means you probably shouldn't apply for that one, sweetheart."

Her mother came into the kitchen and her expression said it all.

"Yes, Mom, I'm looking for a job," Abigail said.

"I didn't say anything."

She didn't have to. Isabelle Jansen's face was the most

expressive her daughter had ever seen. Every emotion, every thought could be conveyed by the small furrow of her brow or the twitch of an eye…

"I know you think I need time to get settled, but the sooner I can find work to keep myself busy, the easier that will be."

"You know yourself better than anyone, sweetheart. I'm just saying there's no hurry."

"I appreciate that." And Abigail did. After leaving Glenwood Falls, she'd only gone back to visit a few times, instead sending plane tickets to her parents to come visit her and Dani in L.A. Her decision to move home as her divorce was being finalized had surprised her parents, but they'd opened their door and arms to her and Dani. They were making this transition as easy on them as possible. And she knew how valuable their support was. She also knew she couldn't use them as a crutch. She needed to get back on her feet and prove to herself this was the right decision, that she could move forward without Dean, as soon as possible. And Dani needed to see that, too.

Abigail hesitated, wondering if she should tell them about the one job in town she *was* interested in. She cleared her throat. "I was actually thinking about applying for a teaching position at the elementary school."

Both of her parents stared at her.

"What? I do have a teaching degree." She'd completed the degree after Dani started school, realizing she might someday want a career of her own.

"Yes, but…you've never actually used it," her mother said.

"Don't they expire?" her father joked.

"Very funny, Dad," she said. "When I registered Dani on Monday, I heard one of the other teachers say they were looking for a substitute teacher that could turn into a full-time fourth grade position when Kelli Fitzgerald goes on maternity leave next month."

"Oh, that's right! I saw Kelli at last month's town meeting—she looked ready to deliver then. She's such a sweet girl, and her husband is one of the nicest men—he helped your dad with the deck last spring…" Her mom's voice trailed on, but Abigail wasn't listening.

Her mother raving about Kelli and other of her former high school friends was something she heard often. Apparently they were all living wonderful, successful lives in Glenwood Falls. None of them had fallen in love with a star athlete or left town six months pregnant…or had to crawl back home nine years later after a bitter divorce.

Nope, no one else. Just her.

Abigail's cell phone ringing was her escape, and she was relieved to see her lawyer's office number lighting up the screen. "I have to take this," she said, heading upstairs to her old bedroom. "Hello?" she said, closing the door behind her.

"Hi, Abigail. How are you?" her lawyer, Olivia Davis, asked, sounding far too busy to really care.

"I'm fine. Everything okay?" The divorce was almost finalized after six months of back and forth with Dean's lawyer. There were just a few things left to sign off on—her proposed custody arrangement and the financial settlement terms. She knew Olivia was fantastic at her job and she'd come highly recommended by several other divorcées she'd known as a hockey wife, but she still worried about whether she'd made the right decision hiring her. Deciding who to put her trust in these days was like deciding between the devil you knew and the devil you didn't.

"Well, I have good news and bad news."

Her marriage of nine years was almost officially over—she wasn't sure there was any real *good* news to be had, but she asked for that first.

"I just received an uncontested document to the custody file," Olivia said.

That actually was good news. She'd been worried Dean would try to fight for custody of Dani, even though she knew with his travel schedule with the L.A. Kings and her history of being their daughter's primary caregiver, his chances of getting it in court would have been slim.

Maybe he knew that, too.

"That's great…"

"Actually, he's even stated that the visitation time is too much, and he is relinquishing all of the time to you."

Abigail frowned. "What does that mean—he doesn't want to see Dani at all?" she asked, sitting on the edge of the bed.

"Hopefully that's not the case. It just means he is leaving the power to decide when and how he sees Dani in your hands. The two of you can arrange something that works…without involving a legal, binding visitation schedule."

Great. So, it would all rest on her shoulders. She would have preferred it didn't. Her own feelings toward Dean were sure to cloud her judgment, and she knew she was going to have to put them aside and do what was best for

Dani. "Okay," she said. So much for good news. Now she really didn't want the bad.

"So, the bad news is—he's contesting the settlement. He is claiming that because you decided to move back to Glenwood Falls, where real estate and the cost of living are cheaper, he shouldn't have to pay what we're asking."

No doubt in most situations, this would be the bad news, but the truth was, Abigail didn't care about the money. Yes, she expected Dean to pay child support to help raise Dani, but she'd never been the materialistic type who enjoyed the flamboyant perks of being a hockey wife. She'd bought the expensive clothes and spent the small fortunes on her hair and makeup because it was what Dean expected, what was needed to fit in with the other hockey wives.

At first, she hadn't felt the need to be part of the group, but she'd quickly learned how lonely life as a professional athlete's spouse could be. Other hockey families understood the sacrifices and the often-stressful lifestyle, and she'd found comfort and security within the close-knit group.

At least she *had* until a few weeks ago, when she hadn't been able to bring herself to log in to the Hockeywives.com site. She was no longer one of them, and she needed stand on her own two feet now. Reaching out for their support didn't seem right. And she also didn't want any information about her new life traveling back to Dean through their hockey-playing husbands.

"Look, don't worry," Olivia said when Abigail was quiet. "I'm sure it's just a delay tactic. He can't possibly believe the courts will rule in his favor on this. The longer he can delay things, the longer he doesn't have to pay the divorce settlement or alimony and child support."

"So, what's next?"

"Well, I'll file the counter and see what happens. But in the meantime, try to feel good about the uncontested custody—you wouldn't believe how often that causes the biggest delay. You're lucky."

Lucky, she thought sadly as she disconnected the call. Strange, she didn't feel lucky. How was she supposed to explain all of this to Dani, who'd had a say in outlining when she wanted to spend time in L.A. with her dad? How could she tell the little girl that her father hadn't wanted to commit to a schedule, to time with her? The last thing their strained relationship needed was Dani thinking this was somehow her fault. Neither did she want to paint Dean as the villain, as much as she resented him for what he'd done, for tearing their family apart and putting her in this situation.

No, *lucky* definitely was not a word she'd use.

She stared at the rings on her left hand. Her mother had said there was no rush, she'd know when she was ready to remove them. She struggled to recall the memories attached to each one—the joy, the love, the excitement she'd felt the day he'd proposed and then six months later at their wedding—but too many other memories—of nights alone, of fights that had left her crying herself to sleep, of his betrayal—had caused the good ones to fade.

She stood and walked toward the dresser, where an old wooden jewelry box with her initials and a flower carved into it sat—a gift from Dean he'd made in woodworking class senior year. She opened the lid and removed the rings, then placed them inside.

Her mother was right. She did know when it was the right time.

*   *   *

Sitting on the tiny bench outside the principal's office at Glenwood Falls Elementary two days later, Abigail felt like a kid who'd been caught skipping class. Everything around her was so familiar, yet once again, she didn't take comfort in it. Years before, she couldn't wait to leave Glenwood Falls, and she'd been filled with illusions of a fantastic, exciting life in L.A.

Things hadn't quite worked out the way she'd planned, and the media attention given to her divorce and the circumstances around it left her no hope of saving face among her former friends and neighbors in the small town. Hell, she suspected half of them had known Dean was cheating on her based on the tabloid photos long before she'd even realized something was wrong.

God, she'd been so blind.

Loving him as much as she did—*had*—had clouded her judgment about everything. She'd just felt so lucky that Dean Underwood had chosen her to ask to the school prom, had picked her to be his girlfriend, and then had proposed when she'd told him she was pregnant. The star athlete could have had any girl in town, but he'd chosen her.

And the offer of an exciting life as a pro athlete's wife had been a dream come true for her. She could be the stay-at-home mom with their daughter while Dani was young and they could travel with him around the world…it had all seemed too good to be true.

And it was.

For the first five years, things had been wonderful, but then Dani started school and Abigail went back to college for her teaching degree. She'd also become more active in the hockey wives' charity for the local hospital, Dreams for Life, and soon they were barely together as a family. Dean traveled with the team. She raised their daughter and helped fundraise for various causes.

And somewhere along the line, he'd started having affairs, and she'd been too busy to notice.

"Abby?" Liz, the principal's receptionist, said as she came out into the hall. The woman had been the school's receptionist when she'd been a student.

She stood. "It's Abigail now." She hadn't been Abby in a long time…and she doubted she'd ever see that girl in the mirror again.

"Okay…well, Principal Breen is ready for you," Liz said, holding the office door open. "Just head on in."

"Thank you." Running a hand along her charcoal pencil skirt, Abigail went inside, feeling exactly as she had years before when she'd been sent to the office for talking too much in class. Her palms damp with sweat, she forced a deep breath.

"Wow. I wasn't sure I was reading it right when I saw you on my schedule this morning—but here you are. Abby Jansen back in Glenwood Falls—no one will believe it," Principal Breen said from her seat behind the big mahogany desk.

Nope. No one. Not even her.

Abigail forced her best smile. "Nice to see you, Principal Breen."

"Have a seat, please," she gestured to the chair across from her.

She sat, looking around the office. The same bookshelf along the wall, the same file cabinet near the window, and the same bamboo tree growing in the corner. Nothing had changed in the office. Everything was exactly the same.

"So…you're interested in the substitute teaching position?"

"Yes." Abigail folded and unfolded her legs, shifting in the seat. This was her first real job interview, as the Dreams For Life charity work had kept her far too busy to apply for a teaching position in L.A. Her heart echoed in her ears and her mind raced. What was she doing here? She wasn't even remotely qualified for this position.

"Do you have a recent resume?"

She swallowed hard. "Actually, I don't have one with me…" She did, but not one she was comfortable producing, despite hours trying to make it sound better. Her mother's "maybe they won't need to see a resume" comment when she'd shown it to her said it all.

Principal Breen's eyebrows joined behind her seafoam-green rimmed glasses. "Okay, well, why don't you start by telling me about any previous teaching experience you have." She reached for her notepad and pen and waited.

How about none? How could she somehow turn her treasurer role on the Dreams for Life charity and her stay-at-home mom position into something this woman would consider an asset? "Well, I haven't taught in any schools…but I do have a degree and I did home-school my daughter, Dani, for a while." Three months while they tried to make traveling with Dean work.

"Okay…"

"And I was involved with the Dreams for Life charity,

which helped a lot of children…" God, she sounded like a moron. She wasn't qualified for this job. Nowhere near it. She might as well mention her after-school newspaper delivery job as well.

"Right." Principal Brown set the pen down and clasped her hands in front of her on the desk. "Well, we were really hoping to hire someone with actual teaching experience."

Shit. She needed this job. She needed something to make her feel like she could actually start building a life for herself and Dani there in Glenwood Falls. She needed her confidence to return. And she needed to know they would be okay without Dean. *She* would be okay without him.

"Principal Breen, please," she said, clutching her hands tightly in her lap. "I know my lack of experience isn't ideal, but I can do this job. Please let me prove that to you." And herself. She hated the sound of begging in her voice, but she wanted—*needed*—this job. It was hard enough moving back home, having everyone in town know the sordid details about her failed marriage, and trying to gain her daughter's confidence in her; she really didn't want to be forced to take the flower delivery position in town. Her already low self-esteem couldn't handle it.

The woman hesitated. "I'd like to help you Abby…"

Please don't say *but*…

She paused and studied her for a moment. "How long are you planning to stay in Glenwood Falls? Is this a permanent move? Or just until you get back on your feet?"

She swallowed hard. "It's a permanent move." She

refused to uproot Dani again. Leaving L.A. and her friends had been tough enough. They were here to stay and to start over.

"Okay. The substitute position will only be a few days a week…as needed."

Her breath caught and she tried to hold her excitement. The woman hadn't quite said yes yet.

"When are you available to…"

"Any time," she said quickly.

Principal Breen nodded, looking as though she already regretted the decision. "All right. We'll try this…but there's no guarantee you'll get the full-time position at the end of next month."

"I understand," she said, but there was no way she wasn't getting it. She'd do whatever it took to prove to Principal Breen she was the right person for the job.

She released a breath, tension seeping from her shoulders. This was a good start to getting her life back on track. Maybe not the one she'd planned, but hopefully one she could someday be proud of.

CHAPTER 2

❧

*A*nother school year. Another season.

Jackson Westmore stapled the new hockey tryout schedule on the bulletin board outside of the gym at Glenwood Falls Elementary.

"Hey, Coach, ready for another championship?" his buddy and the school's gym teacher, Darryl Sutton, said as he passed with a group of ten-year-olds returning from a warm-up run around the school track.

"You bet," Jackson said, stopping one of the bigger boys. "As long as James is still planning to try out."

The taller-than-average, skinny kid nodded.

"As long as he keeps his grades up," Darryl—also the boy's father—said.

"Yes, sir," the boy said, disappearing inside the gym with the rest of the class.

Jackson sympathized. He knew what it was like to

have a parent as a teacher. His mother had taught at the Glenwood High School for over twenty years. It sucked. He and his brothers couldn't get away with anything. And then they'd catch shit at school *and* at home. His sister had had it easy, being the only non-troublemaker of the group.

"I hear the team is going co-ed this year," Darryl said, glancing at the sign-up form where the announcement was posted.

"Yeah…We'll see how it turns out. I'm not sure there are many eight- to ten-year-old girls who will be interested, but you never know," he said with a shrug.

He was actually thrilled by the Junior Hockey League Association's decision to make the Atom/Novice teams a co-ed division. So far in Glenwood Falls, they hadn't had the funding for a girls league, and he knew one in particular who was dying to play. His niece, Taylor, had been on skates since before she could walk; with two uncles in the NHL and him coaching the local Junior team, it seemed only natural for her to be interested in the sport. She was ten, and this would be her last year to play on his team. He couldn't wait to get her out there; she could skate and puck handle better than any boy he'd ever coached.

"I assume Taylor is guaranteed a spot?" Darryl asked.

Jackson grinned. "She'll have to try out like everyone else, but I have a feeling the Glenwood Falls Lightning will have a new female defenseman this season."

"Well, I've seen her play, so I'm all for it, but not everyone feels that way."

Jackson frowned. "Who's having an issue with it?"

Darryl lowered his voice. "James mentioned that

some of the boys…and I suspect it's the boys' fathers' words they're repeating…are not as open-minded about this."

He nodded slowly. Not everyone liked change. He knew that. He just hoped that once the team was finalized based on who could play the game, and not their gender, everyone with reservations would start to feel better. They were kids after all, and the Atom league was the place to have fun while learning the sport. They would start to be more competitive once the talented, promising players moved up to Peewee and then Bantam. "Thanks for the heads-up."

Darryl looked past him down the hall, his expression changing. "Speaking of a heads-up…"

Oh no. He knew in his gut before he even turned around who would be standing there. He'd already heard the rumors she was back. Yet, nothing prepared him for the sight of Abby Jansen, dressed in a slim-fitting suit, her long blond hair loose around her shoulders, her three-inch heels clicking on the tiled floor, walking toward them.

In ten years, she hadn't changed a bit.

And obviously neither had his feelings for her.

Damn.

* * *

Keep walking. Don't stop. Just keep walking.

One expensive Gucci pump in front of the other…Shit. They were both staring at her. "Hi, guys," Abigail said tightly, keeping her gaze on Darryl and ignoring the other man she'd gone to school with.

Wow—what an understated way to describe their relationship, she thought.

"Hi, Abby. How are you?" Darryl asked, looking uncomfortable as he glanced at his friend.

Jackson's gaze was burning a hole through her forehead, but she plastered on the fake smile she'd perfected since news of her divorce had spread all over the country and continued to pretend he didn't exist. "I'm great." Okay, that might be stretching things a little, but she'd just gotten a job, so that counted for something. "How are things?"

"Good…still teaching phys ed."

She nodded politely. He'd inherited the job from his own father when the older man had retired.

"Well…Better get back in there." The awkward tension seemed to be making him squirm, and he opened the gym door and ducked inside. "Great to see you," he said quickly, as the door shut.

Jackson's panicky gaze left her just long enough to glance at his disappearing friend.

Leaving them alone together in the hallway.

She cleared her throat and waited for him to speak first. She had nothing to say to her soon to be ex-husband's best friend, who'd never disguised the fact that he disliked her. All through high school, he'd treated *her* like the third wheel whenever the three of them went anywhere together. She'd even tried setting him up with countless friends, but he'd scared them all off with his jerkish I'm-better-than-everyone attitude. Obviously, he was still chasing them away. She'd heard he was single, and it couldn't be his tall, dark, and handsome looks keeping the women at bay.

She hadn't seen him in years, other than to peek over Dean's shoulder sometimes when the two Skyped. He was taller than she remembered, towering over her, even in her heels, and his broad shoulders and chest revealed he was a lot more muscular than he looked on the computer screen. His midday five o'clock shadow seemed Photoshopped to perfection, and his square, strong jawline erased any trace of the boy she used to go to school with. All he and Dean ever talked about was hockey, and she often wondered if there were any other layers to the friendship besides a shared passion for the sport.

Obviously without hockey as the subject, the guy had little to talk about, she thought as she continued to wait for him to say something.

He stared at the floor, his hands shoved deep in his pockets, rocking back and forth on his heels.

Silence.

Okay then.

Moving around him, she continued down the hall.

His voice stopped her. "I don't believe everything they're saying about Dean in the papers."

Neither had she, but actually seeing her husband in bed with two women was proof enough.

Of course she didn't expect Jackson to see her side. Slowly, she turned back. "Believe what you want, Jackson. I really don't care."

He moved toward her and her spine stiffened. His light blue eyes were dark and judging. "Adultery? Abuse? Come on. We both know Dean is not that guy."

She hadn't believed him capable of the emotional and verbal abuse, either. That had changed the day she'd confronted him about pictures of him and a Dallas Stars cheerleader she'd seen on the front of a supermarket tabloid. He'd gone on the defensive, saying nasty things to make her believe she was the one at fault for even accusing him of anything. Paranoid, stupid, delusional… just some of the angry insults that played on repeat in her mind.

"I'm not having this conversation with you. Or any conversation." They'd barely spoken before, why start now? "Glenwood Falls is big enough. I think we should be able to make these run-ins few and far between if we try hard enough." Though, that might be harder now that she would be spending time at the school, which was right next door to the arena.

"Oh, believe me, I'll try hard enough," he said, his ice-cold stare making her shiver.

The sound of the lunch bell prevented her from saying anything more as instantly they were swarmed by groups of children heading toward the school cafeteria.

Her eyes skimmed the crowd for Dani. Spotting her coming toward them, Abigail smiled—for real for the first time that day. She waved a hand, relieved to have the perfect excuse to end the intense, uncomfortable conversation.

"Mom? What are you doing here?" Dani asked with a frown when she reached her.

Not exactly the warm greeting she'd been hoping for, but at least her daughter was speaking to her. That small victory was short-lived as she noticed Jackson still standing there watching them. Dani had never actually met Jackson, only saw him occasionally on the computer and in Facebook pics. And Abigail wasn't about to make the introduction. If in nine years the two men hadn't felt it necessary, neither did she.

"I came to talk to Principal Breen about a substitute teaching position," she said, wrapping an arm around her daughter's shoulders.

Dani shrugged away.

Her arm fell to her side. She knew none of this was easy on her daughter. Dani was close with her father, despite his frequent long absences, and she was more like him, which made common ground for bonding with her a challenge. Her daughter was too young to understand everything going on, but Abigail had done her best to explain the situation to her. She didn't want her to rely on the tabloids for information. However, she sensed Dani blamed her, at least for the move, and she was determined to make things right with her. "She said I can start next week…whenever they need a substitute." She glanced toward Jackson. Why was he still standing there—listening? "Isn't that wonderful?"

Dani shrugged.

Heat rushed to her cheeks, and she forced herself not to look at Jackson. Moving her daughter farther away, she knelt in front of her. "I'm sorry you're upset, and I know this move is hard on you," she said. "But, I promise things are going to get better now." How often had she said those words to Dani in the last three days? She wondered if it was only her daughter she was trying to convince. "Soon we'll move into our own place, and before long this will start to feel like home." She brushed her daughter's whip-straight dark hair—her father's hair—away from her face and searched her expression for any sign of understanding.

Dani didn't look convinced, but finally, she nodded. "Fine. Whatever," she said simply.

She'd take any agreement she could get at that moment. "Come on. We'll go to the diner on Main Street for lunch." The cafeteria food sucked. Soon enough they would both have to get used to it. But not today.

And she suspected soon enough she would have to get used to seeing Jackson Westmore. But that, too, was something she was more than willing to postpone for as long as possible.

* * *

"Keep your hands away from your body…that's it. You don't want to be looking down at the puck, or you won't have it for long," Jackson said as he skated backward, watching Taylor move across the ice toward the net with the puck.

Tryouts were the following week, and he wanted to make sure his niece would be ready. Darryl's warning about the other dads still troubled him, but what had him off his game was his brief—yet far too long—glimpse of Abby Jansen earlier that day.

She was going to be teaching at the school. Fan-freaking-tastic.

He shook his head, banishing the image of her in her expensive suit, looking more beautiful than ever. He didn't need any new memories of her competing with the old ones.

He moved closer to his niece to steal the puck, but she moved her body between him and the biscuit the way he'd taught her. He smiled. The kid was a natural. "That's good. Where did you learn that?"

"From Uncle Ben," she teased.

"Ha! I taught both of your uncles everything they know." Ironically, that was true. He'd been the first of the three of them to develop an interest in the sport at age four. His older brother, Ben, and his younger brother, Asher, hadn't started playing until several years later.

But, as it turned out, they were both better than he was. That's why they were playing on major league hockey teams and he was still coaching in Glenwood Falls.

Taylor skated faster and shot the puck. It hit the right post.

"You released it too soon," he said, skating up to her and patting her helmet. "Just hold on to it a little longer. You're overeager to score without an assist—maybe you have been learning a thing or two from your Uncle Ben." Ben played for the Colorado Avalanche. He was the top scorer for the team for the last three years, but he didn't know how to share the puck.

Jackson skated by it and scooped it up. Checking his watch, he saw it was after five. They'd been practicing for almost two hours. "Come on, let's go get something to eat."

"Can we go to Slope and Hatch?"

"Craving a Big Valley Mac?" he asked as they sat on the bench to remove their skates.

She took off her helmet and shook her short dark hair. "Is there any other hot dog worth eating?"

He laughed. "You make a good point, kid. Go grab your stuff." As she rushed off toward the locker rooms, he stood, staring out at the ice. Above the blue line hung the local team's championship flags and across from him on the wall was the banner that read WELCOME TO THE HOME OF THE WESTMORE BROTHERS!

Ben and Asher—the source of community pride.

They were the stars of Glenwood Falls—he was just everyone's favorite coach.

ABOUT THE AUTHOR

Jennifer Snow lives in Edmonton, Alberta, with her husband and son. She writes sweet and sexy contemporary romance stories set everywhere from small towns to big cities. After stating in her high school yearbook bio that she wanted to be an author, she set off on the winding, twisting road to make her dream a reality. She is a member of RWA, the Writers' Guild of Alberta, the Canadian Authors Association, and the Film and Visual Arts Association in Edmonton. She has published more than a dozen novels and novellas with many more on the way.

You can learn more at:
   JenniferSnowAuthor.com
   Twitter @jennifersnow18
   Facebook.com/JenniferSnowBooks

Fall in Love with Forever Romance

LONG, TALL COWBOY CHRISTMAS
By Carolyn Brown

A heartwarming holiday read from *USA Today* bestselling author Carolyn Brown. Nash Lamont is a man about as solitary as they come. So what the heck is he doing letting a beautiful widow and her three rambunctious children temporarily move in at Christmas?

Kasey Dawson thought she'd never get over the death of her husband. But her kids have a plan of their own: Nothing will keep them from having a real family again—even if it takes a little help from Santa himself.

Fall in Love with Forever Romance

THE TROUBLE WITH CHRISTMAS
By Debbie Mason

The Trouble with Christmas is the first book in the *USA Today* bestselling Christmas, Colorado series by Debbie Mason. This special reissue edition will feature bonus content never before in print! Resort developer Madison Lane is trying to turn Christmas, Colorado, into a tourist's winter wonderland. But Sheriff Gage McBride is tasked with stopping her from destroying his town. After meeting Madison, he can't decide if she's naughty or nice, but one thing is for certain—Christmas will never be the same again.

Fall in Love with Forever Romance

TOO BEAUTIFUL TO BREAK
By Tessa Bailey

Losing Sage Alexander is not an option for Belmont Clarkson. His heart is hers, has always been hers. He knows she's hiding something from him, but nothing will stand in his way of telling her just how much she means to him—even if saving her from her past ends up costing him everything. Don't miss the final book in Tessa Bailey's Romancing the Clarksons series!

THE CORNER OF FOREVER AND ALWAYS
By Lia Riley

Perfect for readers of Kristan Higgins, Jill Shalvis, and Marina Adair. When princess impersonator Tuesday Knight faces off against Everland mayor Beau Marino to save her theme park from demolition, sparks fly. Will she save Happily Ever After Land only to lose her own happy ever after?